SPAWN OF ROCKET BOY AND THE GEEK GIRLS

Also Edited by Phyllis Irene Radford

Rocket Boy and the Geek Girls
Dragon Lords and Warrior Women
The Shadow Conspiracy, Volumes I, II, and III
Beyond Grimm
Across the Spectrum

Also Edited by Shannon Page

Witches, Bitches & Stitches
The Usual Path to Publication
Book View Cafe 2020 Holiday Anthology
Black-Eyed Peas on New Year's Day: An Anthology of Hope
Murmurs in the Dark (with Marissa Doyle)

SPAWN OF ROCKET BOY AND THE GEEK GIRLS

EDITED BY

PHYLLIS IRENE RADFORD

AND SHANNON PAGE

Spawn of Rocket Boy and the Geek Girls, edited by Phyllis Irene Radford and Shannon Page

Individual story copyright details appear on pages 310-311.

Cover art and design by Marissa Doyle
Interior design by Shannon Page

First Edition

ISBN: 978-1-63632-039-7

www.bookviewcafe.com
Book View Café Publishing Cooperative

CONTENTS

INTRODUCTION

Back in the mists of Time Before Time, Book View Café was a group of geeky women writing science fiction, fantasy, romance—all the good stuff.

Then…(shudder)…a *man* was admitted to BVC's august ranks.

From this extraordinary event, our first-ever anthology was hatched: Rocket Boy had joined the Geek Girls, delivering a spaceship full of rare reprints, hard-to-find favorites, and new tales in a one-of-a-kind story collection.

Now, many moons later, BVC's ranks boast *several* men, and our catalogue features a growing collection of anthologies—a few of which, we realized, needed an update.

Welcome to the first *re*vamped, *re*issued, extra-freshened-up Book View Café anthology: Spawn of Rocket Boy and the Geek Girls! More stories, more spaceships, more fun!

Because, even with boys in our midst, we are *still* writing the good stuff.

-Shannon Page and Phyllis Irene Radford, Editors

SPACE

Kinds of Strangers

Sarah Zettel

Margot Rusch pulled open the hatch that led to the *Forty-Niner*'s sick bay. "Paul?" she asked around the tightness building in her throat. She pulled herself into the sterile, white module, focusing slowly on the center of the bay, not wanting to believe what she saw.

Paul's body, wide-eyed, pale-skinned, limp and lifeless, floated in mid-air. A syringe hovered near his hand, pointing its needle toward the corpse as if making an accusation.

"Oh, Christ." Margot fumbled for a handhold.

The ventilation fans whirred to life. Their faint draft pushed against the corpse, sending it in a slow arc toward the far wall of the module. Margot caught the acrid scent of death's final indignities. Hard-won control shredded inside her, but there was nowhere to turn, no one to blame. There was only herself, the corpse, and the flat, blank screen of the artificial intelligence interface.

"Damn it, Reggie, why didn't you do something!" she demanded, fully aware it was irrational to holler at the AI, but unable to help it.

"I did not know what to do," said Reggie softly from its terminal. "There are no case scenarios for this."

"No, there aren't," agreed Margot, wearily. "No, there sure as hell aren't."

The crew of the *Forty-Niner* had known for three months they were going to die. The seven of them were NASA's pride, returning from the first crewed expedition to the asteroid belt. They had opened a new frontier for humanity, on schedule and under budget. Two and a half years of their four-year mission were a raving success, and now they were headed home.

There had been a few problems, a few red lights. Grit from the asteroid belt had wormed its way into the works on the comm antenna and the radio telescope. No problem. Ed MacEvoy and Jean Kramer replaced the damaged parts in no time. This was a NASA project. They had backups to spare. Even if the reaction control module, which was traditional methane/oxygen rockets used for course corrections, somehow failed completely, all that would mean was cutting the project a little short. A magnetic sail handled the long-distance flight, a gigantic loop of high-temperature superconducting ceramic cable with a continuous stream of charged particles running through it. No matter what else happened, that would get them home.

"Margot?" Jean's voice came down the connector tube. "You okay?"

Margot tightened her grip on the handle and looked at the corpse as it turned lazily in the center of the bay. *No, I am not okay.*

The mag sail, however, had found a new way to fail. Particle discontinuities caused by a combination of radiation and thermal insulation degradation raised the temperature too high and robbed hundreds of kilometers of ceramic cable of its superconductivity.

Once the mag sail had gone, the ship kept moving. Of course, it kept moving with no atmospheric friction to slow it down. But it moved in a slow elliptical orbit going nowhere near its scheduled rendezvous with Earth. They could burn every atom of propellant they carried for the RCM and for the explorer boats, and they'd still be too far away for any of the Mars shuttles to reach by a factor of five. Frantic comm bursts to Houston brought no solutions. The *Forty-Niner* was stranded.

"Margot?" Jean again, calling down the connector.

"I'll be right up." Margot hoped Jean wouldn't hear how Paul's suicide strangled her voice.

Margot looked at the empty syringe suspended in mid-air. '*Drunk all and left no friendly drop to help me after.*' The ancient quote made her swallow hard. *Stop it, Margot. Do not even start going there.*

"Is there another request?" asked Reggie.

Margot bit her lip. "No. No more requests."

She pushed herself into the connector and dragged the hatch shut. She had the vague notion she should have done something for the body—closed its eyes or wrapped a sheet around it, or something, but she couldn't make herself turn around.

Margot's eyes burned. She'd flown four other missions with Paul. She'd sat up all night with him drinking espresso and swapping stories while the bigwigs debated the final crew roster for the *Forty-Niner*. They'd spent long hours on the flight out arguing politics and playing old jazz recordings. She'd thought she knew him, thought he would hang on with the rest of them.

Then again, she'd thought the same of Ed and Tracy.

Tracy Costa, their chief mineralogist, had been the first to go. They hadn't known a thing about it, until Nick had caught a glimpse of the frozen corpse outside one of the port windows. Then, Ed had suffocated himself, even after he'd sworn to Jean he'd never leave her alone in this mess.

Now, Paul.

Margot pulled herself from handhold to handhold up the tubular connector, past its cabinets and access panels. One small, triangular window looked out onto vacuum, the infinitely patient darkness that waited for the rest of them to give up.

Stop it, Margot. She tore her gaze away from the window and concentrated on pulling herself forward.

The *Forty-Niner's* command module was a combination of ship's bridge, comm center, and central observatory. Right now, it held all of the remaining crew members. Their mission commander, Nicholas Deale, sandy-haired, dusky-skinned and dark-eyed, sat at one of Reggie's compact terminals, brooding over what he saw on the flat screen. Tom Merritt, who had gone from a florid, pink man to a paper-white ghost during the last couple of weeks, tapped at the controls for the radio telescope. He was an astronomer and the mission communications specialist. He was the one who made sure they all got their messages from home. The last living crew member was Jean. A few wisps of hair had come loose from her tight brown braid and they floated around her head, making her look even more worried and vulnerable. She stood at another terminal, typing in a perfunctory and distracted cadence.

Margot paused in the threshold, trying to marshal her thoughts and nerves. Nick glanced up at her. Margot opened her mouth, but her throat clamped tight around her words. Tom and Jean both turned to look at her. The remaining blood drained out of Tom's face.

"Paul?" he whispered.

Margot coughed. "Looks like he overdosed himself."

Jean turned her head away, but not before Margot saw the struggle against tears fill her face. Both Nick's hands clenched into fists. Tom just looked at Nick with tired eyes and said, "Well, now what?"

Nick sighed. "Okay, okay." He ran both hands through his hair. "I'll go take care of…the body. Tom, can you put a burst through to mission control? They'll want to notify his family quietly. I'll come up with the letter…."

This was pure Nick. Give everybody something to do, but oversee it all. When they'd reeled in the sail, he hadn't slept for two days helping Ed and Jean go over the cable an inch at a time, trying to find out if any sections were salvageable from which they could jury-rig a kind of storm sail. When that had proven hopeless, he'd still kept everybody as busy as possible. He milked every drop of encouraging news he could out of mission control. Plans were in the works. The whole world was praying for them. Comm bursts came in regularly from friends and family. A rescue attempt would be made. A way home would be found. All they had to do was hang on.

"In the meantime…" Nick went on.

"In the meantime, we wait for the radiation to eat our insides out," said Tom bitterly. "It's hopeless, Nick. We're all dead."

Nick shifted uneasily, crunching Velcro underfoot. "I'm still breathing and I don't plan to stop anytime soon."

A spasm of pure anger crossed Tom's features. "And what are you going to breathe when the scrubbers give out? Huh? What are you going to do when the water's gone? How about when the tumors start up?"

Tom, don't do this, thought Margot, but the words died in her throat, inadequate against the sudden red rage she saw in him. He was afraid of illness, of weakness. Well, weren't they all?

Paul's chief duty had been keeping them all from getting cancer. One of the main hazards of lengthy space flight had always been long-term exposure to hard radiation. The mag sail, when it was functional, had created a shield from charged particles, which slowed the process down. Medical advancements had arisen to cover the damage that could be done by fast neutrons and gamma rays. Paul Luck maintained cultures of regenerative stem cells taken from each member of the crew. Every week, he measured pre-cancer indicators, inky areas of the body. If the indicators were too high, he tracked down the "hot spots" and administered doses of the healthy cultured cells to remind bone, organ and skin how they were supposed to act and viola! Healthy, cancer-free individual.

The Luck system was now, however, permanently down, and the only backup for that was the AI's medical expert system and the remaining crew's emergency training. Right now, that didn't seem like anything close to enough.

"We have time," Nick said evenly. "We do not have to give up. Come on, Tom. What would Carol say if she heard this?" Nick, Margot remembered, had been at Tom's wedding. They were friends, or at least, they had been friends.

"She'd say whatever the NASA shrinks told her to," snapped Tom. "And in the meantime," he drawled the word, "I get to watch her aging ten years for every day we're hanging up here. How much longer do I have to do this to her? How much longer are you going to make your family suffer?"

For the first time, Nick's composure cracked. His face tightened into a mask of pent-up rage and frustration, but his voice stayed level. "My family is going to know I died trying."

Tom looked smug. "At least you admit we're going to die."

"No…" began Jean.

"Help," said a strange, soft voice.

The crew all turned. The voice came from the AI terminal. It was Reggie.

"Incoming signal. No origination. Can't filter. Incoherent system flaw. Error 365…"

A grind and clank reverberated through the hull. Reggie's voice cut off.

"Systems check!" barked Nick.

Margot kicked off the wall and flew to her station at navigation control.

"I got garbage," said Tom from beside her. "Machine language, error babble. Reggie's gone nuts."

Margot shoved her Velcro-bottomed boots into place and typed madly at her keyboard, bringing up the diagnostics. "All good here," she reported. She turned and looked out the main window, searching for the stars and the slightly steadier dots that were the planets. "Confirmed. Positioning systems up and running."

"Engineering looks okay," said Jean. "I'll go check the generators and report back." Nick gave her a sharp nod. She pulled herself free of her station and launched herself down the connector.

"You getting anything coherent?" Nick pushed himself over to hover behind Tom's shoulder.

"Nothing." Margot could just make out the streams of random symbols flashing past on Tom's terminal.

"Reggie, what's happening?" she whispered.

"I don't know," said the voice from her terminal. Margot jerked. "Unable to access exterior communications system. Multiple errors on internal nodes. Code corruption. Error. 34…" The computer voice cut out again in a pulse of static, then another, then silence, followed by another quick static burst.

"Margot, can you see the comm antenna?" asked Tom, his hands still flashing across the keyboard.

Margot pressed her cheek against the cool window, craned her neck, and squinted, trying to see along the *Forty-Niner's* hull. "Barely, yeah."

"Can you make out its orientation?"

Margot squinted again. "Looks about ten degrees off-axis."

"It's moved," said Tom between static bursts. "That was the noise."

"All okay down in the power plant." Jean pulled herself back through the hatch and attached herself to her station. "Well, at least there's nothing new wrong…" She let the sentence trail off. "What is that?"

Margot and the others automatically paused to listen. Margot heard nothing but the steady hum of the ship and the bursts of static from Reggie. Quick pulses, *one, one, two, one, two, one, one, one, two.*

"A pattern?" said Nick.

"Mechanical failure," said Tom. "Has to be. Reggie just crashed."

One, one, two, one.

"You ever hear about anything crashing like this?" asked Margot.

One, two, one.

"Reggie? Level one diagnostic, report," said Nick.

One, one, two.

"Maybe we can get a coherent diagnostic out of one of the other expert systems," Margot suggested. Reggie wasn't a single processor. It was a web-work of six interconnected expert systems, each with their own area of concentration, just like the members of the crew. Terminals in different modules of the ship gave default access to differing expert systems.

"Maybe," said Nick. "Tom can try to track down the fault from here. You and Jean see if you can get an answer out of si…the power plant." Margot was quietly grateful he remembered what else was in sick bay before she had to remind him.

One, one, one.

Jean and Margot pulled themselves down the connector to the engineering compartment. As Jean had reported, all the indicators that had remained functional after they'd lost the sail reported green and go.

"At least it's a different crisis," Jean muttered as she brought up Reggie's terminal, the one she and Ed had spent hours behind when the mag sail went out.

"Remind me to tell you about my grandmother's stint on the old Mir sometime," said Margot. "Now there was an adventure."

Jean actually smiled and Margot felt a wash of gratitude. Someone in here was still who she thought they were.

Jean spoke to the terminal. "Reggie, we've got a massive fault in the exterior communications system. Can you analyze from this system?" As she spoke, Margot hit the intercom button on the wall to carry the answer to the command center.

"Massive disruption and multiple error processing," said Reggie, sounding even more mechanical than usual. "I will attempt to establish interface."

"You hear that?" Margot said to the intercom grill. She could just hear the static pulses coming from the command center as whispering echoes against the walls of the connector.

"Roger," came back Nick's voice.

"I am…getting reports of an external signal," said Reggie. "It is…there is…internal fault, internal fault, internal fault."

Jean shut the terminal's voice down. "What the hell?" she demanded. Margot just shook her head.

"External signal? How is that possible? This can't be a comm burst from Houston."

Margot's gaze drifted to the black triangle of the window. The echoes whispered in ones and twos.

"What's a language with only two components?" Margot asked.

Jean stared at her. "Binary."

"What do we, in essence, transmit from here when we do our comm bursts? What might somebody who didn't know any better try to send back to us?"

Jean's face went nearly as white as Tom's. "Margot, you're crazy."

Margot didn't bother to reply. She just pushed herself back up the connector to the bridge.

"Tom? Did you hear that?"

Tom didn't look up. He had a clipboard and pen in his hands. As the static bursts rang out, he scribbled down a 1 for each single burst and a 0 for each pair. He hung the board in mid-air, as if not caring where it went, and his hands flew across the keyboard. "Oh yeah, I heard it."

Nick was back at his station, typing at his own keyboard. "The engineering ex-systems seem to be intact. Maybe we can get an analysis…" He hit a new series of keys. Around them, the static bursts continued. Margot's temples started to throb in time with the insistent pulses.

"There's something," Tom murmured to the terminal. His voice was tight, and there was an undercurrent in it Margot couldn't identify. "It'll take awhile to find out exactly what's happened. I've got Reggie recording." He looked straight at Nick. "As long as it doesn't crash all the way..."

Margot and Jean also turned to Nick. Margot thought she saw relief shining behind his eyes. *At least now he won't have to find us make-work to do.*

"All right," said Nick. "Tom, you keep working on the analysis of this...whatever it is. Jean, we need you to do a breakdown on Reggie. What's clean and what's contaminated." He turned his dark, relieved eyes to Margot. "I'll take care of Paul. Margot..."

"I'll make sure all the peripherals are at the ready," said Margot. "We don't know what's happening next."

Nick nodded. Margot extracted herself from her station and followed Nick down the connector. She tried not to look as he worked the wheel on the sick bay hatch. She just let herself float past and made her way down to the cargo bay.

The cargo bay was actually a combination cargo hold and staging area. Here they stored the carefully locked down canisters holding the ore samples. Here too was where they suited up for all their extra-vehicular activities. Just outside the airlock, the explorer boats waited, clamped tightly to the hull. They were small, light ships that looked like ungainly box kites stripped of their fabric. The explorers were barely more than frames with straps to hang sample containers or sample gatherers or astronauts from. They'd been designed for asteroid rendezvous and landing. Margot remembered the sensation of childlike glee when she got to take them in. She loved her work, her mission, her life, but that had been sheer fun.

For a brief moment they had thought they might be able to use the explorers to tow the *Forty-Niner* into an orbit that would allow one of the Martian stations to mount a rescue, but Reggie's models had shown it to be impossible. The delta-vee just wasn't there. So the explorers sat out there, and she sat in here, along with the core samplers, the drillers, the explosive charges, doing nothing much but waiting to find out what happened next.

Hang on, Margot. Stay alive one minute longer, and one minute after that. That's the game now, isn't it? Forget how to play and you'll be following Paul, Ed, and Tracy.

She touched the intercom button so she could hear the static bursts and Tom's soft murmuring. It reminded her that something really was happening. A little warmth crept into her heart. A little light stirred in her mind. It was something, Tom had said so. It might just be help. Any kind of help.

Small tasks had kept her busy during the two weeks since they lost the sail, and small tasks kept her busy now. She made sure the seals on the ore carriers maintained their integrity. She ran computer checks on the explorers and made sure the fuel cells on the rovers were all at full capacity, that their tanks were charged, and the seals were tight. Given the state Reggie was in, she was tempted to put on one of the bright yellow hard-suits and go out to do a manual check. She squashed the idea. She might be needed for something in here.

She counted all the air bottles for the suits and checked their pressure. You never knew. With Reggie acting up, they might have to do an EVA to point the antenna back toward Earth. If this last, strange hope proved to be false, she still hadn't said goodbye to her fiancé Jordan, and she wanted to. She didn't want to just leave him in silence.

Reggie's voice, coming from the intercom, startled her out of her thoughts.

"Help," said Reggie. "Me. Help. Me. We. Thee. Help."

Margot flew up the connector. She was the last to reach the command module. She hung in the threshold, listening to Reggie blurt out words one at a time.

"There. Is. Help." said Reggie, clipped and harsh. The words picked up pace. "There is help. Comet. Pull. Tow. Yourself. There is a comet approaching within reach. You can tow yourself toward your worlds using this comet. It is possible. There is help."

Margot felt her jaw drop open.

Tom looked down at his clipboard. "What Reggie says we've got here is a binary transmission from an unknown source. Taking the single pulses as ones and the double pulses as zeroes gave us gibberish, but taking the single pulses as zero and the double pulses as one gave us some version of machine language. The engineering expert sub-system was able to decode it."

Margot felt her mouth go dry. "My God," she whispered. "The seventh cavalry really is made up of little green men."

Tom gripped his pen tightly, obviously resisting the urge to throw it in frustration. "This is impossible, this can't be happening."

Margot shrugged. "Well, it is."

"It can't be," growled Tom. "Aliens who can create a machine language Reggie can read inside of four hours? It couldn't happen."

"Unless they've been listening in on us for awhile," Jean pointed out.

Tom tapped the pen against the clipboard. *One, two, one.* "But how…"

Margot cut him off. She didn't want to hear it anymore. This was help, this was the possibility of life. Why was he trying to screw it up? "We've been beaming all kinds of junk out into space for over a hundred years. Maybe they've been listening that long." She felt his doubt dribbling into the corners of her mind. She shut it out by sheer force of will.

Jean folded her arms tightly across her torso. "At this point, I wouldn't care if it was made up of demons from the seventh circle of Hell, just so long as it's out here."

"Jesus," breathed Nick softly. Then, in a more normal voice

he said, "Okay, Margot, you and Jean are going to have to do an EVA to turn the antenna around so we can send a burst to Houston."

"We can't tell Houston about this," said Jean sharply.

"What?" demanded Tom.

Jean hugged herself even tighter. "They'd think we'd all gone crazy up here."

"What's it matter what they think?" Nick spread his hands. "It's not like they can do anything about it."

"They can tell our families we've all taken the mental crash," said Jean flatly. "I, for one, do not want to make this any worse on my parents."

Nick nodded slowly. "Okay," he said. "We keep this our little secret. But if we do make it back, mission control is going to have a cow."

Tom looked from Nick to Jean and Margot saw something hard and strange behind his eyes. He faced Margot. "This thing with the comet, could we really do something like this?"

Margot's mouth opened and closed. A short-period comet, swinging around the sun. If they caught it on its way back in…if they could attach a line (hundreds of kilometers of unused cable coiled on its drum against the hull of the ship)…theoretically, theoretically, it could pull them into a tighter orbit. The stresses would be incredible. Several gees worth. Would they be too much? How to make the attachment? Couldn't land on a comet, even if the explorers had the delta-vee. Comets were surrounded by dust and debris, they ejected gas jets, ice, and rock. Asteroids were one thing. Asteroids were driftwood bobbing along through the void. Comets were alive and kicking.

But maybe…maybe…

"We'd need to find the thing," she said finally. "We'd need course, distance, speed. We'd need to know if we can use the RCM to push us near enough to take a shot at it. We'd probably need the explorers to do the actual work of attaching the *For-*

ty-Niner to the comet..."

"We could use the mag sail," said Jean. She gnawed slowly on her thumbnail. "All that cable, we could use it as a tow rope. But we'd need a harpoon, or something..."

"A harpoon?" said Tom incredulously.

Jean just nodded. "To attach the tether to the comet. Maybe we could use some of the explosives..."

Nick smiled, just a little. For the first time in days, Margot saw the muscles of his face relax. "Jean, let's get down to engineering and see what we can work up. Tom, you and Margot find our comet." His smile broadened. "And keep an ear out in case the neighbors have more to say."

"No problem," said Margot. She raised her arm and whistled. "Taxi!"

Jean, an old New Yorker, actually laughed at that, and Margot grinned at her. Nick and Jean pulled themselves down the connector. Margot planted her feet on the Velcro patch next to Tom.

"Let's see if we can still get to the database," she said, as she reached over his shoulder for the keys. "We should be able to narrow down..."

Tom did not lift his gaze from the screen. "It's a fake, Margot," he whispered.

Margot's hand froze halfway to the keyboard. "What?"

"Little green men my ass," he spat toward the console. "It's a fake. It's Nick. He's doing this to try to keep us going."

Margot felt the blood drain from her cheeks, and the hope from her heart. "How do you know?"

"I know." For the first time Tom looked at her. "He'd do anything right now to keep us in line, to keep giving orders, just so it doesn't look like he's out of options like the rest of us mere mortals."

Margot looked at his wide, angry blue eyes and saw the man she'd served with swallowed up by a stranger. "You got proof?"

Tom shook his head, but the certainty on his face did not waver. "I checked the logs for gaps, suspicious entries, virus tracks, extra encryptions. Nothing. Nobody on this ship could have made an invisible insertion, except me, or Nick."

"Unless it's not an insertion," said Margot. "Unless it's really a signal."

Tom snorted and contempt filled his soft words. "Now you're talking like Jean. She hasn't been with it since Ed went. Be real, Margot. If E.T. is out there, why isn't he knocking on the door? Why's he sending cryptic messages about comets instead of offering us a lift?"

"It's aliens, I don't know." Margot spread her hands. "Maybe they're methane breathers. Maybe they're too far away. Space is big. Maybe they want to see if we can figure it out for ourselves to see if we're worthy for membership in the Galactic Federation."

Tom's face twitched and Margot got the feeling he was suppressing a sneer. "Okay, if it's aliens, how come I was able to figure out what they were saying so fast? They have a 'NASA Machine Language for Dummies' book with them?"

Margot threw up her hands. "If Nick was faking this, why would he insist on a comm burst to mission control?"

Tom's jaw worked back and forth. "Because it'd look funny if he didn't and he knew Jean'd object and give him an out. She might even be in on it with him."

Margot clenched her fists. "It's a chance, Tom. It's even a decent chance, if we work the simulations right. It doesn't matter where the idea came from…"

"It does matter!" he whispered hoarsely. "It matters that we're being used. It matters that he doesn't trust us to hear him out, so he's got to invent alien overlords."

"So, report him when we get home," said Margot, exasperation filling her breathy exclamation.

"We're not going to get home." Tom slammed his fist against the console. "We're going to die. This is all a stupid game to keep us from killing ourselves too soon. He's determined we are not going to die until he's good and ready."

Margot leaned in close, until she could see every pore in Tom's bloodless white cheeks. "You listen to me," she breathed. "You want to kill yourself? Hit the sick bay. I'm sure Paul left behind something you can O.D. on. Maybe you're right, maybe how we go out is the only choice left. But I think we can use the delta-vee from the comet to tow us into a tighter orbit. I'm going to try, and I may die trying, but that's my choice. What are you going to do? Which part of that stubborn idiot head are you going to listen to? Huh?" She grabbed his collar. "If it is Nick doing this, I agree, it's a stupid ploy. But so what? It's the first good idea we've had in over a month. Are you going to let your pride kill you?"

Tom swatted her hand away. "I am not going to let him treat me like a fool or a child." He lifted up first one foot then the other. He twisted in the air and swam toward the connector. Margot hung her head and let him go.

Give him some time to stew and then go after him. She planted herself squarely in front of his station. "Reggie?"

"Functioning," replied the AI.

"We need to do some speculation here." She rubbed her forehead. "I need you to pull up any databases we've got on comets. Specifically, I need any that are passing within a thousand kilometers of the *Forty-Niner*'s projected position anytime within the next several months."

A static burst sounded from the speaker as if Reggie were coughing. "Several is not specific."

"Six months then. Add in the possibility of a full or partial RCM burn for course correction to bring us within the cometary path. Can you do that?"

Two more quick bursts. "I can try," said Reggie.

"That's all any of us can do right now."

"Searching."

Margot sat back to wait. She listened to the hum of the ship and the sound of her own breathing. No other sounds. She couldn't hear Nick and Jean down in engineering. She couldn't hear Tom anywhere. Worry spiked in the back of her mind. What if he was taking the quick way out? What if he was angry enough to take Nick out instead?

No, she shook her head. *Tom's just on edge. They're friends.*

Were they? She remembered the stranger looking out of Tom's eyes. Would that stranger recognize Nick? Would Nick recognize him? She glanced nervously over her shoulder. No one floated in the connector. She looked back at the screen. Reggie had a list up—names, orbital parameters, current locations, sizes, with an option to display orbital plots and position relative to the *Forty-Niner*. Highlighted at the top was Comet Kowalski-Rice.

Sounds like a breakfast cereal. Margot glanced over her shoulder again. The connector was still empty. The ship was still silent.

Kowalski-Rice was a periodic comet, with a nucleus estimated to be 3 kilometers long and between 1 and 3 kilometers wide. It had passed its aphelion and was headed back toward the Sun. Right now it was 2.9 million kilometers from the *Forty-Niner*, but it was getting closer. Margot brought up the orbital plot and did a quick calculation.

We burn fifty…okay, say sixty to be on the safe side, percent of the remaining propellant, we can bring our orbit within seven hundred-fifty kilometers of the comet. Take about… She ran the equations in her head. She could double check them with Reggie or Nick, whoever turned out to be more reliable. *Bring us there in about 159 hours, with the comet going approximately 2 kilometers per second relative to the ship. This could work. This could work.*

Silence, except for the steady hum of the ship and her own breathing.

Margot swore. *This is no good.* "Reggie? Do you know where Tom is?"

"Tom Merritt is in the sick bay."

"No!" Margot yanked both feet up and kicked off the console. "Nick! Jean!" she shouted. "Sick bay! Now!"

She reached sick bay first. She wrenched the wheel around and threw the hatch open. A little red sphere drifted out toward her face. Margot swatted at it reflexively and it broke against her hand, scattering dark red motes in a dozen directions.

Tom had fastened himself to the examining table and sliced his throat. Clouds of burgundy bubbles rose from his neck, knocking against a pair of scissors and sending them spinning.

"Tom!" Margot dove forward and pressed her fingers against his wound. Panting, she tried to think back to her emergency medical training. Dark red, not bright, oozing, not spurting, missed the carotid artery, cut a bunch of veins...

Tom, you idiot, you're so far gone you can't even kill yourself right.

Events blurred. It seemed like Nick, Jean and Reggie were all shouting at once. A pad got shoved into her hand to help staunch the blood. The table was tilted to elevate his head. Reggie droned on clear and concise directions for covering the long, thin wound with layered sealants. Nick's and Jean's hands shook as they worked. Blood and tears stung Margot's eyes.

When they were done, Tom was still strapped to the table, unconscious and dead white, but breathing. The medical ex-system was obviously still working. Reggie had no problem reading from the various pads and probes they had stuck to him. It was giving him good odds on survival, despite the blood loss.

"Let's get out of here," said Nick. "We can vacuum this up when we've had a chance to catch our breath."

Jean didn't argue, she just headed for the hatch. Margot had the distinct feeling she wanted to crawl into a corner and be quietly sick.

Margot followed Nick and Jean out and swung the hatch shut. She wanted to be able to talk without getting a mouthful of blood.

"God." Nick ran both hands through his hair. "I cannot believe it, I cannot believe he did this." Unfamiliar indecision showed on his face. Margot turned her gaze away. Another stranger. Just one more. Like Tom, like the others.

No! she wanted to scream. *Not you. I know you! You recommended me for this mission. You have a great poker face, and you sing country-western so loud in the shower the soundproofing can't keep it in! You keep all the stats on your kids' sports teams displayed as the default screen on your handheld! Your wife's the only woman you've ever been with! I know Nicholas Alexander Deale!*

But she did not know the person torn with weariness, anger, and doubt who looked out of Nick's eyes. The one who might be a liar on a scale she'd never imagined. How long before that stranger took Nick completely over?

Margot looked at Jean. Blood splotched her face, hands, hair and coveralls. Fear haunted her bruised-looking eyes. Fear brought the stranger. Jean would go next. The stranger would have them all. Tom was right. They were all dead. Only the strangers and Margot Rusch lived.

"What is it, Margot?" asked Nick.

What do I say? Which "it" do I pick? Who let the stranger into Tom? Me or you? She licked her lips. *Well, it does not get me. It does not get me.*

"Nothing." Margot grabbed a handhold and pulled herself toward the command center. "I'm going to find that comet."

After all, that was what the strangers wanted her to do. She had to do what they said. If she didn't…look what they did to Tom. Who knew what they'd do to her?

They do not get me.

"HERE IT COMES, MARGOT." THE voice that used to be Nick's crackled through her helmet's intercom.

Margot turned in her straps, and there it came. Actually, Kowalski-Rice had been visible to the naked eye for the past two days. The comet was ungainly and beautiful at the same time. A dirty snowball tumbling through the darkness surrounded by a sparkling veil fit for an angel's bride. It was huge—a living, shining island, coal black and ice white. Margot's hands tightened on the twin joy stick directional control for the explorer.

They had planned the maneuver out so carefully and modeled it so thoroughly. She had to give the strangers who walked as Nick and Jean credit. They were very good at what they did.

Jean's stranger had cobbled together the "harpoon" from drill shafts, explosives, and hope. The grappling shaft had a timed explosive mounted on it and a solid propellant shell around it. When Margot pulled the pin, the propellant would ignite and burn for one minute to drive the harpoon to the comet. At one minute ten seconds the explosive would blow, driving the barbed head deep into the comet's hide. It had taken all of them to unwind and detach the mag sail cable from the drum and then rewind it, as if they were reeling in a gigantic fishing line. The very end of that cable had been welded to the harpoon using every vacuum glue and tape Jean's stranger could lay her hands on. Jean's stranger had spent hours out on the hull, readjusting the tension on the cable drum so the payout would be smooth.

Margot would launch the harpoon into the comet. The cable would pay out. Once the harpoon struck, the friction of the cable unwinding against the barrel would accelerate the *Forty-Niner*, and Margot in the explorer, which was tethered to the *Forty-Niner* by the cables that used to be the shroud lines for the mag sail. The more the cable unwound, the faster the ships would accelerate. Finally, the cable would run out. The comet would shoot forward with its leash trailing behind it, and the *Forty-Niner* and the strangers would fly toward a braking rendezvous with Mars, and a rescue by NASA.

At least, that's what they said would happen. They might be lying. There was no way to tell. But if Margot refused to go along, they'd probably just kill her. She had to play. She had to act like she believed they were who they said they were. It was her only chance.

She tried to tell herself it didn't matter. She tried to believe what she'd told Tom, who they still, miraculously, let live, that it didn't matter who'd come up with the idea, aliens, the strangers, it didn't matter. If Nick and Jean, and Tracy and Ed, and Paul and even Tom finally, were overcome by the strangers, it didn't really matter. What mattered was getting home. If she could get home, she could warn everyone.

But first she had to get home. She, Margot Rusch, had to get home.

"Better get ready, Margot," said Nick's stranger. "It's all on you."

So it is. And you hate that, don't you? I could mess up all your plans and you know it, but you can't get me. Not out here you can't.

Margot squeezed the stick, goosing the engine. Silently, her little frame ship angled to starboard, sliding gingerly closer to the wandering mountain of coal-black ice and stone. Behind her, the three shining silver tethers that attached the explorer to the *Forty-Niner* paid out into the darkness.

She gave the comet's path a wide berth, but not so wide that she couldn't see how it lumbered, turning and shuddering as sparkling jets shot off its pocked hide.

I can do this. How many asteroids did we skirt? They were all falling too... But not like this. She imagined the comet hissing and rumbling as it dashed forward. *They're making me do this. They don't care if I die.*

Black specks dusted her visor. She wiped at them. She glanced behind to see that the tethers were moving smoothly. The comet was almost in front of her. Black ice, black stone, and the sparkling white coma surmounted the darkness.

Suddenly, the rover shuddered and Margot jerked in her straps. A stone careened off the frame ship and shot past her head.

That was a warning shot. That was them... No, no, they can't get me out here, but the comet can. Keep your mind on the comet, Mar-

got. Don't think about them.

The *Forty-Niner* was below and behind her now. The comet was receding. The comet filled the vacuum, shining like snow blowing in the sunlight. Margot pitched the rover up and around, until the comet was flying away from her, but she was not in the thick of its tail.

For a moment, she was nothing but a pilot and she smiled.

Perfect deflection shot. Fire this baby right up its tailpipe.

The strangers had mounted the harpoon on the explorer's fore starboard landing strut and attached the launch pin to the console. Margot fumbled for the thick, metal pin and its trailing wire.

Well, just call me Ishmael, she thought, suppressing a giggle. *There she is, Captain Ahab! There be the great white whale!*

"Margot..." began Nick's stranger.

"Don't push," she snapped. *Don't push. I might decide not to do this. I could. I could not do this. I could leave the strangers out here. Never have to bring them home. Never have to hurt my friends' families by showing them what's happened.*

But I want to go home. Forgive me, Carol. Margot Rusch has to get home.

Margot gritted her teeth. Ice crystals drifted past her. The comet retreated on its lumbering path, inanimate, or at least oblivious of their presence and their need.

Margot pulled the pin on the harpoon.

The recoil vibrated through the frame. The harpoon shot forward, hard, fast and straight. The tether vanished into the thick of the coma, lost in the shining veil of ice.

A jet of ice crystals exploded into the night. The comet rolled away as if wounded. The tethers on their reel played out into the void. Margot bit her lip. The tether was the key. If it released too fast, got tangled, or broke, it was over, all of it.

"Margot! Report!" demanded Nick's stranger.

"Tether holding steady," replied Margot reflexively. "Payout looks good."

You'll get home. To Nick's home. That's what you care about.

The explorer shuddered. A sudden intense cold burned Margot's shin. A red warning light flashed on her visor screen.

No!

A black gash cut across her gleaming yellow suit. The joints at knee and ankle sealed off automatically. Margot fumbled for the roll of sealant tape on her belt. As she did, the explorer began to slide backward, away from the comet, toward the *Forty-Niner* to the limit of the tether. The movement dragged her back against her straps. Her glove gripped the tape reel. Pain bit deep.

Hang on, hang on. Lose the tape and you're gone. You're all gone. The strangers'll have you if you lose the tape.

The tug grew stronger. Margot felt her body shoved backward to the limits of its straps. A weight pressed hard against her ribs, her throat, her heart. After years of zero gee, the acceleration gripped her hard and squeezed until her breath came fast and shallow.

Ahead of her, the *Forty-Niner* began to swing. A slow, sinuous movement that transmitted itself along the tether. It pulled the explorer to starboard, tilting her personal world, confusing her further, adding to the pain that screamed through every nerve.

Slowly, slowly she pulled the roll of tape from her belt. She grasped it in both clumsy, gloved hands. The explorer shimmied. Her body bounced up, then down, hard enough to jar her. The tape slipped. Margot screamed involuntarily and clung to it so hard she felt the flimsy reel crumple.

"Margot?" Jean's stranger. "Margot? What's happening?"

"Don't unstrap!" came back Nick's stranger. "Jean, stay where you are."

Right, right. Why risk anything for me? I'm not a stranger.

She leaned forward as if leaning into a gale wind. Black spots danced in front of her vision. She saw red through the gash, as if her leg glowed with its pain. She jounced and shuddered. More hits. The explorer was taking more hits from cometary debris. She couldn't steady her hands enough to lay down the tape.

Margot bit her lip until she tasted blood. She pressed the tape reel against the black gash, pushed the release button down and pulled, hard. A strip of clean white tape covered the black scoring.

The red light on her suit display turned green and the joints unsealed. Her suit was whole again.

Margot let herself fall backward, gasping for air, gasping for calm against the pain. Her left leg from ankle to knee would be one gigantic blood blister. But she was alive. The stranger hadn't got her yet. She hugged the tape to her chest. The *Forty-Niner* started swinging slowly back to port. Gravity leaned hard against her. Her heart labored, as if trying to pump sideways. Her stomach heaved. Her whole body strained against the straps.

She closed her eyes and tried to reach outward with every nerve, trying to feel the clamps and catches as she could her fingers and toes, wishing she could hear something, anything, a straining, a snapping. There was only silence and the unbearable pressure driving her ribs into her lungs.

"*Forty-Niner* to Explorer One." Nick's stranger. What did he want? To find out if her stranger had swallowed her yet?

Not yet, Sir. Not yet.

"Margot? Margot, it looks like you're venting something. Report."

Venting? Margot's gaze jerked down to the monitor between her flight sticks. Red lights flashed. She didn't need to read the message. The diagram showed everything. The methane tank had been hit and all her fuel was streaming out into the void, leaving nothing at all for her to use to guide the explorer back to *Forty-Niner*.

She was stuck. She would hang out here until her air ran out. She was dead all over again.

All at once, the vibrations ceased. She was flying smooth and free, gliding like a bird on a sea wind with only the most gentle roll to perturb her flight.

"We have tether release!" cried Jean's stranger.

Margot looked up. A silver line lashed through the clean, sparkling white of the comet.

Tether release. They'd done it. It had worked. The strangers were all on their way home. She looked again at her own fountain of crystals streaming out behind her, a comet's tail in miniature.

That roll'll get worse. They'll have to correct for it. They'll have to fire the rockets and catch me in the blast and tell Jordon and mission control how sorry they were.

Nick's stranger spoke to her again. "Margot, we gotta get you in here. If your fuel's gone, can you haul on the tether? Margot?"

"She's not receiving, Nick. The headset must be out. I gotta get down there."

All gone. Nothing to do. Pain throbbed in her head, crowding out her thoughts.

"Margot, pull!"

She couldn't move. Pain, bright and sharp, burned through her. All she could do was watch the crystal stream of her fuel drift away into the vacuum.

Margot Rusch is dead.

"Margot! Answer me! Pull, Margot!"

She's been dead for weeks.

"Come on, Margot. I got a green on your headset. Now answer me, damnit!"

The stranger wins. She got Margot Rusch after all.

"She didn't even get a chance to say good-by to Jordan. That's the bad part," she murmured.

"Margot?" came back the voice of Nick's stranger. "Margot, this is Nick. We're receiving you. Acknowledge."

Why are they still calling her Margot? They must know the stranger had her by now. She would have liked to know the stranger's name. Maybe she wouldn't mind burning to ash when they fire the correc-

tion burst. Margot Rusch certainly wouldn't mind. Margot Rusch was dead.

The explorer jerked. Mildly curious, Margot looked toward the *Forty-Niner*. A figure in a bright yellow hard-suit leaned out the ship's airlock. Its hands hauled on the tethers, as if they were hauling on curtain cords. The *Forty-Niner* drew minutely closer and the pair of ships began to spin ever so gently around their common center. Margot felt herself leaning against the straps.

"Margot Rusch!" Nick's voice. Nick's stranger? A quick burst fired from the *Forty-Niner*'s port nozzle. The spin slowed.

"Margot Rusch, wake up, you stupid fly-jock, and pull!" Jean now. Jean's stranger? Jean's stranger trying to save Margot Rusch's stranger?

Jean trying to save her? But she was dead, as dead as Ed and Paul and Tracy and Tom.

No, not Tom. Tom's still alive.

What if I'm still alive?

Cold and pain inched up her leg and emptied into her knee, her thigh. Her head spun. Readings flashed in the corner of her helmet. The suit had sealed itself. Blood pressure was elevated, respiration fast, shallow, pulse elevated. Recommend termination of EVA.

"Margot Rusch, help Jean get your butt back in here!" shouted Nick.

Margot leaned as far forward as the straps would let her. Her gloved fingers grappled with the tether and snared some of the slack. Margot pulled. The *Forty-Niner* came a little closer. The suited figure became a little clearer.

"I knew you were still with us!" cried Jean, jubilantly. "Come on, Margot. Pull!"

Margot pulled. Her arms strained, her joints ached. Her suit flashed red warnings. The *Forty-Niner* moved closer. The spin tried to start, but another burst from the engines stalled it out again. Margot's breath grew harsh and echoing in the confining helmet. Her lungs burned. The cold pain reached her hip and started a new path down her fingers. The *Forty-Niner* filled her world now, its white skin, its instrumentation, its black stenciled letters and registry numbers.

And Jean. She could see Jean now, hauling on the tether as if it was her life that depended on it. She could even see her eyes. Her eyes and herself, her soul, looking out through them. Margot knew if she looked at Nick she would see him too. Not strangers, not anymore. Maybe not ever.

They had done what they had done. Maybe Nick had faked that message, maybe they'd had help from unknown friends. They'd sort it all out when they got home. What mattered now was that they would get home, all of them, as they were. Not strangers, just themselves.

Margot grabbed up another length of tether and pulled.

Like Starlight

Alma Alexander

Four of them came to take a world.

Bel was the oldest, although none of them were old—one did not often get the grace of a long life in the ranks of the Resistance. Bel's hair was salt-and-pepper, and his moustache, which he allowed to grow luxuriant over his upper lip, was almost entirely white—but he was no older than maybe thirty-eight, forty. He wasn't their leader, though. That was Dalaina, twenty-one and afire with the passion of her convictions.

She was the one who had volunteered for the mission. The rest of them were there more or less because of her. Bel because he would always be where Dalaina was. Albard because of his technical expertise. And Simme…Simme because he loved Dalaina with all the unrequited passion of the younger and the subordinate for the older, the more accomplished, the beautiful, the flawless. Maybe Dalaina had flaws, in truth—but one would not go to Simme to learn what they were.

Simme was seventeen, his lower lip still full and sometimes petulant like a small boy's. He was afraid, so afraid, that he was at best a hanger-on, at worst a liability for this particular mission. The lower lip sometimes trembled with that fear, but he said nothing of it to anybody, wearing the shreds of pride like a royal cloak and trying not to think about how much its tatters revealed.

Dalaina had more or less crashed the shuttle on the surface of the barren fourth planet of the Syrroi system; there had been something final and defiant in the gesture, a claiming, an announcement that this was, for better or worse, her world now. Whatever came.

They had been expected, of course. The shuttle was scarred already with ion cannon fire from the intercept ships waiting for them just as they had come out of the jump point near Syrroi IV. But Dalaina was a good enough pilot to have guided the craft down to a near perfect landing if she had chosen. Simme was uncomfortably aware of what she had not chosen.

She had, in fact, seemed to go out of her way to draw the attention of the intercept ships to her small craft. It was as though she wanted to announce her coming—which, of course, was ridiculous.

Unless they already knew.

Unless there was a whole story unfolding here of which Simme knew but a fragment of a sentence, a piece of paragraph.

He wondered, several times, what it was that he was giving his life up for. He found himself resenting, for just the briefest of moments, Dalaina the perfect, because of the knowledge she held and must have hoarded, because of the ignorance he was being held in. But then he would remember who she was, what his heart had made her. And it didn't matter, after all.

It was the Resistance who had found the planet, perfect, isolated, abandoned, barren, nobody's until it was claimed by the discoverers. But the Allanton Republic operated under the premise that everything belonged to it, and that included a barren planet—which they claimed only because someone else wanted it.

Not that they meant to do anything with it, or put it to any useful purpose themselves. The entire system was largely inimical to human life; it boasted twelve planets, no fewer than five of them alien and noxious gas giants, three of them shriveled cinders in tight orbits too close to the sun, one a poisoned planet with a sulfurous atmosphere and a pressure that would bend a human back with the burden of carrying the yellow air. That left one, Syrroi IV—there was nothing on it, really, except a barren reddish desert under a thin atmosphere churned by an endless keening wind.

Terraforming any of these places would have been difficult, time-consuming and prohibitively expensive, which was why the system had been left so severely alone for so long. But the Republic had got wind that the Resistance was going to make landfall anyway. It might have been easier to let them do so, and then destroy the base they established—but it was less wasteful of resources, all around, if they were simply not allowed near the place at all. In any event, the Republic was being kind, even to its rebels. If they, the all-powerful and wealthy Republic, did not have the resources to make the planet habitable, where would the Resistance find any?

But before Syrroi, there had been another landfall, one that the Republic did not know about, one that even Simme was left largely in ignorance of. All he knew, all anyone in the rank-and-file knew, was that there had been a world. Somewhere. And on it there had been Something. Something which had smiled on the Resistance explorers.

Syrroi was suddenly a prize.

That was why Dalaina was here. Why *all* of them were here. She was carrying something, something that would make Syrroi IV into Home.

Simme was the grunt with the gun on this mission. He knew no real details. Albard had been brought along because there were technical things that needed to be done. Dalaina was the leader. Bel was her shadow. She knew, and she had crashed the shuttle.

Whatever it was she had brought here, it had better be something good because none of them were going back.

She and Albard had disappeared shortly after they had loped away from the wreck of the shuttle, gasping in the thin air, and had returned hours later, dusty, pale, exhausted. In the meantime, Bel the silent and young Simme had been left to dodge the occasional fire from some orbiting nemesis which had pinpointed their crash site and was trying to finish the job. It had been Bel who had found shelter, ducking into a crack between boulders and discovering the cave beyond. The others would come to them there, following the signal from the device that Bel carried—but Simme still could not help lingering at the lip of the cave, his shoulders tight with anxiety, waiting for a glimpse of them, the certainty that they were all right.

He was appalled that he completely missed them, with Dalaina almost surprising him into shooting instinctively when she loomed up beside him from behind the boulder concealing the cave entrance. Bel met her eyes with a questioning glance under a raised eyebrow, as she ducked inside; in response, she had just nodded. Albard, following her into the cave, had merely looked around to find a place to curl up and go to sleep. Dalaina herself withdrew, with only a small smile and a half-whispered word of greeting to Simme. Alone with Bel, again, Simme finally roused from his patient silence.

"What was it they did? What do they have, Bel?" he asked, resigned from the outset to his questions being mere pebbles dropped into the pool of silence.

"The Watchers gave us something," Bel said immediately, much to Simme's surprise. "They went to install it."

"Install it where? What does it do?"

"If I knew the answer to either of those questions I would tell you. I don't. All I know is, it's a way to live out here. Some sort of technology to give us *our* air, *our* pressure. The world we are used to. Home."

A barrage of fire exploded not too far away from the cave mouth. Simme ducked as rocks the size of his head tumbled just outside the cave entrance. The land shook. "Whatever they placed…it isn't going to live long enough, not if they keep this up. Nor are we."

"I am told it fends for itself," Bel said. "There is protection."

"But…only one?" Simme said, in desperation. "And how would anyone get here to live with this thing? While…while *they* are out there with their guns? If they had never learned that we were here…if we could plant a dozen of these things, a hundred…maybe we'd have a world for us to live on, plan on…but just one…?"

"But who said it was just one?" A soft voice spoke from behind them. Dalaina stood in a cavern archway, shaking dust and debris from her hair.

"We brought only one, didn't we?"

"Yes," Dalaina said, "but there were others."

"Others?"

"Others. While the Republic chased us, knowing what I brought…or what they think I brought…there were others. There are those dozens you wanted, Simme. They are all over the surface of this world. They are everywhere. And the Republic does not know they are there."

Simme gaped. "So you never *had* one?"

"Oh, I did—but it was never meant to survive, this one of all of them. All of the machines that will bring this world to life. This was the decoy that will let the others live. In a while we will try and make for one of them, while they pound this place back to the dust it had always been."

Simme stared at the sky, brooding with the eyes of his enemies, then back at the serene faces of his friends.

"We were the price, weren't we?"

"Yes." Dalaina cupped her hand around his cheek for a moment, a gentle caress. "We are the will o'the wisp in the darkness leading the hunter deeper into the swamp. But beyond the swamp…we'll be free to go to the stars from this place, Simme. This is the place where we stand."

We're going to die, Simme thought, and it was quite a dispassionate thought, without an ounce of fear or pathos in it. That was just the way it was.

"We'll leave at full dark," Dalaina said. "In the meantime, we can only wait."

"Coffee?" asked Bel, practically, breaking into Simme's thoughts.

"Thank you," said Dalaina.

Simme just nodded, moving quietly to the cavern entrance and peering outside where it was starting to get dark—a sort of quick, violet, alien twilight had wrapped itself around everything and the edge of true night was already visible on the horizon.

It was real coffee—how, he didn't know, but Bel had all kinds of hidden talents, it seemed—but it was real coffee, and Bel brought it to him where he stood staring into the darkening sky. He held two cups, passing one to Simme, cradling the other in his own large hands, stirring the contents of his own with a thin metal rod. The motion had the odd quality of spell-casting, the steady, constant clockwise motion making a tiny whirlpool in the cup. Something bright shimmered in the dark liquid every now and then, at the edges of Simme's vision, like starlight against black space.

"What are you cooking up there, Bel?" Simme asked.

Bel stood there for a moment in enigmatic silence.

"The future," he replied at length, slowly, stirring the stars.

Pixie Crystals

Irene Radford writing as C.F. Bentley

In the annals of the Confederated Star Systems, the following events never happened and will not be acknowledged by any participants.

"Pixies. You think pixies have invaded the *First Contact Café.*" Admiral Pamela Marella, spymaster for the Confederated Star Systems, buried her face into her palms, elbows propped on her desk. "You've had some crazy ideas in your life, Jake Devlin, especially since you took up with Sissy, High Priestess of Harmony, and found *religion.*"

"Actually, Pammy, the high priestess in question refuses to acknowledge this new alien life form as real." General Jake Devlin lounged against the door jamb of her secret office, the one no one, not even Jake, was supposed to know about. His responsibilities as commander of this space station might weigh heavily on his shoulders, but he still cut a roguishly dashing figure, tall and lanky, with impressive abs and shoulders. He'd been her best spy once. Then he met that pesky high priestess and became useless to covert intelligence.

"So why are you telling *me* that pixies have invaded wing 25C?" She looked up, hoping he was simply playing a practical joke. The acolytes to the high priestess, that Jake treated as if they were his daughters, were notorious for such things.

"Because, dear Pammy, as spymaster it is your job to observe and record before first contact of new alien species."

Jake was the only person alive who got away with calling her "Pammy." Well, maybe Sissy and her acolytes might.

But no one else. No One!

"Okay, I'll play along. Show me the recordings." Pamela leaned back in her chair and prepared for the worst.

Jake touched a button on his wrist link and aimed it at the multiple screens built in to Pamela's desktop.

Suddenly the entire desk exploded in a mass of random pixels, then zoomed out until the individual bits of color resolved into a face. A cerulean blue face with hot, harem-pink hair. Pointed chin, ears, and up-tilted eyes stared back at her. The classic image of a pixie from one of her childhood storybooks.

She blinked and shook her head to clear it of one of her earliest memories. Long ago memories when magic was possible and reality was of her own making. Now she believed only what she could document. This recording appeared to be documentation.

"Maybe we should just give this place to the Dragons of D'Or who think they hold a nonexistent mortgage and therefore own the place, and let them handle all the mysticism and fairytales that are taking over," she muttered, not caring if Jake heard her or not.

When she looked back, the blue face had moved away from examining the security monitors to flit back to the center of the room on impossibly flimsy, neon green wings. It wore absolutely nothing, no clothes at all, not even a loin cloth to cover its—*his*—privates. "Did he take fashion lessons from the Dragons of D'Or?" she asked, not knowing what else to say. They'd only recently banished the banker dragons from the space station. Those large, obnoxious lizards took pride in parading in the altogether showing off battle/mating scars as points of honor.

"Yeah, I noticed the lack of clothing. Almost enough to make a mere mortal like me jealous. But that's not important. Zoom out again so you can see the entire area around the lift shaft." Jake touched another place on his link. The images shrank and the view expanded.

Six upright, pointed structures placed in a circle around the lift sprang into view.

"What are they made of?" Pamela leaned closer, tapping the icon to enlarge a specific area.

"Junk," Jake said.

"I can see that. Bits and pieces of construction material, and crystal shards, and even some leaves from the orange tree in the hydroponics garden. What are they doing?" She half stood and craned her neck to see if an upside down perspective made more sense.

A thrill of shock rippled down her spine. "Jake, is this…is this…?"

"Yeah, they stole the black Badger Metal crystal stars right off my uniform collar. The most expensive things I own. And the first gift Sissy gave me."

"Not to mention that when Badger Metal is added to a crystal matrix it augments communication waves exponentially through hyperspace. We can talk to each other almost instantaneously across light years," she gasped in awe. She'd lusted over those stars—Sissy had taken them right off her ceremonial beaded veil—for years. Pamela could do so much more in organizing her field operatives with those stars, or even shards from them.

Then a new thought pierced her awestruck brain. "Jake, are they building communications towers?"

"Could be. Could be." His face remained professionally blank, which meant she'd surprised him with that idea. "Wanna go look in person?" He aimed for the door, automatically checking the pockets within pockets within pockets of his everyday black uniform. He always had at least three perpetually sharp Badger Metal blades on him somewhere.

She mimicked him, adding various projectile, energy, and throwing weapons to empty places in her own "Civilian" professionally casual jacket and trousers she'd made into her own uniform without being a uniform. That's what spymasters did.

Her wing looked abandoned on any station sensor but actually bustled with activity. She checked the sensor so that they showed the lift stopped, the continuously rotating platforms idle and gathering dust. Then silently she and Jake stepped onto the next moving platform and traveled upward to the zero G station hub. Their route took them across three tram stops to the 25C wing. A quick review of the station map showed this wing and the two adjacent ones, 25A and 25B, were empty, but warming and filled with atmosphere. No airlock above the blast doors so the incoming aliens breathed something non-toxic. The place was ready for the arrival of a diplomatic mission from…from…

"Am I reading this right, Jake?" she asked, slapping her forehead in dismay.

"Diplomatic mission consisting of three ambassadors, each with three mates, and three assistants, from Ælbion. Please tell me that isn't pronounced Elven."

"Have they arrived?"

"No. Their ship hasn't even broken hyperspace, and shouldn't until day after tomorrow."

"This is taking on all the symptoms of a cosmic joke," Pamela grumbled.

"Yeah, I know." Jake looked ecstatic rather than dismayed. "Isn't it great?"

Pamela stepped onto the next rotating platform headed down into the dark depths of the wing. Jake followed, squeezing into the confined space of the lift beside her.

"Do you suppose these critters are ancient refugees from

Earth?" he whispered.

"No." But those pictures in her storybooks…

"I've got one of the improved universal translators. I wonder if the memory will play back an ancient Earth language, like Anglo-Saxon or some such."

"You are getting too caught up in this, Jake. Think like the trained military tactician and pilot you are, not the mystic consort of a high priestess."

"Part of being a mystic consort to Sissy is awakening a sense of wonder in life. All life, even alien life. Finding that joy again is very important. You should try it sometime, Pammy."

Light leaked upward in the lift shaft.

"This wing is supposed to be dark," Jake whispered, reaching for a mini blaster holstered on his belt above his right hip.

Pamela toyed with her own version in the patch pocket of her suit jacket.

Down through the first two levels of light gravity they rode the lift, the light growing ever brighter. Pamela's eyes adjusted as they descended. She broadened her stance, ready to leap or run the moment they reached LG4, the first level with heavy enough gravity that humans couldn't fly. The docking bay for this wing lay below LG5 as a transition to MG, medium gravity.

Jake stepped off the platform and moved forward two steps, giving Pamela room to follow. The lift continued its perpetual rotation down into the docking bay before returning upward to the hub. To catch the upward lift they would have to walk around to the other side of the mechanism. Or take the spiral stairs that wound around the shaft.

Something buzzed Pamela's hair. She swatted at it as she would an errant mosquito if she were dirtside. "Did you import insects for the hydroponics garden?" she whispered to Jake.

He ducked another buzzing thing before replying. "Yes. And the pixies were in the garden if they found orange leaves. Probably didn't close the screens when they left."

Another buzz circled Pamela's head three times. She stood very, very still, as she'd been taught as a child at summer camp to avoid bee stings.

The *thing* paused and hovered in front of her nose. Her eyes crossed trying to focus on it. "Should have brought my reading glasses," she growled. Jake was the only one who knew she needed help reading, not enough to take three days off work for corrective surgery.

The buzz took up a different cadence.

"Stay still, Pammy. I think it's talking." Jake held the palm-sized translation gadget level with the blurry, flapping pixie.

Loud squawking static blasted from the translation unit.

Pamela flinched at the irritating noise.

Jake dialed back the volume.

Still static. No words.

"We are trying to understand you." He spoke slowly and distinctly into the device. "Please speak more words so that this machine can learn from you."

More static. It came out in an angry and emphatic tone.

Pamela had a sudden urge to flee. Pressure built up in her chest and her feet itched to run.

"Maybe we should go and come back with a telepath?" she suggested, inching backward and around the lift to the upward-moving platforms.

"Not without my stars," Jake said. He looked around frantically until his gaze caught the distinctive black gleam of Badger Metal crystals in the tallest pile of junk behind and to his right. He backed toward it.

Inch by inch he edged away from Pamela and the pixie—for lack of a better word. The alien ignored him. As long as he kept his movement slow and fluid, he seemed a natural part of the landscape, a broad open space that should have been a neutral grey with portable partitions stacked on the deck awaiting assignment to separate the lobby of the lift area from rooms. The incoming aliens could arrange those partitions to their needs.

Then it hit Pamela. The pixies had painted the walls with tiny streaks of green. It reminded her of paintings she'd seen of open meadows with pinpricks of color that might be wildflowers.

Then Jake shifted the universal translator, which wasn't so universal after all, to his left hand and reached with his right.

Ten pixies materialized in front of him, swooping in from all directions so rapidly, Pamela barely noticed their movement.

Jake, idiot that he was lately, kept moving his hand until he grasped one of two elusive black stars between two fingers.

A scarlet, emerald, and purple pixie dove for that hand.

"Ouch! Oh, ow, ow, ow, ow." He jerked his hand away and started sucking on the back, near the thumb joint. "The damn beast bit me." But he clutched the star between two fingers.

The pressure in Pamela's chest increased along with the itch in her feet. An incredible sense of violation overwhelmed her.

MINE!

"We have to leave now, Jake. We'll come back with a telepath," she said as calmly as she could. "An empath would be better."

Pamela paced Jake's office while he moved icons around on his desktop with his left hand. As a pilot he'd had to become ambidextrous to manipulate the controls. His right hand was currently occupied by his wife. Short, wispy, and mousy (sometimes), she did what she did best, take care of Jake. Within seconds of Jake sitting at his desk, she appeared with disinfectant, antibiotic patches, and bandages.

"What do you mean there are no available telepaths? Last I looked, we had twenty-four registered on board," Jake yelled at the database on his center screen.

"You sent them all back to Earth," Sissy reminded him. "Except for three who are still trying to decipher the Maril language."

"I'll take those. Similar situation: initiate communication with a totally alien race," Pamela replied.

"No. My daughter is part of that team. I will not expose her to those rabid pixies." Jake thumped his desk with a clenched fist. Icons bounced, rearranged themselves and settled into a new order.

"Oh! Pammy, you've got to see this." He pointed to a screen showing the pixies in 25C.

Sissy leaned over Jake from behind, hand resting lightly on his shoulder.

Disgusting. Any time they were together, they touched, as if reattaching their other half.

Pamela looked at the screen anyway. The pixies were there, all right. And seemed to have multiplied in the ten minutes since she and Jake had left them. And the junk towers! They'd added a cross bar connecting two of them at the top. Another arced plank lay on the deck between two others. The top pieces seemed to have been woven together with bits of ripped bright red and sparkling cloth from…from her favorite formal diplomatic evening gown. The one that was lined with fine titanium mesh for added protection from projectiles and blades. It also had pockets secreted among the flowing drapery for weapons of her own.

"There's your other Badger Metal star, Jake." Pamela pointed to a bit of black glitter that scintillated differently from her red sequins.

"Look there, they are embedding the Badger Metal in the exact center of the lintel. The other one was in the center of an upright 180 degrees from it." Jake pulled up a calculator and began sliding numbers around in arcane patterns.

"I'll go get Martha," Sissy said as she squeezed his shoulder before departing.

Jake broke his deep concentration long enough to tilt his head far enough to kiss her fingers before she withdrew.

"Pammy, get me the coordinates of 25C LG4."

"How precise?" She opened a new screen on his desk and began searching maps and tactical displays.

"To the millimeter of the center of that circle of junk towers," he murmured distractedly.

"I need my own computer."

"Don't care where you get the numbers, just send them to me within the next thirty seconds."

Pamela hunched over the screen and typed an encrypted command that linked her desk to this one. Easy. She did it all the time, usually from her desk so she could monitor what he was up to.

"I changed my encryption this morning. You won't find anything interesting with that string of numbers," he said, as if asking for cream and two sugars in his coffee. He took it black.

She fed the system another string of numbers and the tactical display she wanted popped into view.

"Wow, I can't get resolution that good and I run this place." Jake whistled as he scanned her display. His right hand added the coordinates he wanted while admiring the rest of the view.

"You only think you run this place," Pamela replied. She watched as he triangulated the coordinates for the center of the pixie towers, then projected outward.

The computer churned and processed, throwing long strings of alphanumeric codes onto the screen at random intervals. Pamela recognized *some* of them.

"Is the trajectory headed for Earth?" She frantically enlarged graphs and star maps on her own section of the desktop.

"Looks like," Jake said on a long exhale. "From this distance I can't get any closer than northern hemisphere."

"Maybe I can narrow it." Pamela called up her own secret (supposedly) com towers in Europe, North America, and Siberia. Then she layered satellite views and maps over their displays. "Europe," she muttered. "Northwest Europe."

"England." Jake refined her data. A long pause.

"Is that Stonehenge?" Pamela pointed at the ancient monument, preserved inside a stasis field, and off limits to all but the most privileged of researchers. Thousands of years of research and archeologists, spiritualists, and conspiracy theorists still did not know its full purpose or how it was built.

"Yeah, that's the mother of all standing stone monuments, though there's an older one in a different configuration in Turkey," Jake replied. "And I've seen similar structures on a dozen different planets, but never in a space station."

The hatch to the outer office irised open to admit Sissy and fourteen-year-old Martha, the telepath Jake had adopted last year.

"You coming, Pammy? Or are you going to monitor this from the safety of your own office?" Jake asked as he moved to join the two newcomers.

"I'm coming. You couldn't keep me away." She had trouble reconciling the beneficent and friendly pixies in her storybooks with the angry, malevolent, thieving pests in 25C. Her favorite dress might be ruined. But she'd be damned if she left it with the monsters.

Jake rubbed at the bite wound on his hand as if he agreed with her. He still had an incredibly valuable and emotionally significant star-shaped Badger Metal crystal to retrieve.

They explained the situation to Martha while they traversed the station to the infested wing. She nodded and smiled until Jake came to the part about the bite.

"Let me see the holos," Martha said, slipping her arm through Jake's. Their close relationship still amazed Pamela. One would almost think he was her biological father and not just an adopted one. "Pammy?" she asked, using Jake's insolent nickname, "what did you feel when you tried to get close to the towers?"

"What does that matter?" Pamela stilled, unwilling to expose this invasion of her privacy.

"That scary?" Martha asked impudently.

Damn, her telepathic powers heightened and honed every time Pamela encountered the girl. A single telepath within the ranks of her spies would be *the* most useful tool and a powerful weapon. Power-lust invaded her so fiercely she almost couldn't see where she set her feet. Dangerous! They approached the constantly moving platforms of the lift. A tumble here could leave her broken and bleeding. Useless.

But this girl had ethics about invading other people's minds. Pamela's thoughts about the chest pressure and urge to flee must have been very close to the surface. Martha would probe no deeper without permission or dire emergency.

Did this invasion of pixies classify as an emergency?

Jake pressed his wound tightly, as if to contain pain.

The lift descended into 25C more rapidly than Pamela wanted. Her mind told her that the mechanism moved at the same speed as ever, but her guts wanted to linger, and delay.

"Incoming!" Jake ducked and rolled off the lift.

A half second later Pamela heard the buzz and felt the brush of feather-light wings against her cheek. In her peripheral vision she caught an impression of bared teeth in the middle of a puke-green face.

Pressure built inside her chest with twice the intensity as her previous trip here. As she mimicked Jake in avoiding a fierce bite, she noted the holographic number displayed on the walls of the lift LG3, a full level above the towers under construction.

"Sissy!" Jake screamed as his wife and daughter disappeared downward in the relentless rotation of the lift. He jumped to his feet and grabbed the railing of the spiral staircase in one fluid motion. Without a pause he perched on that railing and let gravity propel him downward almost as quickly as the lift.

Pamela followed him. She knew that if she walked down the steps she'd have time to give in to the compulsion to flee.

She slid around the last curve before the spiral and the lift terminated at blast doors, separating this portion from higher gravity, in time to watch Sissy and Martha step off the lift, pictures of feminine calm. Jake leaped free and flung himself between his family and the towers—which appeared to have grown in the short time since she'd watched them from Jake's office. Her gaze flicked to the glint of black Badger Metal crystal embedded in one tower, then shifted to the red sequins woven throughout all six towers. Added to those features, she saw six helmet lights beloved by maintenance workers the galaxy wide. The pests liked their bling.

Martha stopped two steps away from the lift and held up both hands, palm out, level with her ears.

The pixies held their positions, wings working to keep them in place. One by one, two dozen of them at least dropped to the deck in a close circle around the telepathic girl.

Jake and Sissy froze in place. Pamela did too, though the pressure on her lungs and the itch in her feet really wanted her to turn around and leave the other three to handle the situation.

"Dad, can you try the translator again? I'm getting lots of sharp syllables and very few images," Martha said.

Slowly, Jake drew out the palm-sized device and thumbed up the volume.

Static gave way to harsh, throat-gargling consonants.

"I understand some German," Pamela admitted. "That sounds close. But I can't find any one word there that I recognize."

A second later, the translator repeated her words in the same throat-ripping gargle.

"That's progress, of sorts," Pamela said.

The pixies rose in a flurry of wings, weaving rapidly among themselves in a pattern too complex for Pamela to discern. Only there was a pattern.

"Martha, can you project a nice peaceful image to calm them down?" Sissy whispered.

"Like what?" The girl sounded frustrated.

"Flowers. You like roses," Jake urged her.

Pamela had set up monitors near the circle of rose bushes in the hydroponics garden. Martha spent a lot of time there "meditating." Whatever that meant.

The translator erupted with noise. Martha backed up, hiding her head beneath her crossed arms. "Roses, evil. Bad, bad, bad," she said, sounding more than a little panicky. Then she followed up with a series of explosive sneezes.

"I think the pixies are allergic to roses," Pamela said, finally finding the courage to step down from the last stair and onto the deck. Her left hand fingered a mini blaster in her jacket pocket.

Sissy put her arms around Martha and pulled her face into her shoulder.

"Well, that didn't work," Jake agreed, moving to wrap both his wife and daughter in a protective hug.

"Wait," Martha said, looking up and around. "Who is supposed to move into this wing?"

"A new race we haven't met before, the Ælbion," Jake said.

Pamela tried to follow the agitated pixies' flight path. It looked…it looked like classic piloting evasive maneuvers, the kind taught at the academy. Everyone knew those tactics and predicted them with accuracy. She taught her operatives to use their imaginations and not be so predictable. Now. Jake had taught her the value of that strategy.

"A-ee-l-bee-n?" Martha tried the name phonetically.

The pixies didn't vary their pattern at all.

"Martha, try El-ven," Pamela suggested.

She'd barely finished the last sound when the pixies exploded with a loud chatter that made her throat ache just thinking about replicating the words.

The pixies began circling each tower in a giant spiral. Her ears popped with changing air pressure. The remaining cross lintels levitated into place without anyone touching them. Something about the flight path and flapping wings must create an energy field.

Then the pressure in her chest doubled. She had to drop to her knees to keep breathing. Why weren't the others affected? Wait, Jake panted shallowly. Sissy and Martha, however, were so focused on understanding the pixies, if they felt the same chest pressure, they ignored it.

"Wh…what are they doing?" Pamela gasped.

"It's not like that at all!" Martha shouted as she stamped her foot and placed tightly clenched fists on her adolescently slim hips.

"What is like that?" Pamela ground out.

"You're just selfish bullies with no manners," Martha continued her tirade.

Then she had to duck and cover, dragging Sissy down with her.

"We've got to get out of here, fast," Sissy said. "They don't like us at all." She dragged Martha toward the lift.

Martha turned back at the last second and shouted at the pixies in their own language. Pamela didn't need to know the words to recognize insults.

The pixies knew it too and…and blew raspberries at their retreating backs from safety behind the towers.

They made it back to Jake's office in record time. He'd left the monitors recording.

Pamela planted herself in his chair and flipped icons around to suit her own work routine. Jake spent his attention on comforting Sissy and Martha. He did it well. Fine. That left the desk and computing power to Pamela.

"Um…Jake, you need to see this." She had to rest her head against the back of the chair.

When she dared open her eyes, she found Jake hunched over the desk, propped on his elbows, hands flat against the reflective surface. "That can't be! We have to figure out how they are doing this!"

"Their message is beaming back to their planet of origin and using the home beacon to bounce their signal out into the galaxy to all of their colonies," Martha said. She sounded exhausted. Sissy guided her to one of the guest chairs. The gel pads shifted to conform to her slight body.

"What are they saying?" Pamela asked as she tracked the energy pulses emanating from wing 25C of the *First Contact Café*. The message moved with the speed of a Badger Metal-enhanced ansible. Near instantaneous across thousands of light years. If she had access to that kind of communications network, she could run the entire Confederated Star Systems from her desk.

The searing white light paused when it reached the ancient monument known to humans as Stonehenge. Some of the original stones had fallen, others broken and repurposed into building material. Still the energy circled, around and around much as the pixies had circled their miniature replica. Ten circles, she counted them without blinking, they moved too quickly to take the chance of missing something.

"This is too much," Jake said. One of his fingers traced the images on the desktop. The solid beam of light and energy separated into a dozen strands and began weaving a complex pattern around and around the monument. "That's the same flight pattern we watched the pixies fly."

"You noticed," Pamela said, trying to mask her awe with dry humor.

"Yeah, I noticed. I wonder if the pixies learned it from the academy or if our military learned it from the pixies?"

"Don't wonder, just watch," Pamela ordered.

"No safe haven," Martha murmured.

Pamela didn't dare look toward the girl. The strands of energy had woven their fabric of communication and separated once more, each shooting out into space in a different direction.

"Where's it going?" Jake asked.

"You said you'd seen similar monuments on a dozen different planets?"

Jake nodded, his eyes crossed as he thought through the implications. "Twelve strands of energy, each in a different direction. I bet if we plotted the trajectory they'd end at those monuments.

"No safe haven," Martha repeated. "Humans infest space. Humans bring killer roses. Elves making peace with them. No safe haven. Get out now!"

The memory of cherished picture books from an innocent childhood crumbled in Pamela's mind.

TECHNOLOGY

The Genius Prize

Marie Brennan

There are abundant records of the Twentieth Annual Metzger-Patel Genius Prize championship in 2131. Everything from the entry forms for each Contestant Team, to the judges' notes on each creation, to the home videos filmed by proud parents, to the helicopter footage of the aftermath.

Finding out what happened isn't the hard part.

Believing it is.

After the conclusion of the nineteenth championship, Immis Chae interviewed Anjale Metzger for *Globeline.* Metzger and Tahira Patel usually retired out of the public eye after the competition was over, but Patel had given a similar interview after the ninth year, and this time it was Metzger's turn.

"It's become a cliché," the interviewer says in the recording, smiling under the broadcast lights, "but the entries this year really were bigger and better than ever—with an emphasis on bigger. What are you going to do for the twentieth anniversary of the

Genius Prize? How are you going to make it stand out, when escalation has become the expected norm for your competition?"

Metzger is less fond of the camera than her wife, but she looks crisp and collected in her tailored silk suit, the grey threading through the black of her mathematically precise cornrows almost more decorative than a sign of age. She does not smile. "Well, Immis, in part, that is up to our contestants. It's their creations that the world tunes in to see, and so if those are more impressive every year, that's because these young people keep on coming up with new and more astonishing innovations. But yes, Tahira and I have plans for the twentieth anniversary, just like we did for the tenth. This time we'd like to look back at the history of the prize and honor those who have come before—and that's all I can say for now."

Chae faces the nearest floating camera, and their smile grows wider. "You heard it here, folks: next year you won't just see *one* Genius Prize, but twenty years' worth. I'm sure it will be spectacular."

THE CAMERA IMAGE FROM THE warehouse in Bamako rocks unsteadily as a parran-alloy arm slams into the wall. "Careful!" Akua Fonghoro shouts, as if her teammate Kisi Abouta is deliberately being careless.

Their mecha staggers drunkenly. "I'm trying!" Kisi shouts back, even though the microphone inside the suit picks up every whisper with perfect clarity. "It's just—this thing—won't—"

The days of simple humanoid shapes are long gone. Everyone knows that Dr. Metzger and her judges score the entries on more than just size, power, agility. Anybody can slap together a mechanical suit, piston-driven arms and legs and a thundering engine to make it go; without style, you're no better than the average middle-class tinkerer in their garage.

The device lurching with a stiff-legged gait toward the cinderblock wall has the head and beak of a skeletal pterosaur, and wings that are extending and retracting in a stuttering rhythm. They aren't used to fly like a bird; no amount of flapping up and down could lift the mass of machinery beneath them, even with modern lightweight alloys. That's what the spinjets are for.

"Breathe," Ye Tangara says from a prudent distance, as one of the spinjets fires briefly, incinerating a stack of fiber rods. "Like you practiced."

Panting comes over the loudspeakers. Kisi manages to turn aside before she runs headfirst into the wall. "Okay. I think I'm getting the hang—"

The left wing shoots out full-force and slams against the cinderblocks. Kisi's curse is lost within the grinding screech of the collision.

Almost out of frame, she stops the mecha and levers back the top of the pterosaur's skull, exposing her face, which leaks sweat like a crushed sponge. "I swear, I'm going to just rip that thing out of here. We did fine without it before. Why do we need it now?"

"Because," Akua says, as Ye brings Kisi water and mops off her face. "What we've got was good enough to win the Songhali Nationals, but not the Genius Prize. *Everybody* there is going to have a Truong sympathy net. Without one, you won't be able to keep up."

"And with one, I'll fall on my face and be the laughingstock of the world." But Kisi nods away the last of the water and claps her mecha shut again. The machine hums as the sympathy net activates, and the wings rattle shut, unevenly. The loudspeakers pick up her voice again, restored to its usual focus and cool. Nobody lacking in those qualities makes it to the three rounds of the Genius Prize, much less through them.

"I have two months," Kisi says as she stumbles out of the camera's view. "I'll get this."

"GOD, THAT STUFF STINKS."

For all that the robotics teams mock the bioengineers as being "squishy" and not knowing which end of a computer is up, the truth is that the bios know their way around a program or two. They couldn't possibly design their handcrafted genomes, much less produce them, if they didn't.

But it is true that they're more prone to being careless. Chango Benitez used his laptop to call his parents back in Guatemala, and while the camera is off now, he forgot to disable the audio pickup afterward. With enhancement, it's possible to make out his team's entire conversation, right up until the point where Miguel Cobar asks if he remembered to kill the mic and Chango swears, running for his computer.

Before that happens, their team leader and kaiju handler speaks. "I don't care what it smells like, as long as it works." Rico Sarabia's bitter words are undercut by a gagging noise. "Okay, maybe I care a little."

Faint noises register on the mic as he fills the cartridge, loads it into the hypospray, and hooks up the pressure hose. Their organism, a creature best described as an armor-plated, six-armed gorilla with the many-rowed teeth of a shark, is only vulnerable to such a device in one location, but the boys have it well-trained; there is no sound of shuffling, and only a small grunt of complaint, as Rico crawls between its legs, levers up one of the armor plates, and shoots a dose of cutting-edge chemistry into the creature's bloodstream.

"We should have done this months ago," Miguel says as Rico crawls back out. "I can't believe we lost, man. This is our only chance to redeem ourselves."

The Tlachi Institute is the most respected secondary school for biological sciences in the world. They've won fourteen of the last thirty Patel Bioengineering Tournaments, dating back to before the foundation of the Genius Prize. For Rico and his friends to lose the Central American Regional Championships to the Nicaraguan national team was humiliating. Had the Nicaraguans not been disqualified after the fact for outside assistance—a consultation with the leader's aunt at the Shinrasen Center, not covered up quite well enough—Rico, Miguel, and Chango would be staying home this year.

The Tlachi team's chat logs, subpoenaed during the later investigation, reveal that Rico was the one who successfully argued against using obsequium on their kaiju before regionals. Although ruled legal by Dr. Patel and the advisory board of her tournament, he felt the agent was not "in the spirit of things," and preferred to direct his kaiju the old-fashioned way, with shouted commands and hand signals.

He changed his tune after the Nicaraguans' obsequium-dosed three-headed serpent dodged every one of their gorilla's six arms, got it in a pin, and nearly put one head's fangs through its skull. There's another hypospray hiss on the audio from Chango's laptop as Rico doses himself with dominatio, the companion drug to obsequium.

Scruples don't last long in the face of defeat.

EVERY YEAR, THERE ARE NEW developments. More efficient engines. A carbon nanotube splice that makes the bones lighter and more resilient. Stabilizer systems that mean the mecha spend less time knocking each other over. Fast-coagulating blood. What starts out as secret tech becomes standard military issue, then the plaything of the rich, then fodder for teenagers working in their garages and backyards and high school bio labs.

Many of those things are invented by past winners of the Genius Prize. Some of the new techniques make their debut in the competition. After all, that's why Metzger and Patel founded their respective championships: to encourage innovation, to find and nurture the brightest young minds in their respective fields.

As for why they joined those championships together, pitting the top wonders of each side against one another in a no-holds-barred fighting extravaganza?

They've answered that question a thousand times in a thousand interviews. A polished answer, focus-tested and vetted by lawyers as being non-prosecutable. But Tahira Patel gave the real answer once, when she'd had a bit too much sake at a reception in Tokyo.

"Because it's *fun*."

What Anjale Meztger meant about history becomes clear during the inaugural parade of the Twentieth Annual Metzger-Patel Genius Prize.

Although not quite as extravagant as the opening ceremonies of the Olympics, the Genius Prize parade is still quite astonishing. For the billions of people worldwide who only tune in to the realms of high school competitive robotics and bioengineering during the third week of June, it's their first chance to see the competitors: massive robots and equally massive kaiju, shaped to look like creations out of science fiction or national folklore or someone's worst nightmare, all stomping or rolling or slithering or flying around the arena where they will soon be demonstrating what they're capable of.

When the masking field drops, revealing the stage at the center of the arena, Metzger and Patel are not alone. Together with the usual array of judges, officials, and security forces, they have the winning entries from the previous nineteen years of both their respective competitions.

The effect is initially comical. In the early days, the standards for what teenagers might be expected to create were a good deal lower than they are today. It is a tradition almost as old as the Genius Prize itself to bemoan the loss of those simpler, more innocent days, before the attention of recruiters and the sizable cash award drove the teams to ever-more ambitious heights. The top mecha from the first year of the competition is little more than human-sized—essentially just a souped-up exoskeleton. The top kaiju from that year isn't even present in person, having died of lung failure six months after the competition. It is represented instead by one of its ninth-generation offspring, having displayed a capacity for budding that surprised its designers as much as anyone else.

But with each subsequent year, the creations get more impressive. Simple human-shaped mecha give way to things with more arms, more legs, more spikes. The kaiju leave nature behind and take hybrid forms even the ancient Greeks never conceived of.

And they get bigger.

A *lot* bigger.

The winners from the previous year—a scythe-armed Cuisinart with no discernible head and a creature that resembles the love child of a squid and a rhinoceros—dwarf Metzger and Patel, towering nearly forty feet tall. The technology for creating such things may fit into a suburban basement, but the creations themselves do not.

So in the end, the effect is exactly as the two women intended. As laughably simple as the early entries may seem, they're the foundation for a progression that has escalated through the years. They make clear the sheer magnitude of what Metzger and Patel have wrought.

In the footage of that evening, there are close-up shots of all the individuals who would become so important a few days later: the Songhali team of Akua, Ye, and Kisi; the Tlachi team of Chango, Miguel, and Rico; the Canadian hacker Tiennot Ahenakew, nearly the only member of his team to survive; Nevali Jones, the head of security for the event; and, in a panning shot across the stands, the Canthorpe twins.

In the focus piece that ran prior to the nineteenth championship, ambition burns within Arthur and Arnold Canthorpe like a flame. You can see it blazing in their eyes, feel the heat of it in every gesture.

"We've been planning this since we were six," Arthur says, slinging one arm around his twin brother. "Eleven years of work. This is the year it's gonna pay off."

From outside the frame, the interviewer asks, "Why did you decide to split up? Why not join forces, work together on the same team? Then you could both win the Genius Prize."

Arnold laughs. "Because we want *all* the prizes. The way we've got it set up, Arthur will win the Metzger Robotics Championship, and I'll win the Patel Bioengineering Tournament. Then we'll face off in the final round, and whoever walks away with the Genius Prize, it'll still be a Canthorpe."

Their confidence is infectious. You can see it in your mind's eye: Arthur Canthorpe holding the robotics trophy, Arnold Canthorpe the one for bioengineering, and between them, the enormous twined helix and gearing of the Genius Prize. The interviewer says, "It's quite a plan. Aren't you competitive with each other at all?"

Arthur laughs. It's indistinguishable from his brother's laugh; their hairstyles are identical, save for the direction of the part. They worked hard to create their public image, the cooperative opposition of the Canthorpe twins. "Oh, sure," he says, and lets go of his brother to punch him gently in the shoulder. "I'm going to kick his—"

Although the courtesy filter transforms his final word to "butt," anyone who reads lips can tell what he really said.

There are no interviews with the twins after their defeat. Although most leaders of losing teams are gracious enough to speak at least briefly with reporters, the Canthorpes left in a fury before the dust had even settled.

INVESTIGATORS SCOURED ALL THE RECORDS of the first few days of the twentieth competition, not because they were unclear on what happened, but because they wanted to answer the question: could it have been prevented?

The answer, of course, is *yes*. There were countless opportunities for someone to notice what was going on and put a stop to it before the chaos began. But those opportunities all came in the months between the nineteenth and the twentieth competitions—not at the event itself. The government of the Rocky Mountains Federated States, exceedingly eager to pin responsibility for the disaster on as many people as possible, did its very best to flay Nevali Jones alive for being negligent, but the truth is that she wasn't. By the time the various competitors arrived at the stadium outside Aspen that had been chosen to host that year's Genius Prize, there was nothing she could be expected to see, no action she ought to have known to take. Not until the trouble began.

The documents from the investigation describe the first few days as utterly routine, the recordings showing nothing suspicious. Demonstration trials for each of the kaiju, each of the mecha, in alternating turns. The panels of judges inspect them up close, questioning the teams who built or bred them, conducting various tests. Then they back off to a safe distance while the team leaders put their creations through their paces. The robotics pilots climb into their mecha; the bioengineering handlers shepherd their beasts along like proud owners at a dog show.

But the differences are visible. With the aid of a Truong sympathy net, the linkage between the mecha pilots and their suits is far more fluid than before, the mechanisms responding to thought instead of controls. With a fresh injection of obsequium rendering them docile, the kaiju almost seem to have a telepathic link with their dominatio-dosed handlers, never hesitating, never balking.

Even knowing what will happen, it's mesmerizing to see. More people tuned in to watch the first round than ever before, just to enjoy the balletic dance of these creations across the arena.

As usual, the judges choose eight in each category to progress to the second round. This is the point at which the whole world starts watching, because who can resist the appeal of watching giant robots slam each other with titanic force, giant beasts tear each other apart? It's better than a movie, because it isn't scripted; it's better than the Olympics, because it's mecha vs. monsters. Metzger and Patel judge this round themselves, basing their choices not simply on the brute question of which entry can beat up the other entries, but on subtleties of movement, speed, elegant engineering.

If there's one downside to the creation of the Genius Prize, it's that it has taken a little of the shine from the awards—the lesser awards, the preliminary awards. People these days use a whole host of deprecatory words to refer to the Metzger Robotics Championship and the Patel Bioengineering Tournament, so thoroughly have they been subsumed into the spectacle of the final round. You can even see it in the faces of the winners, Kisi and her Songhali teammates, Rico and his Tlachi friends: they're happy, of course they're happy, but they're also thinking ahead to the next day. And so are all of the losers, because it's happened before that an entry has lost the individual competition, but won the final prize.

This is where the real fun usually begins, the temptation that led Metzger and Patel to combine their two events into one. The top eight finalists from each category—those still in good enough shape to move, after a night of frantic surgery and repair—march into the arena, for a grand melee of metal against flesh.

In the year 2131, this is when the chaos starts.

THERE IS NO FOOTAGE OF how it happened, of course. The Canthorpe twins were far too clever for that. They both placed a close second in their respective competitions, and came near to winning the Genius Prize itself; no one ever accused them of being stupid. They made sure the cameras and microphones where they settled in to work transmitted only what the twins wanted them to.

But it's possible to re-create it from the evidence. Arthur found a security vulnerability in the Truong sympathy net about one month after Truong Industries hired him, and chose not to report this to his employers. Arnold had the more difficult challenge, contaminating an entire production batch of obsequium with a custom-designed virus—and in fact, one of the kaiju entries was dosed from an earlier batch, and failed to be suborned as expected.

Every single recording of the main event agrees: precisely thirty seconds into the melee, the twins take over.

Fifteen of the titanic figures thudding and whirring and flying toward one another across the huge arena stagger to a halt. The sixteenth, the French scorpion that has escaped the trap, pulls up short a moment later; its handler has noticed the sudden stillness, and thinks someone has given a signal to abort the competition.

In unison, the fifteen under Canthorpe control wheel to face the box from which Metzger and Patel are watching. Every loudspeaker in the arena, every mecha's external output, and quite a few personal devices that have been insufficiently shielded, suddenly boom out the identical voices of Arthur and Arnold Canthorpe, speaking in eerie (and pre-recorded) unison.

"Peoples of the world," the twins declare into the growing silence. "Last year, Anjale Metzger and Tahira Patel judged our creations inferior. Insufficient. Unworthy of their respective awards, and of the Genius Prize itself. They judged *us* unworthy. We have come here today to show them—to show all of you—how wrong they were."

The French handler, Amina Beausoleil, breaks the stillness. Her scorpion wheels and charges the nearest kaiju.

Some people later claim that Amina thought she could win the Genius Prize while everyone else's backs were quite literally turned. But with eight mecha and seven kaiju under Canthorpe control, she had to know her creature didn't stand a chance. Footage from a thousand angles shows the scorpion spitting a tangling web at the legs at the Greater Irish kaiju that sends it crashing to the ground, but Japan's teddy-bear-shaped mecha breathes fire that crisps the web into ash—fire-breathing still being popular for its visual effect, even though it's easy to engineer and useless against any competitive creation. The whip arm of the Brazilian mecha duels briefly with the scorpion's extendable tail, but three seconds later it's over. A camera in one of the exit tunnels from the field shows that Amina abandoned her charge the instant the rest of the entries turned on her beast, running for cover—an action that certainly saved her life.

During this brief fight, one of the mecha begins to spasm. Then another, then another, until all of them have twitched and then fallen still.

Only when that is done do they turn against their surroundings, unleashing their firepower on the shielded stands that surround them.

Credit goes to the Songhali team for observing appropriate safety standards, and installing a purely mechanical hatch release in their pterosaur. Thanks to this, Kisi is able to pop open her construct and dive free after Arthur takes it over. Not all of the other pilots were as diligent, and so they remain trapped, helpless passengers in their own creations, as the Canthorpe twins begin to wreak vengeance for what they saw as their unfair defeat the previous year.

The teammates of the pilots, and all of the kaiju engineers, are on the field. They know first-hand exactly how destructive their creations can be. A few of them waste precious seconds trying to regain control; others realize the futility, and begin fleeing immediately.

Nevali Jones is in the judges' box with Metzger and Patel at the start of the attack. Her body cam shows the first rocket exploding against the front window, and (contrary to those who would like to accuse her of negligence or incompetence) less than two seconds go by before she takes action. The judges' box is defended, of course, because accidents have happened before. But anything that offers visibility to the outside world has certain innate vulnerabilities to focused attack, and so you can hear Jones shouting for Metzger, Patel, and their various guests to retreat to the much more heavily fortified chamber behind. She covers their retreat herself, even though frail flesh isn't much of a shield against a kaiju or a mecha; her own body armor is only rated to resist threats up to Hellstop rockets, Class B plasma drills, and fluoroantimonic acid.

Once the dignitaries are secured, she descends to the arena below, shouting orders to her subordinates as she goes.

Chango, as the Tlachi team's tactical coordinator, had a drone circling the field so he could advise Rico in handling their kaiju. Its auto-tether drags it after him when he and a dozen others retreat into one of the tunnels, and so unlike most of the drones in the air when the Canthorpes took over, it escapes the destruction outside long enough to memorialize what comes next.

The shot is from above, but the figures are recognizable. From the Tlachi team, Chango and Rico; Miguel has escaped, but via a different tunnel. From the Songhali team, Kisi, Akua, and Ye. From the Canadian team, Tiennot; all three members of the Brazilian team; two from the Pakistani team; from the Sinai team, Muhammed Najjar, badly injured by shrapnel; and Yankton Robins, an arena employee responsible for supplying food to the kaiju.

Akua immediately begins applying first aid to Muhammed. Most of the others are shouting in a medley of languages; isolation analysis later teases out their words, the majority of which are profanities supposedly unsuitable to their tender years. Then Kisi's voice rises above them all. (Her words, and most of the subsequent conversations, are in Kotava.) "What the hell is going on out there?"

The Canthorpes' message is still broadcasting. Despite the noise from outside, it echoes through the tunnel in which the group shelters.

"Who else has the capacity to hijack the sympathy nets in all the mecha built by the newest crop of supposed geniuses?" the twins boast. "Who else can brainwash kaiju that supposedly answer to no one but their handlers? The display of coordination and skill you see before you now—"

"What fucking coordination?" Kisi yells toward the mouth of the tunnel. The flames consuming that end of the field are not visible in the drone's view, but their light dances across the huddled figures. "You're destroying everything!"

Tiennot stands up from his crouch against the wall. "Listen to the message! The ambient sound—it's pre-recorded, not live. I don't think this was supposed to happen."

Rico answers him with a well-chosen vulgarity in Spanish, then says, "Who cares what was supposed to happen? There are people dead out there!"

(At the moment he says it, the death toll stands at thirty-four, all individuals who were on the field when this began. It will climb fast as the stadium's shielding begins to fail.)

Tiennot's hands flap in the air, beating out a swift rhythm as his mind focuses on the problem. "The sympathy nets. He hijacked them—must have been Arthur. But one mind can't control eight at once. He must have daisy-chained them together, so that he's controlling one and that controls the next and so on—but that only works if he can maintain the focus necessary to stop sensory input from washing back through the chain. Did you see them spasm? He must have let that slip on the first link. Then he'd be hit by the second, and his odds of resisting that are lower, so—"

He doesn't finish the sentence, but he doesn't have to. The image of dominoes falling is so clear, it might as well be on the video feed.

Chango and Rico are kaiju crafters. They've never worked with sympathy nets. "What does that *mean*?" Rico demands.

Kisi slams her hand against the wall. "It means Arthur Canthorpe has gone insane. Taking all the mecha with him."

"What about that *comemierdas* Arnold?" Chango says, gesticulating wildly toward the tunnel entrance. "What's his excuse?"

An explosion cuts short any answer the others might have given. The shock wave knocks Chango's drone into a wall, destroying it. The next record of this group comes from inside the west loading dock, whose security barriers Tiennot has hacked. By this point Akua has taken Muhammed toward Infirmary Station D, and two of the Brazilians, along with Yankton Robins, have chosen to flee into the surrounding mountains, hoping to find safety there. Thanks to Robins, all three will make it to Aspen, the nearest town. Others who try the same escape do not fare so well.

"We've got to do something," Rico says. "We can't just let a pair of insane losers rampage around with kaiju and mecha—*our* kaiju and mecha." He says that last part with venomous fury.

"What do you think we can do?" Ye asks wildly. "Throw wrenches at them? Carve them apart with welding torches? We built ours to be indestructible!"

One of the Pakistanis says, "The contest authorities have their own kaiju and mecha—"

"Which also use sympathy nets," Tiennot says, with bitter amusement.

Chango nods. "And obsequium, I'm sure. They have all the best tech before we do, unless we invent it ourselves."

Ye snorts. "Right. So all we have to do is invent some brand new bit of tech out of whatever we've got in our pockets."

While all of this is going on, Kisi drifts a few steps away from the group. At first her posture is limp and hopeless, her movements dazed. But as Ye speaks, she straightens, her gaze going into the distance.

"No," Kisi says, not looking at any of them. "Not something new."

In the tunnels under the arena stands, Nevali Jones is hunting Canthorpes.

They have prepared for this, of course. She's already walked into several booby traps, not because she failed to see them before they triggered, but because she cannot afford to take the time to disarm them. Instead she trusts in her armor. It is now blackened and smoldering, the silencers destroyed, such that each step she takes clangs against the concrete floor.

The final defense is a good deal subtler. It has been growing for weeks, seeded by Arnold Canthorpe via an "accidental" spill the janitor did not realize should have been cleaned with hydrochloric acid.

By the time Nevali Jones walks into it, the creature has grown to coat the hallway in something that will pass for concrete, if you don't stab it to see if it will bleed.

It's smart, too. It lets her get halfway down the hall, halfway to the door of the generator room where the Canthorpes are holed up, before it moves.

Then the entire corridor comes to life and closes in on her like a fist.

TIENNOT THROWS THE SWITCH IN the west loading dock. The lights come on in rows, a gunfire volley of illumination rattling from the near end to the far, revealing in true color what, until that point, had been recorded only in infrared.

The mecha stand silent along one wall. The cages facing them from the other wall are quiet only because there are sound dampeners on each one; Metzger and Patel wanted all attention on the new entries for the Genius Prize, not the old ones. But they're there: kaiju and the descendants of kaiju, and the mecha they once battled.

"You've got to be kidding me," Chango says in Spanish, before collecting his wits and switching back to Kotava. "None of those things can stand up to what's out there!"

"They're all we've got," Kisi says. "And they don't have sympathy nets or obsequium."

Ye utters an oath in Igbo and runs down the line to the robotic winner from six years before. "He's here! Anansi is here!"

The construct in front of her can only be called a spider as a courtesy toward its eight legs; unlike the French scorpion that died on the field a little while ago, it does not spin webs. But its Nigerian creators named it for the famous West African spider god, and so that is the name by which the world knows it. Although the two countries have been longtime rivals, Songhali robotics students have a great deal of respect for Anansi, whose sheer agility and ability to climb larger mecha to find a better angle of attack made for a thrilling display in 2125.

"Do you even know how to pilot that thing?" Chango demands.

Kisi doesn't look at him. All her attention is on Anansi. "I've watched the recordings of the Nigerians. We tried building our own six-legged mecha a few years ago—couldn't resolve some center of gravity issues with the weaponry. But that won't be a problem here."

Meanwhile, Rico is studying the various kaiju. Nine of them are Tlachi creations, the legacy of a long tradition of victorious teams. His gaze lights on the 2128 winner: La Diestra, who resembles nothing so much as a deinonychus the size of a tyrannosaurus rex. She, too, is memorable—albeit for a different reason.

Tiennot makes a sound like he choked on his tongue. "You can't be serious."

"What choice do we have?" Rico asks.

The ensuing silence breaks Kisi's attention away from Anansi. Her gaze meets Rico's. Then she says, "Oh."

Finally Rico says, "We need more than just us."

Kisi nods and faces the Pakistanis. "You in?" She doesn't even wait for their answer before she adds, "Ye, round up anybody you can find. Pilots, handlers—anybody brave enough to try. But hurry."

Outside, the destruction is mounting.

The recruiter for the Shinrasen Center left his standing camera rig in his private box. The various explosions have shaken it out of its original alignment, leaving it pointed at the mouth of one of the tunnels—the one nearest to the west loading dock.

It records, with astonishing clarity, the moment when the tide turns.

Rico charges out first, mounted bareback atop La Diestra. The huge, dinosaurian kaiju—the only one ever to win while carrying her handler—provides cover for fast-moving Anansi, whose faceted pilot bubble refracts the face of Kisi, bellowing a war cry. Behind them comes a herd of other mecha and kaiju, winners of the previous competitions, piloted and directed by more than a dozen brave contestants.

It is the grandest grand melee the Genius Prize has ever seen. Anansi swarms up the back of the Canadian grizzly-shark and blows open the hatch; two legs reach in, snag Tiennot's compatriot Miigwan, and drop her to the waiting arms of a small naga kaiju below. Rico on La Diestra kites several of the Canthorpes' enslaved mecha around the field, and one of them falls into a pit dug by the infamous Tlachi-crafted Mole Man from the 2117 competition. (He is not under anyone's control; he is simply burrowing for the sheer joy of it, as he does whenever given access to dirt.) Anansi leaps from the grizzly-shark across to the Lovecraftian monstrosity the Norwegians brought, then leaps again just as the Japanese teddy bear breathes fire across its supposed ally. The Holy Angel of 2120 defends a large portion of the stands, where the collapsing structure has trapped several thousand spectators.

Chango was right. Very few of the previous winners can hope to stand up against the most recent entries; even Anansi and La Diestra are outmatched. But the young people who have taken the field can and do save lives, covering the evacuation of the stadium, and giving the crazed Canthorpes something to focus on other than mass slaughter.

And Kisi manages more. When three of Anansi's legs are crushed by her own pterodactyl, leaving that construct helpless on the field, she doesn't hesitate. She leaves the pilot's compartment and climbs the pterodactyl's leg while it finishes smashing the Nigerian spider. Like most mecha, it's built to tackle things its own size; it can't grab Kisi, and has no weaponry it can point so close to its own body. When she arrives under its jaw, Arthur Canthorpe can't even see her on the mecha's external sensors.

The Songhali team installed the sympathy net only after their national championships. It's an add-on, not integrated into the frame the way it would have been had they built it in from the start.

Ye's toolbelt is around Kisi's waist. Clinging to the outside of the pterodactyl even as it turns its attention to the rest of the field, she removes the panel on the underside of its jaw and shorts out the sympathy net. The pterodactyl stops dead.

The hatch is still open, left that way during Kisi's earlier escape. She climbs back inside, and as the spinjets fire and the pterodactyl takes flight, the interior mic picks up her next words.

"I'll show you who's a genius."

The lens of Nevali Jones's body cam is smeared with blood and ectoplasm, but it still shows the furious, horrified, defiant face of Arnold Canthorpe when she blows the door off its hinges, and the twitching body of Arthur Canthorpe on the floor, overwhelmed by the sensory input of too many sympathy nets at once.

She doesn't bother with speech. She just stuns Arnold, then Arthur, and then shoots them both again for good measure.

On the field above, the remaining enemy mecha stop. The remaining enemy kaiju stagger and fall.

The arena is silent, except for the crackle of fire, and then the agonizing, metallic screech of La Diestra finishing what she started: tearing the arm off the Japanese teddy bear.

Wheeling overhead, the Songhali pterodactyl lets out a victorious cry.

Out of respect for the dead, there was no competition in 2132.

Metzger and Patel gave no personal interviews during that time. They testified before judges and committees, gave public statements, and spoke privately with the families of those who had lost loved ones. They donated enormous sums to charity. And they made sure the heroes of the day were honored as they deserved, from Nevali Jones down to Yankton Robins and an arena janitor who led fleeing spectators to the shelter of a supply closet—anyone who helped save lives. Kisi Abouta and Rico Sarabia were named the joint winners of the Genius Prize: the first time the award was given to two individuals from separate teams.

They shared the cash with everyone who had helped them that day.

A little over one year after the disaster, Metzger and Patel appeared together on Immis Chae's show. After a brief review of the previous year's tragedy, Chae cuts straight to the question on everyone's mind.

"Will the Genius Prize continue?"

Patel glances at Metzger and says, "My wife and I still believe in the principles that led us to create our respective competitions, and the Genius Prize itself. But it's undeniable that the entries have grown far beyond anything we envisioned when we started out."

"And with that," Metzger says, "the danger has grown as well."

Chae says, "So you plan to end it?"

It's a sensible idea, but you can hear the disappointment in their voice. Metzger smiles. "Not exactly. We'll be back in 2133…

"… but we'll be taking it in a different direction," Patel finishes.

In unison, they reach into their pockets and set two objects on the table before them, neither more than three inches tall.

"Miniaturization."

Rolling Steel: A Pre-Apocalyptic Love Story

Jay Lake and Shannon Page

Rough Beast slouched toward the Bethlehem steel mill. Tons of fresh hot metal in there, every cobber and new chum from the Allegheny to the Delaware knew that. Even Topper, the old cat-eyed bastard with steel cables for fingers and a brain stewed in barium-laced æther, knew which way the good stuff lay, for all that he couldn't tell up from down on days ending with a /y/.

He's a bad man, our Topper. Used to run child-soldiers over the St. Lawrence to the Froggies during the Quebec-and-Michigan War. *La troisième mutinerie*, the Quebecoise called it in one of their endless prayers to St. Jude, for if ever a cause was lost surely it is theirs. Wolfe had put paid to their ambitions at the Plains of Abraham two centuries earlier, but no Frenchman ever born minded much dying for the romance of a shattered heart.

And there was no heart so shattered as that of a patriot whose country has been brought to ground.

And so we have Topper, driven bird-mad in the trenches of

the Somme when it would have been kinder for him to have just died. Came home he did to the quack attentions of the New Friends of Sweet Reason, got caught up in the Technocracy movement as exhibit A, and finally fell apart as the country itself did in Roosevelt's dying days.

Now there's Wehrmacht units on the loose from Nova Scotia to New Jersey, the South has risen again (and again), the Federals are barely hanging on in the Mississippi basin, issuing wireless dispatches from Washington-on-the-Rails while the Great Madness takes anyone stupid enough to be caught outside at night anywhere between the Wabash and Pamlico Sound.

Only those who started mad can stand the stuff, and move faster by night than any prayerful man might by day. Especially Topper in his *Rough Beast*, which once upon a time was a machine meant to kill other machines before he made so much more of it, oh so much more.

"Metal, my pretty," he whispered, patting with a clattering crackle of steel the crawler's upholstered dashboard between the engraving of Percy Bysshe Shelley and the platinum-dipped weasel skull with the rhinestone eyes. Only one of those two had he killed, Topper, and some days he knew the difference. He squinted into the depths of night through the prism that made up *Rough Beast*'s forward vision block, watching for the mill which loomed close, its fires never banked.

Fate and fortune walked on the greased knuckles of Topper's war machine, as never they had since Poland's borders collapsed in the first of the lightning wars.

I PATROLLED THE UNQUIET STREETS south of the steel mill, cussing as I walked back and forth in my own precious allotted square block of turf, practically wearing channels in the concrete with my steel-heeled stilettos. "Bastards," I muttered, thinking of the

Best Sister and her Little Chums. Well, 'bitches,' technically, but I didn't fancy using such a term of endearment when referring to their ilk.

"Bastards," I growled, as I turned the corner for the seventeen-thousand-and-thirty-second time, only this time I was thinking of my crib mates, the ones who had sniffed out some sort of rupture in my soul and handed me this godforsaken turf as my undue reward.

"Bastard!" I screamed, jamming to a halt as the ferocious machine loomed before me. Hadn't heard the fucker coming at all. My NKVD surplus large-bore riot gun was already raised and trained on the madman coming up from a top hatch, red-lacquered nail rattling against the trigger as my finger trembled with desire. Then I saw it was Topper.

Which didn't change my assessment of the situation, or my epithet. But I did lower the gun, and hike up my leather miniskirt an inch or two.

The gibbering fool grinned down at me, leaning over the console in a halo of actinic light to stare down the front of my corset. I set my shoulders back to improve his view and leered right back up at him.

"Going my way, big boy?" I called out.

"Bethlehem, Bethlehem, Bethlehem!" he chanted, his eyes rolling in his head. Oops, there went the tiny whisper of sanity I'd detected a moment ago. I danced back a step, just in case the worms in his brain told him to gas up that monstrous vehicle and put paid to the sexiest thing he was likely to see all day—any day.

My heels tapped on the sidewalk as I leaned against the wall of the foundry behind me. "And what are you going to do when you get there, mm?"

"Steal," Topper said, letting the word do its double duty.

"Stable." Another word doing double duty. He stared down at the woman. Someone from another lifetime, Topper knows with animal cunning and vestiges of functional memory.

He has had many lifetimes, our Topper. Lived them all together inside one much-mended head, until his name has become legion because he is many. Swine out of Garaden could not be more multiplicitous than this man. But even through the palimpsest of his personality, this woman emerges like a slave ship out of an African fog bank.

"Coming with?" Topper asked. He gunned his twinned diesels for emphasis. *Rough Beast* shivered like a dog about to piss. The woman looked scared but determined, a combination which even Topper cannot ignore.

He locked down the upper hatch, set the brakes, pegged the clutches, disarmed the antipersonnel charges on the outer hull, and crawled back between the ammo cans and the fuel bags to undog the ventral hatch. As he twisted the clamps, Topper hoped the woman hadn't run away or been jumped or something. He can't protect her from up here. *Rough Beast* is made for salvage runs and fighting heavy metal, not personnel escort.

Topper is confused about a lot of things, but he's not confused about what his crawler does.

The woman was still outside, armed and dangerous. And that was just her looks. Dark hair swept back from an aristocratic face. Pretty teeth, which Topper remembers from white rooms full of screams. She had a big gun, too, a riot weapon meant for stopping dogs or people caught in the Great Madness.

"You're going to the plant," she said.

It was not a question.

"In," Topper ordered by way of a non-answer.

Indecision flicked across her face like a trout in a mountain stream, then she climbed the metal steps he'd dropped down for her. *Rough Beast* had ground clearance that would give an arborist's ladder a bad case of envy.

Distant gunfire echoed as Topper dogged the hatch, but the incoming wasn't to their address. He wormed back up to the driver's station, leaving the woman to follow or not as she chose.

The crawler got moving with a shuddering lurch which foretold trouble for the portside throw bearings. He could rebuild. He just needed some high-grade ingots to trade out for the finished parts. That was how he took care of everything on this monster.

A single man wasn't meant to maintain and operate something like *Rough Beast.* Not even a single man as profoundly unalone as Topper.

The woman squirmed into the radio operator's seat behind him. That surprised Topper, he'd already forgotten about her. No radio, never had been one, but there was part of a sandwich rack out of an automat right in front of her face, as if she could plot their course in egg salad and bologna and trimmed crusts.

"So." Her gun thumped briefly against the floor. He noted she was smart enough to clip it to the seat pedestal. "When did they let you out?"

Topper had to think that one over for a while. Finally he said, "Ain't sure they have yet."

Call it boredom if you like. I won't dispute it if you do, not at all. Boredom, ennui, a sense of adventure left unaddressed for far too long—any of that could explain why I left my post and crawled up into that oil-dripping beastie with the lunatic pilot.

When I'm summoned before Best Friend and her bitches to explain myself, though—and you know I will be—we won't be talking about any ennui bullshit. No, I'll be spinning some tale about surveillance and undercover and getting on the inside of the enemy camp and all that sort of yak.

To support this notion, and also because I was damned curious, I slithered up the ladder at the behest of the grisly creature. (Hey, don't let it be said I never plan ahead.) I'd known Topper before, of course; knew him before he was the raving lunatic we'd all come to know and love in the Madness. Not that he was ever entirely sane.

Who is, any more?

I knew him because I'd been part of the crew that had taken him down, during the last round of the world-shifting adventures. We'd taken him hard, real hard, even before handing him over to the New Friends for, shall we say, readjustment therapy. I'd never expected to see him again. Which was shame, in its way.

So here he was, grinding up my street on his way to god-knows-what kind of tomfoolery down at the plant. Didn't even bother to deny it. Invited me aboard.

How could I resist?

I settled in behind him, looking around everywhere, trying to take it all in before he came to whatever shred of senses might have been left him by the New Friends and booted me out of there. Because, right, surveillance. Remember? I kept my right hand close to the NKVD riot gun in case Mr. Topper decided to get cute. But he had already started the monster rolling again, ignoring me completely.

He answered my question well enough, I suppose. All things being equal, you never really do get out, do you?

I fell silent after that, wishing the asylum refugee had thought to put windows back at my seat. What was I supposed to do with A-4 and D-0? I'd had a lovely lunch already, thank you very much. The rats are fat and sassy, this part of town.

Oh, Jesus, just kidding. What do I look like? I don't eat rats. You think this figure comes from eating street sludge like rats?

Feral cats, now: that's where it's at. Yum yum, meow yum. Excellent diced and stir-fried, with tree ears and a sprinkling of hoisin sauce right at the end.

After a particularly difficult highway crossing, Topper's mind wanders back to the woman. She was muttering under her breath now. Something about rats and cats and someone named Hawser Ann. He could smell her breath even in the diesel-and-metal reek of the crawler.

Cats was right in there. Topper cackled. He'd had a cat once, lived in the bed with him in the pale green room with the telephone that whispered secret vices in his ear-of-virtue, and blessings in his ear-of-vice. He knew what had happened to that cat too, every time he blinked his eye.

Our Topper spent some quality time under the close personal care of Doctor Sergei S. Bryukhonenko, after the good doctor B. had fled the collapse of the Eastern Front and wound up under a New Friends of Sweet Reason ban working out of a former mental hospital in the quiet fields near Yellow Springs, Ohio. The fields were quiet then because of the gas pooling in the low-lying watersheds which killed off everything with a central nervous system.

Dr. Bryukhonenko had been the beneficiary of good pressure seals and a number of human canaries chained to stakes in a three-mile radius around the hilltop facility. Our Topper had been the beneficiary of Dr. Bryukhonenko's newfound health and safety.

Until the psychosurgeries began.

Now he saw in strange shades of gray, a world of movement and chiaroscuro, relying on childhood memories of paintboxes and flower gardens to fill in the colors. Topper still knows the curve of a woman's breast from the rounded nose of a bullet—he's not *that* far gone—but so much else slides past the greased corners of memory, electroshock therapy, and deep conditioning, as if he were a human carpet afflicted with flea's eggs.

"Food?" he asked the woman. A gap yawned before the crawler, smoke crawling up out of some nether hole in the Pennsylvania soil. Mine fire? Enemy attack? Wrath of God? He navigated around it while one of his inner selves listened to her answer.

"Is that a request or an offer?" She began suggestively polishing the barrel of her riot gun.

"Dunno," Topper said. "Thought you might have some catsmeat." He felt vaguely like a cannibal for asking. Then his attention was distracted by the towering stacks of the mill, his destination. Someone flew a small aircraft close above them. He resisted the urge to jump up into the air and swat at it.

For all Topper knows, he might be able to do just that. Muscles he didn't know he had creaked at the thought.

"Rowr," the woman growled.

He wondered if she would purr, as well.

"You don't remember me, do you?" I asked the lunatic, after he'd failed to respond to my clever sally about the cat. I'd even growled to remind him. Good times. But I'm not even going to tell you about the look on his face when I did that, now.

Suffice it to say, crazy or not, the man had a strange charisma. And not because I was hard up, either. Not that I was ready to hop into the sack with him. Not right then. Not even the floor of this machine, or up against the wall of the mill. Not me.

The mill! A squinting straining gaze through what I could see of the forward view told me we were almost there, though Topper hadn't even been paying attention to the road. "Road"—such as it was, of course. The route, more like.

"Harridan Three, Harridan Three, do you copy?" a small voice crackled from my satchel. Damn, it must be one of the bitches in that plane buzzing overhead. Checking up on me. They don't trust me to wipe my own ass, any more.

Of course I couldn't respond, not overtly. But if I didn't send her on her merry way, she'd land that overgrown horsefly right in our path, and…well, let's just say I didn't fancy being two feet behind Topper when he was suddenly beset by Sisters in a well-armed aircraft, attempting to halt his forward progress.

"Nice rig you got here, Topper," I said instead. "I especially like the seats. Ooh, comfy."

He tore his attention away from peering up at the sky and stared at me. A droplet of slobber formed in the V at the lowest point of his lip and hung there. "Seats?" he finally asked.

"Yep," I said loudly, patting the foul cracked vinyl next to me. "These seats right here, in this-here vehicle you're driving me around in. Yep. Love it."

"Harridan Three, we copy," came the voice in my bag. It was Lena: bad news. And she was clearly pissed.

But the drone of the plane engine faded, and then the mill loomed large.

Too large.

"Stop!" I screamed, just as this abortion of a tank crashed through the wall.

Topper came round to paying attention to what he should be doing just after a few dozen tons of masonry bounced off the roof. That plane had buzzed off, but it had dropped him a present on the way out.

He spun *Rough Beast* left, just to confuse anyone who might be sighting in on him. From the sound of things, the crawler was now taking out another portion of the mill's outer wall. The hull pounded and shuddered, a brick rain.

"Where's the map?" he screamed over the deafening war.

She shook her head. *Useless bitch,* he thought. Bring a girl on a picnic, she doesn't even remember napkins. Topper keyed off the antipersonnel charges ringing the upper hatch and jacked his chair for a look. He let his feet do the driving.

Thing about a cat's eye is it sees in darkness. Not the pitch black of coal mines or a politician's soul, but places where a human being would stand blinking and wondering which way to the egress. The very bad Dr. Bryukhonenko had built a neural jumper block so the input from the cat's eyes jammed swollen and dry into Topper's skull could be made sensible—sense-in-light for a man who lives in the endless nonsense of his own head.

All of which meant that with the Bethlehem mill running on blackout except for the glow from the Bessemers further down the compound, only Topper could see what was going on. The defenders had to rely on triangulation and their own knowledge of the terrain. Topper was ignoring the terrain in favor of the direct approach.

"Damned loading yard ought to be down here somewhere."

Rails had been torn up a long time ago—their fixed routes were useless in this age of rolling borders and continuous sabotage—but the rail yard was still useful space.

Having gotten something resembling his bearings, Topper spun *Rough Beast* around. The wide open area had been *behind* him.

A woman was screaming from down near his waist. She sounded familiar. He jacked the chair low and looked around.

"Marie," Topper said, pleased as hell to see her. "What are you doing here in San Diego?"

The look on Marie's face was almost frightening. The gun in her hand worried him more, though. When had she learned to shoot?

Outside, the aircraft buzz had come back. *Fucking spotters,* he thought. "Whoops, got to go," he said, "bad guys up above. Hold that fire till we need it, kiddo."

By the time Topper was back out of the hatch and heating up the solenoids in the remotely-operated turrets, he'd forgotten what he'd gone down for. Until a gunshot echoed from inside the hull of his crawler.

Bastard flipped completely out on me after the impact. I mean, I shouldn't have been surprised, but it wasn't like I'd been having a peaceful day up till then, so I was a bit, well, off guard.

Hey. It happens.

Once the machine (not to mention Lena's bomb) rendered the wall of the mill into so many smithereens, it lurched but didn't stop, instead simply veering off to the left a bit. Or maybe that was Topper, yanking on the wheel. Anyway, that's the part that rattled me more than anything else. I was airborne a good two seconds, then crashed to the slimy floor of the tank-thing at his feet.

At least I held onto my gun.

Which stood me in good stead once I'd recovered enough to think again. The freak was looming over me, again paying no attention to the road, or corridor, or whatever it was we were driving down at the moment...yeah, another wall, I think...interior wall. It was hard to tell, jammed underneath two hundred and fifty pounds of insane manflesh.

I waved the gun at him. "Back off, Topper, I mean it!"

He called me Marie.

Oh god.

Waving the gun again, I tried to look sufficiently menacing. This was no doubt undermined by his view down the front of the corset. He grinned, and mumbled something about San Diego. What the fuck?

Maybe I was still screaming or something, because just then Lena decided she'd had enough. "Harridan three, we're coming in. You're relieved from duty effective immediately. Surrender your weapon to the personnel who will be approaching the tank once we bring it to a halt."

I almost laughed. How exactly were they expecting to do that?

A burst of machine gun fire came from above, mixed in with the aircraft engine. Oh, that's how. At least it got Topper's attention. He yanked his eyeballs away from my girls and scrabbled up top.

Unfortunately, I didn't want Lena to take his attention. Nor did I want to "surrender" anything to any goddamned "personnel" inside Bethlehem. "Topper!" I yelled, but he was beyond hearing me.

I took a shot in his general direction, careful not to aim for anything vital. Like around the middle. Riot loads weren't *supposed* to be fatal.

What? Just thinking ahead here. He'd cleaned up nicely once before. Who's to say it couldn't happen again? Girl can't be too picky these days.

Good. That got his fleeting attention once more. He slithered back down below and stood before me. "Marie?"

"Not Marie," I said. Then I reached down and toggled my radio to blessed silence so we could talk privately. "Grace, and don't you forget it, you moron."

"Grace..." The name slid off his pink tongue, making it sound dirty. "Graaace."

Oh good lord. We were in for a long night.

TOPPER STUTTERED. THAT'S WHAT THE doctor had called it—not Bryukhonenko the surgeon, but that New Friends woman with three moles on her chin that always made him think of Jules Verne's *War of the Worlds* for some reason.

Threes, all evil things came in threes. That's why men and women stayed in pairs. That's why a woman had two tits, a man had two nuts, everyone had two eyes, two ears, two hands, two legs, two nostrils, two lungs for the love of God.

Threes. And the stutters always came in threes. Dr. Roseglove, that was her name, like she had thorns turned inward to her hands, tiny red-brown spikes to pierce the skin, an Orchidglove would have been a very different doctor indeed, or a Lilly-of-the-Valleyglove and when he stuttered he lost *time*, he lost *control*, he lost his *marker* in the place of life.

Bad things. Threes. A woman named Marie, not Grace. But he'd known Marie? Had she been a twin? Or worse, a triplet? Was Grace her middle name, her secret name, her confirmation name, her gang name, her spymaster's handle?

She was shouting. Outside something was bombing. His thigh hurt like fucking hell where something bad had happened.

Adrenaline, he thought, a moment of clarity amid the stutter. *Adrenaline and a pressure bandage, before I die of assassination.*

Why would anyone want to kill our Topper? Even he cannot answer that. Well, other than all the people he's killed over the years, of course, but very few of them have anything to say about it now. Dead is dead, and no one's got relatives no more, not in this fragged world.

She's still yelling, this woman, but he's ignoring her in single-minded pursuit of his wound. He doesn't worry so much about the scattered pellets embedded in the flesh of his leg. They will either kill him or they won't.

Topper jacked up into his open hatch. *Rough Beast* wasn't equipped for anti-air operations. An angry woman loose with a riot gun down below was a problem. Amplified voices and high explosives outside were a bigger problem.

He left his stutter behind when he realized that his enemies had come to ground. Obliging of them. *Rough Beast* was very well equipped for anti-personnel operations.

A beefy woman stood in the red glare between shadows cast by his own arc lights, shouting for someone named Jason Adair to stand down. Topper didn't know any Jason Adair, not since before the wars began when he might once have answered to that name, so he activated the electrically controlled chin turret that looked like a fuel junction and could surprise an unwary, beefy woman and turned this one into a spray of blood and cloth.

Then he ground the crawler straight toward the ducted fan aircraft grounded before him. Topper admired the engineering of the thing—innovative, frightening, probably stolen from the Germans—until *Rough Beast* crushed it to scrap.

He wasn't sure which was more annoying: Marie screaming from below or some woman screaming from the crushed cockpit of the aircraft. In either case it didn't matter. The metal yard was ahead, and that was his purpose here.

OKAY.

Fuck.

Breathe. Just get hold of yourself: breathe, bitch.

'Cause when Topper took out Lena and her bodyguard du jour, *not to mention the whole fucking aircraft* thank you very much, well, okay, it sent me into a bit of a spin.

So maybe I shot him again. Just a little bit. I'm really not sure, frankly. Everything got kind of crazy and blurry there for a few minutes. Like maybe there were psychotic drugs floating in the air around Topper.

No, I didn't mean anti-psychotic drugs. That would have helped. I meant what I said. Pay attention, I'm not going to say it again.

It didn't make a damn bit of difference to his apparent sanity, or lack thereof. I mean the shooting-him-again part, if it happened. The drugs, I have no idea. That was just a metaphor kind of thing. I was making a comparison, one thing to another.

Although who knows?

Anyway, my sanity, however. Well…like I said, I lost a few minutes there. Once everything was tracking again, I saw that the aircraft was a pile of oily rubble behind us, and Topper was rolling the tank forward, muttering about Germans.

He never stopped with the verbiage, that one. If only any of it made the smallest bit of sense. I'd love to see him across a poker table. Looked like every thought was immediately broadcast.

Not that I was likely to be playing poker again any time soon. Anyway, Lena had my deck of cards. Probably they were ground into the mud behind us, too.

Mud and oil and blood and…

Don't think about it. *Don't think about it!*

I clipped my riot gun back into the rack beside the seat, just in case I was tempted to use it again. Because the part of my brain that had been functioning throughout the little misadventure of the past few minutes had just presented me with the irrefutable fact that my fate was now tied to that of this overgrown monkey, the one now drooling and gibbering and steering this massive bit of machinery towards what had to be the biggest metal yard I'd ever seen.

In other words: no more Sisters, not for me, not here, not now. By climbing aboard this contraption, I'd thrown my lot in with Topper.

God, I *hoped* he still cleaned up nicely.

I sidled forward in the cab, or at least something reasonably approximating sidling. Tough to do when the thing was rolling and grinding and rocking back and forth, throwing me from side to side like a hamster in a blender.

"Marie!" he said, catching sight of me. He gave me a delighted smile.

I fell into the copilot's seat beside him, or whatever you'd call it. Jump seat. Small bit of cushioning in a vast expanse of well lubricated metal parts and pieces. "Grace," I said, in a friendly and conversational tone.

"Marie-Grace?"

"Just Grace. Remember, sweetheart, how we went over this?"

He kept staring at me. "Well—never mind that, anyway. Just watch where you're driving, okay?"

"Driving, doing, zooming, duckling," he said. But his head wafted back in the general direction of forward.

"Good boy," I said. "Just keep doing what you're doing." Sooner or later, some of this was going to make sense. For now, he just had to keep us alive.

"W-74," Topper sang out. "Tungsten steel. Hard as a shield, cuts like a blade, keep it sharp, never be late…Burma Shave!"

Marie-Grace Just Grace snorted at him. He was pretty sure she'd shot him a bit earlier, but she had a nice smile. Maybe he'd been wounded by one of the dizzy bitches from that airplane.

Bullets fell on *Rough Beast*'s hull like lead rain. The locals were getting to it. But now he was in the metal yard, the El Dorado of this Pennsylvania hellhole.

"Here, Missy Marie-Grace Just Grace," Topper said, handing her down a gas mask. "Wear this a while and don't get nothing on your skin." He paused, solicitous as a fragment from some long-forgotten safety briefing (back when "safety" and "briefing" were applicable concepts) emerged into his forebrain like pack ice on a midnight river. "You weren't planning to have no children, were you?"

"Not right *now*," she squealed.

Topper wasn't sure that Marie-Grace Just Grace had taken the real point of the question, but duty had been discharged. He pressed the big red button labeled "DO NOT PRESS." It was wired just below a portrait of Bing Crosby with a Hitler moustache.

Several loud, ominous thumps echoed from the outside of the crawler's hull. This was followed by a hissing noise. Topper belatedly remembered to pull on his own gas mask, then wondered what he'd done with the chemical suit.

The part of him that was sane enough to keep the rest of the traveling circus alive watched the sweep second hand on the dashboard clock—Swiss timing in a genuine hand carved Chinese ivory casing, and possibly the most valuable thing aboard *Rough Beast*. Topper liked his treasures portable. He was a man who'd left more towns under more clouds than Seattle saw in a year.

One hundred and eighty seconds later he bailed out into the dissipating yellow fog. Defending fire had stopped, except for the occasional stutter of a weapon discharged as a finger shriveled too tightly in death. That hardly counted, though Topper knew a bullet was a bullet no matter who had fired it.

He wasn't moving right. The dizzy bitch really *had* shot him. Couldn't have been something too fierce, or his leg would be shattered. Riot gun with rubber loads, maybe? Who the hell would hang around a Pennsylvania mill town at night armed with sublethal munitions? That was like bringing a housewife to a bullfight.

Ahead of Topper were thirty-six pallets of high grade tungsten steel. Finest kind, ready for shipment to the manufactories of Detroit and Fort Wayne. Or ripe for the jacking by an enterprising man with good intelligence and solid orders.

Or woman, he reminded himself. Topper turned to stare at *Rough Beast*, wondering what he'd been thinking and which part of him had been thinking it. Her head poked up now, insect-eyed and blank-faced in the gas mask.

An electric turret whined as she brought one of the Bofors to bear on him.

"Screw you," Topper shouted, and began dragging the cargo chains out. It was hijacking time. He didn't have what it took to die again right now.

✦

After monkey-boy propositioned me a few times, I knew we were getting somewhere. Excellent. I could work with that.

The discussion of children, however, was a tad premature. I almost said something, but then he pressed some big goddamn red button and all manner of excitement began.

No, the other kind of excitement.

That all changed once he'd killed everyone within a ten-mile radius of the tank. Or so it seemed, anyway, given the swath of destruction all around us. After that, he turned back to me, with a terrible, deeply insane look about him.

I mean, he'd been insane all along. I knew that. You might have even said it was part of his charm. But I'd just watched him kill everyone I worked for, lived with, fucked and fought. Then I'd watched him kill everyone at the mill I was supposedly defending. Then he turned and looked at me.

"Now or never, baby," I said to myself, cranking one of his cannon turrets to point at him. That ought to put the fear into him.

All he did was proposition me a third time, then turn away and start fooling with a tangle of chains.

I threw my riot gun at him. Insane I can handle. Inconsistency: that makes me crazy.

"Mary Grace Just Grace," he babbled on, as he started spreading the chains out on the gravel in front of us. He ignored the riot gun completely, after glancing at it. I clambered down out of the tank and retrieved it, but it was too big to hold if I was going to help him get the pallets aboard.

Sure, I helped him. He could barely move the damn things. I was in far too deep to back out now. Might as well get our business done in here and get the hell out. Then we could talk about children, or whatever the fuck he wanted.

Men. Can't live with 'em, can't stake 'em out for the vultures. Though some of them might be improved. Including this crazy old bastard.

He was my last ticket.

Topper yanked the cold steel out of the charnel house of the mill one quarter-ton ingot at a time. The winches could handle the load, no problem—they were made for much heavier work than this, naval-grade hardware salvaged off a captured Kriegsmarine surface raider which had been broken in a gray-market yard hidden up the Rappahannock.

The girl helped. She was small, and weak, and not half-rebuilt out of spare parts and Soviet medicine, but she was tough and smart. Topper wondered how he knew her. Good-looking, too, and not just in an any-woman-in-a-war-zone way.

Somehow having his hands on all this hard-case metal was bring him back into himself. Memories spiraled in kaleidoscope paths to land in partially assembled chiaroscuros somewhere deep in our Topper's head. Like how a real person might think, it occurred to him, coherent images and more than a little bit of focused recall stitching together into timelines.

He wanted to turn away from some of them—deeply unpleasant, unpleasantly deep, or just infused with a stunning sadness for the boy and man someone with his name and face might once have been.

It was her, he realized. Not the metal. Not the dead. Not the distant thump of artillery and first drone of engines gone raiding in the cold, smoky sky. Not the screaming cats and bleeding eye sockets of memory. Not the white coats and wire-rimmed spectacles which had dominated so much of the intervening years.

Her.

Topper stepped closer, subtle as a pork roast in a synagogue, and sniffed.

"What the hell are you doing, you cre—" she shouted, then stopped when she got a good look at his face.

"M…Grace," Topper said, and looked her full in the eyes. He could fall into that pooled, dark amber forever, he realized.

Something was waiting to be born here beneath the shadow of *Rough Beast*, behind the walls of Bethlehem. He could feel it stirring inside him.

A soul. Hope. Affection.

Love?

He closed his eyes and breathed her in. She struck him all the way down into the lizard brain, scent and smell wired by million years of evolution and a hundred thousand generations of hairless apes dropping from the trees to say, *this one. This is the one.*

Before he could open his eyes again, she kissed him.

Somewhere inside the shattered Japanese puzzle box of his head, he was made whole.

"Let's get the last of this stuff on board," Topper said, rough but gentle as he drew her into his arms. "Then we're gonna say screw it to the Sisterhood and the New Friends and the Federals and the Wehrmacht and go be alone together. There's freemen in the Alleghenies would pay good money for our cargo, and hire us to raid for them."

His mind was dancing with visions of a quiet cabin, an open sky, and skin exposed for no purpose more sinister than a long slow trail of the tongue.

God, it was like being a kid again.

For the first time in his life, Topper had woken up.

YEAH. SO. OKAY, I KISSED him. Like I said, I'd kind of run out of options at that point.

But it was more than that. Much more.

When Topper turned and looked at me, really looked at me; when he got my name right; when the man that lived somewhere underneath all the layers of insanity our world had thrust at him suddenly bled through and took charge…I kissed him.

And when he pulled me into his arms and I caught the scent of him—the real, true scent, beyond the oil and blood and gasoline and the rank sweat of fear and battle—it hit me right below the belt.

Yeah, there. I meant what I said. How do you think things *become* clichés, anyway?

"Right," I said. "Last load and we're out of here."

And we rumbled off into the sunset. Sunrise. Whatever: I'm telling the story here, okay? The light changed and took us with it into a different world.

Alien Voices

Irene Radford

"*J'accuté comme...*" my nurse whispered to the trailing student nurse.

I heard that the last three patients who had this surgery went insane and committed suicide, I translated in my head. My many years in the ballet studio had forced me to learn French. I understood every dire word she said.

The student nurse proved that she had heard the same rumor. *They left notes saying the alien voices from the nanobots...*

"Enough idle gossip." The surgeon's looming presence in the doorway to my private hospital room cut short the women's whispered confidences.

"Mademoiselle de la Marachand must rest without anxiety." He spoke in English for my benefit, but with a decided French accent. He'd been practicing medicine for many years in this Caribbean haven for money launderers, drug smugglers, and off-the-wall medicine.

I'd done a lot of research on him and his unique treatment for worn-out knees before committing to this strange and peculiar treatment. The AMA said it was unsafe and ineffective.

For me and other athletes staring at the end of a too-short career, his new technique looked like a miracle.

At twenty-eight I'd neared the pinnacle of success in the world of ballet. At twenty-nine I was close to losing it all because my knees were torn to shreds by the dance.

Faced with the prospect of never again melding my soul with movement and music into the glorious art of ballet, I searched for options. Even now, with the cold steel cage of the bed frame around me, my body twitched with the need to move with the canned calypso music filtering through the hospital.

Without dance the music was incomplete. Without dance I was less than half a person.

The drowse of pre-surgery drugs could not remove my need to dance.

"So will I kill myself?" I asked the surgeon as he lifted my gown to look at the markings made by the nurses on my knees. Perhaps the conversation I'd overheard was merely the product of my overactive imagination under the influence of those drugs.

"You speak French?" His eyebrows went up. He placed a warm hand on my foot. "Do not worry your pretty head about what these ignorant cabbages bandy about," Dr. Bertrand reassured me. "They merely seek to thrill each other with tales of science fiction."

So, I had not imagined the whispered conversation.

"I do not fear voices." Could these alien voices be worse than those of the mad choreographers, dictatorial ballet masters, and critics who thought they were God?

"Yes," Dr. Bertrand chuckled. "I have heard that dancers do not fear. You welcome pain as a necessary part of your art."

"If it doesn't hurt, you aren't doing it right." I tried to grin but the drugs were making my face as well as my tongue numb.

"If you had not avoided treatment to your poor abused knees for so long, you would not require such drastic measures."

"If I'd undergone corrective surgery sooner—a stopgap at

best—I would have missed three of the most important years of my career. I might never have danced again."

"Ah, but soon, I shall put that all right. My nanobots will repair all the damage you have inflicted upon your knees and keep repairing it for many years to come."

"How long can you promise me?"

"My nanobots will last longer than the rest of your body. When you die of old age, your knees will remain as limber and strong as those of a teenager."

"When can I dance again?"

"You will need a few weeks for the nanobots to work. Then you will feel the youth pouring into you. But you must rebuild slowly so you do not overtax the ability of the 'bots to keep up with new damage."

"I'm scheduled to open in London in eight weeks."

"Eight weeks?" Dr. Bertrand shook his head and clicked his tongue. "Possibly you will be better by then, but I cannot promise peak performance in eight weeks."

"We'll see about that," I said. The music played as I let the drugs carry me off. I could hear the music. I tried to move to the music. To dance.

Always, the dance.

Two days later, before breakfast, I ignored my physical therapist's orders and rose up on tiptoe to test my balance. A big smile creased my face as I realized that Dr. Bertrand's treatment had indeed worked a miracle. Pain-free, except for a tightness around the small incisions, I raised my arms and spun in a circle.

My body swayed and threatened to tumble. I caught myself on the bed railing and forced my feet to stay under me.

Someone sighed in relief. I looked around for the source of the whoosh of air through clenched teeth.

I was alone.

Perhaps I had made the sound. I certainly was relieved that I had not landed upon the still-healing surgery incisions around my kneecaps.

A few hours after that I tried again and accomplished five steps and a turn on tiptoe, then five steps back to the bed.

Étienne, the physical therapist, whisked me away to his gymnasium—or torture chamber—as the aides cleared away the lunch trays.

"You are a lot more limber this afternoon," he said as he pushed my bent leg toward my chest.

I smiled at him but said nothing.

"Tell me when the muscles *begin* to protest," Étienne said as he pressed a little harder against my leg. I loved the way his French accent slid from his mouth, almost like music. I could dance to his voice.

I let my kneecap brush my breasts before I squeaked a protest. Étienne gently straightened my leg and let it rest upon the hard therapy bench. In truth I'd felt the burn in my thigh fifteen inches before I said anything. I needed to push myself harder and faster than either he or Dr. Bertrand thought prudent.

In my experience, all medical people were far too conservative. They didn't *want* athletes—including dancers—back at peak performance as soon as we could manage. We ceased to pay for their services when we felt ourselves healed, long before they were ready to release us and our checking accounts.

"That was amazing, Mademoiselle. But you really should not press so hard," Étienne said, shaking his head. He stood back, hands on hips, a stern frown upon his face.

"I am a dancer. I do not interpret pain in the same way you do." I tried to temper my excuse with a flirtatious smile. Hard-nosed critics had been known to change their reviews when I smiled like that.

"Then allow me to judge the intensity of your therapy. The

nanobots need more time to repair the damage to your bone, ligaments, and cartilage before you begin to stress them. Even miracles need time." He stalked out of the gymnasium-like room.

Before the orderly could arrive with my wheelchair to take me back to my room, I rolled off the bench to the treadmill. I used the handrails as a barre.

Long habit settled my posture into a classic *première* position to begin a ballet warmup, heels together, toes pointed out, left arm hanging down in a slight curve with fingertips at the top of my thighs, right hand resting lightly on the improvised barre. The mirror opposite me reflected my long legs, narrow waist, long dark hair pinned up in a ponytail. I smiled at the figure I cut, even wearing baggy sweats.

Except my feet pointed straight forward.

I forced them to turn outward along with my thighs and knees. My kneecap should face the same direction as my toes. Both should line up with my shoulder.

I sighed in relief when I achieved an almost normal *premièr*e position.

No! someone—someones?—shouted into my mind.

My feet and knees whipped forward of their own accord. My left knee buckled. I clung to the railing with both hands, desperate to master my rebellious body.

I inched myself back to standing. Then I eased my feet and legs outward until toes, knees, and shoulders again aligned. Then before my muscles could protest and change my position, I bent my knees into a *demi-plié*, forcing my heels to remain on the floor.

Sharp pains shot from my knees into my brain. It felt as if someone drove daggers directly into my temples, again and again in rhythm with my elevated pulse.

I collapsed onto the floor, pressing the heels of my palms into my eyes. The moment I pressed my body against the floor the pain stopped. But the memory remained. I cowered there for many long moments, whimpering.

The orderly found me curled up in a fetal position. He carried me back to my room.

For the rest of the day I contemplated my situation from the confines of my bed. I let the nurses and Étienne do what they needed to do without protest, without interest. My entire focus and concentration riveted upon the overheard conversation just before the surgery.

Alien voices? Nanobots inside my body. *Alien voices!*

My mind looped around and around the problem. Could it be? Could the mad surgeon with his miracle procedure have done more? Much, much more?

The nanobots repaired damage. The doctor had hinted that they could even recognize new damage as it occurred.

Was the leap to recognizing *potential* damage too far?

From there might they not need to discourage behavior that *could* lead to potential damage?

No, I reasoned. That was madness.

Madness. Had the nurse used that word?

I WAITED AND COUNTED THE hours until after midnight. The rehab wing grew quiet. The PTs and doctors went home. The other patients slept. Occasionally a nurse walked the corridors on her rounds. I could listen to my head without interference.

With as little bending and twisting as possible, I rolled from my bed and stood. So far, so good. The knees did not protest. I took one step, then two in the direction of the bathroom. Still no reaction from the *things* inside me.

I turned my feet and knees outward—not the full ninety degree angle I wanted, but enough to suggest a ballet stance.

Ten steps, then twelve. My knees felt a little shaky. A little hum of concern in my nape. I grabbed a towel bar for support. My knees stayed steady. The hum went away.

While I was in there I might as well take care of business. The elevated seat of the john was a blessing in my condition. Once more, I turned my knees and feet outward and lifted my heels several times. My calf muscle welcomed the stretch and release.

Grab bars in all the right places helped me stand again. I left my legs turned out and rose up on tiptoe. Slowly, ever so slowly, I lifted my right arm forward and up to *cinquième en haut*. Then I released the bar and lifted my left arm.

The hum in my head started up. I pretended it was music and stepped forward on tiptoe. The hum grew louder.

I overrode it by singing a jaunty little waltz. "One, two, step. One, two, step."

The hum matched the lilt in my mind.

Arms still up, I dropped to both feet, flat in a modified fifth position, all the while singing. On each third beat I took one step forward on the right toe and brought the left up into fifth position, toes aligned, heels facing opposite directions. Then I came down on the count of three, still in fifth position, heel to toe and toe to heel.

Six times I performed this simple exercise. Six times the aliens hummed along with me, so caught up in the music and the lovely stretch of calf, thigh, and back muscles that they didn't notice how I moved.

Then they noticed. "Straight, straight, straight," they screamed at me.

My feet and knees jerked to an ugly front face and without my will, marched me back to bed. The moment I placed both hands on the side bar, my legs gave out. I had to drag my tired body onto the mattress.

A smile tugged at my mouth as I drifted off to sleep.

For the next three days, every time I had a little privacy in the bathroom, I repeated the exercise, singing my favorite ballet waltzes ever louder to drown out the nanobots' protests. Each day they took a little longer before forcing me back into their version of a normal stance.

By the end of the week I managed a few *pliés*—bends—and *tendues*—stretches—even a quick *ronde de jambe*—a circle of the leg.

"I want a practice room complete with barre, mirror, and sound system," I demanded of Dr. Bertrand on the following Tuesday. A week and a day after the surgery. Time was running out. Seven weeks to the opening in London. Seven weeks to tame the voices in my head.

"This is too early," he replied, setting his jaw stubbornly.

"Étienne has told you that I can walk the entire length of the corridor without aid. The time has come," I insisted. I paced my little hospital room, my legs stiff in the exaggerated step of the dancer.

"No."

"Yes!"

"No. You will damage yourself beyond the ability of the nanobots to repair."

"I have paid you a great deal of money for this treatment. I still owe you half the fee. If I cannot dance, I cannot pay. You will not get the second half of your fee." I could be just as stubborn as he. I softened the demand with a smile and a gentle touch to his hand. "I *must* dance."

"You may use the physical therapy room. But only if Étienne supervises," the doctor conceded as he dropped a light kiss on my forehead. "When you fail, then you will know that I know how the nanobots work in your body better than you do."

I did not retort with the "Oh, yeah?" that burned on my tongue.

The hum in the back of my neck began the moment I took my place at the barre Étienne installed in his beloved PT room. The treadmill, weight bench, and other arcane accessories of his trade were all pushed against the back wall, out of my way.

"Adagio in 4/4 time," I called to the computerized music system.

The slow melodic tune drifted over the hidden speakers. I let the sound fill me as I drew deep breaths. The nanos picked up the count. Carefully I ran through gentle *pliés* in first, second, fourth, and fifth positions. Blood coursed through my muscles, giving them warmth and flexibility. I reveled in the stretch and burn. Then I pushed into deeper *grand pliés*.

Ah! the nanos sighed.

I pushed a little deeper.

Not so much yet, they insisted and shot fire from my knees to my head.

I backed off, but continued through my routine warmup. The microscopic robots let me know when I went too far. We compromised on the *grand battements*, leg lifts. I managed to bring my leg level with my hip, half as elevated as I considered beautiful and necessary, much, much higher than the nanobots thought feasible.

"How in the hell," I asked Étienne, "do you work with football players who have to kick up to their shoulder level?" I mopped perspiration off my brow and neck.

Football players do not demand the precise placement of hip with a full turnout as you. The answer came not from Étienne, who remained focused on my motions, but from inside my head.

A full coherent sentence from the bots. I raised my eyebrows in speculation. Was there more here than an invisible guardian of my cartilage? They seemed to be gaining in sentience. True sentience meant consciousness and appreciation for beauty.

My hope and spirits rose.

Until I moved to the center of the room and asked for a waltz.

Too much! Too much! the bots screamed. My knees collapsed.

Étienne clucked his tongue and lifted me into a waiting wheelchair. "We told you not to push yourself too far," he gloated.

I turned my face away from his glower. "I will try again tomorrow."

"But..."

"I did not fail today. I just could not do as much as I wanted. Dr. Bertrand said I could practice until I failed. I did not fail."

The nanobots needed to love my dance. To know why I had to dance. Why the world needed dance and beauty and art.

Eat, eat, eat! THE ALIENS inside my head insisted.

I stared aghast at the mounds of yams, a tiny green salad drowning in oily dressing, a large portion of fruit salad dripping mayonnaise, and a slab of beef covered in rich Béarnaise sauce. And on a side plate a piece of six-layer *gateau chocolat*, complete with gooey icing.

"You want me to eat this crap?" I nearly gagged at the thought of putting so much fat into my body at one time.

"Well, of course. This is what the doctor ordered for you," the kitchen aide sniffed. "This is how *les Américains* eat!" She flounced out of my room.

"Too much fat," I snorted and pushed everything aside but the salad. I scraped off as much of the fat-filled dressing as I could.

You must eat. We need fuel to work on your body.

I held to my guns as I nibbled the salad.

Please?

Suddenly I was not in control.

The meat disappeared down my throat faster than I expected. That tasted so good, I wanted more. Never since I had begun to dance professionally at the age of fifteen had I so craved food.

The yams too, the nanobots reminded me.

"But the sauce?"

It will not hurt you. And as if reading my mind, *It will not detract from your muscle mass.*

"Promise?"

Promise.

So I ate the yams and sauce as well.

"Nice to see that your appetite has returned," Dr. Bertrand remarked. He entered my room just as I finished the last forkful of super sweet gateau.

"Let's just monitor the activity of my nanobots after your workout today. There should be a slight increase in activity as you rebuild your strength." He attached sticky pads to either side of each knee and then stuck wires to the brackets on each pad. The wires led to a handheld monitor the size of my smartphone.

The gadget clicked and hummed to itself, much like the nanos hummed in the back of my head. We'd been through this procedure every day since my surgery and rehab.

Dr. Bertrand frowned. "I have never seen activity at these levels. If I did not know better, I'd say I'd given you four treatments, not one. I don't see how the number of nanobots I gave you can generate these readings."

The monitor began beeping to a lilting Andalusian tune. *En Aranjuez Con Tu Amor*, by Joquin Rodrigo I thought. A nice piece, easy to dance to.

"You said the nanobots had self-repair and replication capabilities to give them longevity." I tried to look innocent. As long as the nanobots appreciated music and let me dance they could replicate themselves a thousand times over.

"No dance for you tomorrow," Dr. Bertrand said through his frown. "You did too much. The nanos won't be able to keep up with repairs if you keep pushing yourself like this."

"I'm checking myself out and going home tomorrow," I replied icily.

"You can't! You aren't ready. You'll collapse before you get to the airport."

The monitor buzzed and beeped then returned to a much slower pulsing tone, the tone it should have had before I had exposed the nanobots to music.

I smiled sweetly at Dr. Bertrand. The nanos had completed their repair job for the day.

For three days the nanos kept me anchored to the barre while I worked.

When they finally released me for some true dance—after a good warmup at the barre of course—I almost shouted with joy.

"Computer, *Woodland Rhapsody* by Alexander," I called to the music system. The lilting strains of my favorite piece of music in the world drifted out from the speakers, a New Age piece played on synthesizer and uilleann pipes.

I began the slow twisting moves of the dance created especially for me two years ago, just after my first bout of tendinitis. The work had become my signature piece. I always ended solo performances with this dance. I always received multiple standing ovations and dozens of bouquets of roses when I performed it.

The adulation was nice but did not compare to the sheer joy of dancing to this music.

Tears came to my eyes as the music overwhelmed me. I became the dance, the music, the art.

By the time I completed the triumphant celebration at the end, my ears rang and sweat dripped from every pore of my body. My heart beat too rapidly.

"Now you know," I told the nanobots, "why humanity craves art. Existence is chaos, conflict and fear. Art is the flower bud of beauty that allows us to step back from the horrors of life so we can find the hope and joy in living."

I exulted in finally being close to what I was meant to be. Only one more step remained in my recovery.

Inside me, the nanos wept with awe.

We have spent some time working on your pelvic muscles, the nanos informed me as I entered the dressing room of a private studio in London.

"What's wrong with my pelvis?" I sank onto one of the benches and began digging leg warmers and pointe shoes out of my bag.

I was due to open at the Royal Albert Hall in just two weeks. I needed to get into rehearsals in the next day or two at the latest. But I didn't want anyone to see my first venture onto pointe. Certainly the nanos would protest. The argument might take several hours. But I knew how to convince them.

A lifetime of carrying your bags and books and things on the same hip. Then an imbalance in your posture—you tighten your butt but neglect your abs. You had pushed the joints out of alignment. We have corrected that and stimulated the muscles so that they hold.

"Oh. A lifetime of bad habits. Thank you for correcting it. I'll work on eliminating those bad habits." I loved this new relationship with my nanos. I'd found that I could finally indulge my appetite without gaining weight. The nanos put every calorie to good use. They'd added firmness to my breasts, eliminating the beginnings of sag. My skin felt fresher and more elastic all over my body.

I arched my feet within the pointe shoes and tied the ribbons securely.

A strange numbing silence took over the back of my neck.

I slipped from the dressing room into the studio and took my position at the barre. No time to waste putting music in the CD player in the corner. I had to do this before the nanos became suspicious and closed me down. I'd just have to hum along to my warmup routine.

The silence in my head spread through my shoulders and arms as I dipped into my first round of *pliés*.

Biting my lip, for concentration, I rose out of the bend and continued stretching up and up until my feet rolled to a full point within the special shoes.

Fire lanced through all of the delicate bones and muscles from toe to knee and upward.

NO! You can't do this.

"I will do this. The dance is not complete without pointe shoes. The lines of my body are asymmetrical unless I continue the line of my feet into a full point." I dropped down to flat. The fire went away.

I tried again.

The pain increased and rose up to my hips and into my heart and lungs.

Gasping for breath, I bent double.

The moment my heels touched the ground the pain reduced to a burning ache. Air rushed back into my lungs.

"Let's try something else." I marched over to the portable CD player in the corner and shoved in a disc. By the time I returned to the barre, the nanos had begun to hum along.

Hoping I'd lulled them into submission, I tried again.

They reacted more violently. I collapsed onto the floor, straining to breathe through the pain.

We cannot allow you to damage yourself beyond our ability to repair you.

"Then get busy and replicate a bunch more of you. I will do this. The dance is not complete unless I go on pointe. My career is finished if I can't dance *en pointe.* Without my career, I am nothing."

Silence.

When I could bear to stand up again, I tried one more time to rise up *en pointe.*

This time the nanos reduced me to puddle of pain and tears. I had to crawl back to the dressing room.

Inside the studio the music continued its lonesome routine, playing for the dance without a dancer.

✦

Alone in the dead of night, I sat on the bed of my furnished flat and stared at the bottle of pain pills Dr. Bertrand had given me. Sixty of the big green caplets with the unpronounceable name. Heavy duty medication, barely legal in the U.S., and certainly not in the dosage and numbers in that bottle. Enough to last me an entire month if I took the prescribed amount of one with breakfast and another when I went to bed.

Was it enough?

I arched my feet one more time.

No reaction from the nanos.

I stood up and stretched into a long arabesque.

Still no reaction.

I reached for my pointe shoes.

The nanos collapsed every muscle in my body.

Crying for all my lost hopes and dreams, crying for the end of my art and dance, crying for the end of me, I crawled back onto the bed.

The bottle of pills still stood on the nightstand. A big glass of water sat beside it.

Choking on my tears, I shook six pills into my hand and reached for the water.

What are you doing? the nanos asked in alarm.

"The only thing I can do. You won't let me dance. Without my art, my life is reduced to mere existence. There is no hope, no joy, no beauty."

You may dance, just not with those torture devices.

"That is the only way I can perform ballet. The dance is not complete without an audience."

Then invent a new form of dance, a less destructive form that does not require turnout or pointe shoes.

"They call that modern dance. I find it ugly."

I swallowed one pill.

It went down sideways and stuck in my throat. I gagged and drank more water until it cleared.

Damn. Now I'd have to get more water to take the rest of the pills.

One is enough.

"No it isn't. Not to end the pain in here." I slammed my fist into my heart. A new spate of tears blurred my vision as I refilled the glass of water.

You will damage yourself. We cannot allow that.

"You have damaged my identity, my very soul to the point of no return." I tried to put another pill into my mouth and found my hand shaking so badly I dropped them all.

Cursing, I crawled around on the floor seeking them out.

You will end your existence if you take all those pills.

"And your point would be?" I found four. That should do the job. And there were others in the bottle. If my hands stopped shaking long enough to open the childproof cap.

You cannot mean to end your existence! they cried in alarm.

"I mean precisely to do that." I managed to get a second pill into my mouth.

But, but…

I'd never known the nanos to splutter.

It didn't matter any longer. I had to do this. I grasped the glass of water firmly.

"Without the dance, I am nothing. All of the pain, and agony, cutting myself off from friends, denying myself the pleasure of a movie, or an art museum, or a loving relationship… I endured all of that because it interfered with my dancing. Now I have nothing. I am nothing."

If you kill yourself, then we will die too.

"So? What good are you if you won't let me dance?" I got the glass as far as my mouth.

Then my hand clenched so tightly the glass shattered. Water sprayed all over me. The precious pill dropped to the floor once more.

Blood ran down my hand and dripped on the floor from half

a dozen glass cuts.

"Now look what you made me do."

We cannot allow you to terminate yourself or us.

"I'll find a way." I picked up one of the larger pieces of glass. Big enough and sharp enough. I aimed it over the big artery in my wrist. I remembered reading somewhere that those who were serious about their suicide slashed lengthwise, along the artery. Cutting crosswise was only a gesture by those who cried for help.

I watched my blood pulse in my wrist and poised it to slash lengthwise.

Is destroying your body with pointe shoes more important than living?

"Dancing *en pointe* is an essential part of the dance…of living." I brought the glass shard closer to my wrist, bracing myself against the pain I knew would come. The final pain I must endure.

If we let you dance en pointe *will you continue to live?*

"Dancing to the ultimate is life to me. Without the pointe shoes I cannot perform, I cannot complete the art of dance without an audience."

A huge sigh of resignation ran through my body.

Clean up the broken glass, then sleep. We must replicate ourselves one hundred times over to accommodate your art. For the sake of beauty.

Crying in relief, I obeyed and flushed the last of the pills down the toilet. The nanos had given me another chance to live.

"DONNA, YOU'VE NEVER LOOKED MORE radiant!" Lucien, the company director, gushed as he gathered me in a hug tight enough to disrupt the layers of blue chiffon that constituted my costume.

"It's all that time I spent in bed recuperating from surgery," I lied by way of explanation. He'd never understand the sentient nanobots in my system that kept my body looking and performing like a twenty-year-old.

"I watched the rehearsal this afternoon. 'Rhapsody' was positively poignant. You've added new dimension to your work." He held me at arm's length inspecting my new costume, complete with a crown of flowers, wisps of green leaves about the chiffon, and fluttery wings on a flexible wire. My fairy costume.

"Your knees working okay?" Lucien had known me to dance through excruciating pain without admitting it.

"Better than new. The procedure worked miracles."

"How long will it last? This company needs you dancing. Our receipts were way down during your absence. Audiences just do not react to your understudy the same way they love you."

He'd recommended conventional surgical techniques when the tendinitis first hit me three years ago. Those procedures were really only temporary pain relief. Joints never were the same afterward.

"My knees will outlive you." I smiled graciously at the white-haired gentleman of a certain age. He'd been around so long no one dared ask how old he was, and yet he had more energy and stamina than a dozen dancers put together.

In fact, he'd pointed me toward Dr. Bertrand and his controversial techniques when my pain became so acute I could not walk.

I wondered…

"But will your knees outlive you? That is the important part."

I smiled enigmatically.

"Time for you to go on, Donna." He kissed my cheek. "*Merde*," he whispered the universal "Good luck" of all dancers. Though why we said "Shit" to each other in French I'll never know.

"I have to go easy on the jumps," I apologized.

No jumps, the nanos nearly screamed in my ear.

"There are no jumps in this dance." Lucien looked puzzled.

"I've added a small *tourjeté* and *pas de chat*." Next week I'd make those little jumps bigger. Then we'd go for the truly magnificent *grand jeté* leaps I had once been famous for.

We won't let you undo all our repairs with jumps and leaps and such.

"That's what you think," I told the nanos sotto voce.

"Did you say something?" Lucien asked.

"Just a little mantra to psych myself up for my premiere."

No jumps.

"We'll see about that." I could out-stubborn mad ballet masters, cranky conductors, and insistent bean counters like Lucien. What were a few nanobots to a true dancer?

"If I don't jump, leap, and turn, the dance is not complete."

We must complete the dance. To dance is to live.

Exactly!

ALIENS

Its Own Reward

Katharine Kerr

Early on a Tuesday morning Lieutenant Mitsu Morgan of the San Francisco Police Homicide Division slides two steaming bowls of apple-cinnamon oatmeal out of the microwave and plops them down in front of her kids. Alan and Trish barely notice, since they're fighting over the remote for the TV, which drones about weather on the opposite wall. Mitsu slops milk over the cereal, slops a little into her coffee, then intervenes.

"Trish! His turn. You got *Doctor Blast-off*."

With one last whine on a dying fall Trish surrenders the remote. Mitsu checks the time—another hour before she's due down at the Hall of Justice, less before Trish needs to get to her live tutorial. While she wonders if her current daycare person will make it on time, she pours herself more coffee and the kids juice. Synth music floods the kitchen.

"Down!"

The music drops to a tolerable level. On the huge screen a consumer tape-crawl show is gearing itself up, the Admart Experience, or so this one terms itself.

"Alan, love, why are you watching this?"

"Cause Dad promised to buy me a jetboard for the lake this summer if I could find a good one used."

"Ah. Well, you know, I wouldn't put a lot of energy into it. Your dad sometimes has trouble remembering things."

Alan grins and holds up a comp stick.

"I got it in writing."

Mitsu laughs and hands dribbling Trish a paper napkin. Alan shoves the stick into his notebook's slot and sits poised, vulture-like, over the record button.

"Something good comes on, I'm gonna bank it for Dad to watch later."

On the TV the music fades to a mutter. While Mitsu shoves dishes into the washer and sorts the piles of school junk and old mail that always seem to fetch up onto kitchen counters, she finds herself watching bits and pieces of the show, an endless loop of homemade ads. Nervous sapients, both human and lizzie, stand in front of home holocams and stumble through their spiels while their unwanted material goods sit sullenly beside them, old zap ovens and comp units, collections of twentieth century Elvis plates, camping equipment, fiber-hide luggage, nearly-new lamps in the shape of Saturn and its rings, and every now and then a really peculiar object, such as an alabaster globe on a Lucite stand. Down in one corner of the screen lot numbers flash while across the top, the station's link code hangs, gleaming pink and begging viewers to call toll-free and bid. Finally, just when Mitsu wonders if her kids might be better off watching sex and violence, a pale blue void swirls and forms into the long thin oval of a Val Chiri Gan face. She stops working to stare.

Under a thatch of black hair, a huge brow-ridge proclaims him male, and he wears faceted jewels inlaid directly into that sweep of cartilage so that they protrude through the thin gray skin in a pattern of sparkle and scars. His tiny eyes gleam golden: he's from a northern clan, then. For a long time he merely stares into the cam lens, his thin slit of a mouth working, driven by some deep feeling. That he would show feeling shocks her as much as his appearance on this advertising channel. Mitsu speaks out of sheer instinct.

"Alan, record this."

He hits the button on his notebook. At last the Val Chiri raises a speaker-unit in his top-right three-clawed hand and presses it to his long, ridged throat. No Val Chiri mouth can produce more than a few American sounds, any more than a human one can cope with the Gan-Girun syllabary.

"I acknowledge all who watch and listen." The formal greeting sounds grotesquely appropriate. "By the time this my image speaks to you, I shall be dead. I record this message at 2000 hours of March the nineteen in the year forty-one of our common era known as the time in which our people have met one another. I apologize to this city of San Francisco for the trouble my murdering shall cause to be upon its police officers. I have drawn up what is termed here a will, which shall be made public once my death is discovered, so that all may read its provisions and know I speak truth. One of the provisions of that will is this: to the San Francisco Police Force, for the sole purpose of giving to whomever it should be who provides the evidence that produces the discovering of my murderer's identity, I bequeath as I say four times forty-four times four again kilograms of pure gold."

On the screen the Val Chiri pauses, as if allowing his listeners a chance at an expletive.

"That's lots," Trish says. "Right?"

"Multo lots, love," Mitsu says. "Now please, let's listen."

"I cannot say who will be murdering me, or I would save all much inconvenience. I do hope that this reward will be bringing forth witnesses and informants."

The Val Chiri lowers the voice unit and stares once again into the lens. Then he touches his eye-ridge with one finger of his top-left hand and speaks what seems to be a single sentence in his own language.

Mitsu cannot understand one word.

The void swirls, then reforms itself into a living-den, where a female lizzie in a purple sarong is trying to sell her old incubators. Mitsu reaches over the table and punches the stop button on Alan's notebook.

"Sorry, love, but I gotta have that flat. Go get yourself a new one out of my office."

"But Mom! It's the one with Dad's promise on it!"

Mitsu stops herself from venting her feelings.

"Well, rats," she says instead. "Tell you what. If he tries to back out, I'll break my own rule and interfere. That's the best I can do. I got no idea if anyone down at work's recorded this message, and it'll take all day to subpoena the crawl station."

"You mean this is a case?" Alan's eyes grow wide. "I thought that dude was just some actor dubbed over or something."

"Nope. I got this sinking feeling it's all real."

And what's more, she thinks, *it'll be mine to handle*. Although Mitsu's never been to deep space, she's traveled out of the gravity well to a watch station a couple of times, and by some perverse logic on the part of the higher-ups, cases involving aliens always come to her. Alan slides the flat out and hands it over. Mitsu tucks it into the shirt pocket of her uniform, grabs Trish's bowl just as Trish tries to pick it up and drink the last of the milk out of it.

"You have a glass, and there's more milk on the table."

The CopComm unit at her belt begins to beep hysterically. The doorbell rings. Mitsu sets down the sticky bowl.

"That must be Elena. Trish, love, go answer it. I gotta take this call. Alan, turn off the TV. Now!"

Without one word of back-talk they follow orders. It will be the last satisfying moment of Mitsu's day.

✦

The Val Chiri Gan delegation has rented two floors of the New Palace Hotel down on lower Market Street. Three pink ziggurats joined by ramps and enclosed bridges, it hunkers around a triangular courtyard that, at the moment, swarms with police. Mitsu's partner is waiting for her at the gold-veined synthmarble registration desk in Building One—Sergeant Bill Hoffman, a skinny blond Cauc with a perpetually runny nose. Not even gene transplants can cure his allergies to the yellow skies of Earth.

"We got the area cordoned off," he announces. "No one speaks much American up there, but I did find one guy. Jeez, Morgan, these people are weird. I bet they really are psychics, just like you always hear."

"Medic team on the job yet? The lab dudes?"

"Sure are."

"Well, let's go up. See what we can see."

Mitsu strides off across the lobby toward a bank of bronze-colored turbolifts. Bill trots after.

"You don't think they're psychic, huh?" he says.

"Think it's a lot of bull."

"But I saw this special, it was on one of the nets. *The Secret World of the Val Chiri Gan.* Come on, they wouldn't spend a whole hour on a special if it wasn't true."

"Bill, sometimes I wonder how you got into police work."

Bill opens his mouth to answer, shuts it fast, and contents himself with a scowl.

The turbolift drops them at a white corridor carpeted in white. The air is hot, sticky with artificial humidity and the spicy scent of Val Chiri. The first thing Mitsu notices is that all the doors to the various rooms have been removed; the second, that huge potted tree ferns of a kind she's never seen before make a green and random maze out of the halls. Val Chiri Gan males drift from room to room or stand under the ferns and stare. Since they're a small people, maybe 1.2 meters on average, they seem to scuttle whenever they move on their four lower appendages, which can be either arms or legs depending on need. They always hold their heads and top arms upright on double-jointed torsos, and since they're draped and swathed in layers of cloth, mostly blue and a metallic gold, Mitsu finds herself thinking of beetles. Sharply she reminds herself that they're as warm-blooded as she is, mammals of a sort, and intelligent as all hell.

As they walk down the hall, dodging ferns and pedestrians alike, she glances into rooms. Hanging panels of multicolored cloth, a scatter of tubular cushions, big wooden boxes, small and shiny brass things, more ferns—no real furniture to speak of, only Val Chiri males, standing and talking in low chirps and mutters, sitting and staring at nothing. Occasionally someone looks up and waves an upper arm, a gesture mimicking the human one and meant to be friendly. She waves back and keeps walking. The scent, a mix of something like cinnamon, something like roses, and the tang of an open sea, seems to billow around them. Beside her, Bill sneezes, stops to blow his nose and snort. His eyes are bright red.

"You want to go take over on the street?"

"Thanks, sir, but no. I'll be okay." He's fishing in the cargo pocket of his walking shorts. "Brought a lot of Kleenex and some pills."

At a T-junction the corridor ends. One arm of the T leads to an open doorway, where a cop stands glowering.

"The master suite." Bill waves a Kleenex in its direction. "Where the murdered dude lived with his...well, I guess it's his family. There sure are a lot of them."

"The victim was high-status, then."

"You bet. That reminds me. Got a call from Washington."

"Washington? Jeezus christ."

"Yeah. They sounded hysterical. You're supposed to call them back once you got something real to tell them. Turns out that these people are here to dicker over the terraforming project on Venus."

"And without their engineers, it's no go?"

"Yep. We gotta be real careful. Can't cause a diplomatic incident, no matter what the cost, the guy said."

"Okay, I gotcha. Let's be real nice and polite."

Down at the opposite end of the T, sapients and 'bots crowd round a pair of double doors, med techs, the pathologist, a big anti-grav flat of equipment, three beat cops dressed in regulation blue. In among them, swathed in gold lamé, a Val Chiri is standing on his lowest legs to make himself look taller. His bluish-gray hair has been swept up in a plume as well. Around his neck like a necklace hangs a speaker-unit.

"Those doors lead outside, don't they?" Mitsu asks.

"To one of the enclosed bridges, and the bridge leads to the other building, so the doors are never locked."

"So anyone could have come through there last night?"

"You bet."

"And the corpse was found?"

"Just on the other side of those doors. Kind of slumped up against them, like he was trying to get back in."

As they approach, the pathologist hurries over to give her report. The murdered sape died at some time between 0000 and 0400 hours of multiple stab wounds from a thin curved blade. One wound, inflicted from the front, pierced the main heart. For the others, which seem to have been made after death, the knife entered from the back between the shoulder blades and grazed the secondary heart.

"I get the impression that he reflexively twisted round to grab at the door handles," she finishes up. "But he would have been dead before he could touch them. There's blood on the corpse's forehead, too. He might have cut himself as he fell into the door."

"These wounds on his back?" Mitsu says. "Made by someone in a rage?"

"Good guess, lieutenant. Why else stab a dead man?"

With the rustle of cloth-of-gold, the Val Chiri with the speaker-unit joins them. He folds his top four legs over his torso and bows to Mitsu, then puts the box back into position.

"You are the officer in charge?"

"Sure am. Thank you for being willing to humble yourself by translating our unworthy words into your tongue."

"I will endeavor to do so to the limit of my poor powers." He bobs his head rapidly. "But there is something I must be making clear at the very beginning of your most excellent investigation. We cannot surrender to you the body of our leader. We must have it here tonight for the traditional ceremony."

"Well, sir, I'd never interfere with someone's religious beliefs, but couldn't we pick it up for the autopsy after the ceremony?"

"That will be impossible. I cannot say why."

"Well, then, we'll do the autopsy and return it to you for the ceremony."

"That will be impossible. I cannot say why."

Mitsu decides that arguing can wait till later.

"Well, let's start getting some information."

Bill brings out his notebook and turns it on.

"Now, sir, if you'll just give me the victim's full name, and yours as well."

"I cannot do so. Honored lieutenant, you are not of Chiri Gan. You are doubtless not understanding what you are asking. I am sure in my many cells, deep as you say, that you do not understand how you are giving offense by asking for such a personal thing as a name."

"Most certainly I mean no offense, honored translator. But our courts of law will demand names."

"But honored lieutenant, will this matter truly become dragged into a public court?"

If Washington's involved, he has a point.

"Okay, Bill, *for now*, put the victim down as M.M. Murdered Male."

"And you may describe me as Brother of M.M., and we are

Clan Milac' Abri." The Val Chiri bobs his head again. "Honored lieutenant, you display tact and understanding worthy of diplomats."

In the conversation that follows Mitsu needs every shred of those qualities that she possesses. Formal compliments, circumlocutions, evasions, hints, and half-truths—she hears them all, but never a simple statement, though at the same time, never an outright lie. Her other dealings with Val Chiri have convinced her of their essential honesty, which is why, she supposes, they've developed such elaborate ways of hedging the truth, just as, she's sure, Brother of M.M. is hedging now. She's willing to bet a chance at promotion that he either knows or thinks he knows the identity of the murderer, not, of course, that he's going to tell her. What he does talk about, at great length, is the structure of the clan, more than they ever would have thought to ask or wanted to know. Finally, after a frustrating hour, she cuts him short.

"Tell me, honored voice of Clan Milac' Abri, if these things we are recording are true. The murdered male, former First Man of your clan, left his suite last night at about 1800 hours. None knew where he might be going, because it was not their position in life to question him. I, however, guess that he went to the public studio of the Admart show in order to record his message. One of my assistants will confirm or deny that fact. However, he never returned to the suite. In the morning, about 0600 hours, First Wife went to search for him, as was indeed part of her position after so long an absence. He had recently been ill, too, and she was worried because of that. She found him in none of the rooms of the suite and came out into the hallway here. Something struck her about the outside doors, and she opened them to find her husband's body. When she screamed, Second Wife and First Son heard her and came to help. First Son told the women to leave the body as they found it and sent Third Son, who had also joined them by then, to fetch you, Second Man of Clan Milac' Abri. You then called the police."

"That is correct, honored lieutenant."

"May I ask you why you called us?"

He stiffens, glancing this way and that.

"It was the correct thing to do."

"Certainly, but Val Chiri tend to solve these problems on their own, when they can."

"It was the message." He seems to be forcing himself to look her in the eye. "Third Son saw it during its first showing on that execrable television program. Soon the police would have called without doubting."

"Thank you for being so frank. Will you accompany me to look at your brother's corpse? Or will that be too painful?"

"I have seen it once. I can look again."

The med-techs have laid the murdered man flat on the floor of the connecting bridge. Colored shadows fall across him from the stained-glass insets in the bridge walls. The Brother joins her as she flips the end of the sheet back for a look at the victim's face. For a moment Mitsu mistakes the smear of dry orange blood across his brow-ridge for a shadow.

"Hey, wait," she says. "One of the jewels is missing. A diamond, I think it was."

"You are correct, honored lieutenant. It was a white diamond." Automatically he touches his own brow ridge, where a single red jewel glimmers. "It is part of First Man's station in life to carry the wealth of the clan within his body. The rest of us carry only a few gems of little value, for use in emergencies, I think your word is."

"I see. Looks like that diamond got pried out with the point of a sharp knife. Like maybe the one that killed him."

"Perhaps this is merely robbery? Yes, that must be it. That jewel was worth very many of your dollars. Perhaps one of your poor people was overwhelmed by his need to care for his family."

"Do you really think that your brother's murderer had only money on his mind? If so, he would have taken all the jewels."

Brother turns pale and studies the floor. Because she needs him, Mitsu lets him off the hook. She goes to a window and looks out and down. Identical bridges run between the two buildings at every other floor, so that it would be the easiest thing in the world for someone to do the murder here at Building One, rush back to Building Two, take a lift down and cross back to Building One again. She realizes then that she's sure the murderer was another Val Chiri. Whom else would Brother bother to protect?

"Now then, honored voice, I need to speak to First Wife. I want to know what made her open those doors."

"What you ask is impossible. No male from outside her clan may speak to a Val Chiri wife."

"Honored voice, I happen to be female."

Apparently, comic surprise is one of those things that cuts across cultural boundaries. Brother's eyes bulge, and he opens and shuts his mouth several times very fast.

"Honored lieutenant, I am guilty of shame and horrifying insult. I pray with all my hearts that you will be forgiving me for this terrible, terrible mistake. You sapients who are not of Chiri Gan—you look so much alike, male and female both. I will escort you to speak with First Wife."

"You are forgiven, honored voice. Bill, give me that recorder, okay? Get the med techs' final report, make sure the photo guys have double the usual number of record shots, and then get the corpse on a gurney. No need to let him lie out here."

Brother thanks her wordlessly with a low and curling bow.

In a group of other women, First Wife sits in the innermost room of the suite, a white cube hung with red and blue banners and littered with objects: piles of metallic bowls and flat shapes, wooden boxes, fiber-hide sacks, lengths of cloth, cushions, all tumbled and scattered about. She herself wears white gauze and sits silent and immobile on an upturned wooden chest. Her female face, smooth and hairless, nearly featureless except for the tiny eyes, the lipless slit of mouth, is so pale, so utterly closed that

Mitsu finds herself thinking of that strange alabaster globe she saw on the morning's AdMart. All around First Wife the other females alternately curl up into balls like some jointed beetle, then stretch out again, holding their arms up to the Val Chiri idea of heaven, perhaps, and shrieking out a tone so high-pitched that Mitsu's ears can barely register it. At a word from Brother, they stop and flee, scuttling off into the other rooms of the suite.

"I will tell her that you are female," Brother remarks. "And that you wish to help us avenge her husband."

While he speaks, Mitsu kneels to get on the same level with First Wife, who turns her head slowly to face her. Under the white drapery, her top four arms are clutched round her torso.

"Ask her about the doors, honored voice. I don't want to intrude on her mourning any longer than I can help."

They speak together briefly.

"She wants only to know when her husband's body will be returned to her."

"Once I know who murdered him, she may have the body back."

Another exchange, and it seems that First Wife's angry about something, from the way that her arms unclasp and lash back and forth. Mitsu can only assume that the woman's half-mad with grief.

"She does not remember about the doors, she says. They are not important, she says. She is First Wife. She is used to having her wishes fulfilled."

"I see. Well, honored voice, if she remembers this detail later, perhaps she might send one of her sons to tell me?"

"They are not her sons, honored lieutenant. They are his sons. She is the one who gave them birth, yes, but he pouched them during their growing into children."

Mitsu sits back on her heels and reproaches herself for forgetting again. Marsupials. These people are marsupials, and the males produce milk as easily as the females. For some reason she always finds these facts hard to remember.

"Of course, honored voice, and you have my apology for my mistake."

The pale face of First Wife turns once again to her own. The golden eyes sweep over her, the voice softens when she speaks.

"She offers you sympathy, honored lieutenant, that you have no husband and no clan and must work among males."

"Then thank her for me. Huh, interesting. Tell me, honored voice, do your women sometimes do male work, then? If they have to, I mean?"

Instead of answering her directly, Brother relays the question to First Wife, who answers slowly, gravely, and he translates the same way.

"Only in situations of great shame, when their husbands and their clan are dead or utterly and completely without honor, and then, only the most menial of work. She wishes you to know that it is a terrible, terrible thing for the daughter of a man to bear such a shame." He pauses as First Wife says something more. "She says she does not mean to insult you, of course. It is your father's shame that he could not provide for you, not yours."

"And your husband did pouch daughters?"

Brother translates; First Wife inclines her head slightly yes in a mimic of a human gesture and holds up a single finger. So. They have an only daughter. When Mitsu looks into her golden eyes, she finds them still impassive, but she knows that she's been given a clue, a big clue, in the only way that First Wife will be allowed to do so, hidden among female things.

Mitsu meets the daughter a few minutes later, in fact, when she and Brother come out of the suite. The med-techs have laid the body, draped in a morgue sheet, onto a gurney, which now stands, guarded by a pair of officers, in the corridor between the outside doors and the suite. Bill waits nearby, talking with one of the officers. When she hears the word "psionics," Mitsu has no compunctions about interrupting.

"Bill, I need a comp unit and a place to work on-site."

"Manager's already thought of that." Bill gives her a keycard. "We got one opposite the turbo doors on the third floor. He says they keep a few business rooms set up for guests."

From down the corridor Mitsu hears a shriek. She can think of it no other way, than that the shriek, a high-pitched howl of mourning, comes like a living thing, carrying the Val Chiri Gan female along with it. All dressed in flowing white, she rushes to the gurney to raise herself up on her lowest legs and throw herself on the body.

"First Daughter," Brother says. "She is First Wife to Chief Navigator. They and their Second Wife live on the floor below."

First Daughter has clawed back the sheet to cradle her father's head in her upper-most hands. Still sobbing, she begins to rock back and forth.

"Honored lieutenant, you must release us the body of my brother. The women will be in this pain of grief until the ceremony is performed."

Mitsu is too busy watching the daughter to answer. She falls silent, shakes herself to pull herself under control, and rests her father's head on the gurney again. Mitsu walks over and points to the spot where the jewel is missing. The daughter looks, then freezes, crouches, her eyes widening, her breath coming in a long sob. She pulls herself away and drops to race down the hall toward the lift. When Bill starts to follow, Mitsu grabs his arm.

"Let her go. I got what I needed."

Just as First Daughter reaches the lift, a Val Chiri male steps out of it. First Daughter drops flat onto the carpet at his feet. Snarling and muttering, he grabs her top arms and hauls her up, shoves her into the lift, and steps in quickly after her. The doors hiss shut.

"That was Chief Navigator." Brother is shaking all over as he speaks. "She never should have left her rooms. I mean, there are males up here who are not clan males!"

"Is that the only reason he was so angry, honored voice? That missing jewel? It seemed to mean a lot to her."

Brother makes a sound under his breath, partly a sob, partly a chitter of rage.

"Theft is always bad." He hesitates for a long while. "Especially of clan property."

"You know, sir, if we solve this case quickly, like this afternoon, then we won't need to do an autopsy. You can hold your ceremony whenever you want."

For a moment the Val Chiri neither moves nor speaks.

"I have endeavored to assist you in all matters, to the limit of my poor station in life and among our people."

"Of course, honored voice. I do believe you've fulfilled your station in every detail."

The office that the hotel manager's given them turns out to be small but serviceable, with two chairs, a desk, and a good comp link station built right into the wall. It's also sound-proofed, as Bill immediately remarks.

"Sir?" he goes on. "While you were talking to the head wife, Washington called again. Want you to call them back on a secure line right away. They're getting real worried."

"Tough. What do you bet they're going to tell us to sweep this under the rug? We're going to have to do it, too. But I want to know what happened before I start sweeping."

Nodding agreement, Bill grabs another Kleenex and blows his nose hard. Mitsu sits down at the link station and logs into the main police comp at the Hall of Justice, then has Bill feed in everything he's noted as well as her recording of the original AdMart message. The CompHQ in turn has a couple of reports for her, one about the victim's background and his clan, the other about his movements of the night before. He did indeed go down to the AdMart studio to use one of their automated recording booths, then returned to the hotel and gave the night clerk a manila envelope to be put into the safe.

"Looked like papers." The recording officer on screen is reading from his notes. "Might be the will he talked about, lieutenant. We're getting a warrant for it now. The clerk logged the package into the safe at 2146 hours, gave the victim a time-stamped receipt, and watched him get into the turbolifts."

The report ends there. Mitsu feeds an analysis sub-routine into the comp, sets it to isolating that sentence of the original message that was in the language of the Val Chiri Gan, then does some hard thinking. A couple of missing hours there, maybe more, between that receipt and his time of death, but First Wife swears and Mitsu's inclined to believe her that he never returned to the suite.

"Family," she says aloud. "Bill, how many human murders come down to problems between family members or close friends?"

"'Bout ninety percent. But these people aren't human, sir."

"Good point, but about how much of our time did old Honored Translator spend talking about his clan?"

Bill grins.

"Ninety percent, yeah."

On screen, a message comes up. The sentence has been isolated and transcribed into the American alphabet. Since Mitsu still doesn't understand one word, she accesses the police ROM library. She's looking for some very specific facts, and once she finds them, she feeds her gleanings into the case file, clears the screen, and enters a handful of keywords to play around with.

"Shame, daughter, a weird name, virtue, jealousy, polygamy, vengeance, provide for, no testimony against." Bill reads them off. "Against what, sir?"

"No spouse can be forced to testify against his or her spouse. That's our law, not theirs, but they'd agree with the principle, I bet."

"Okay. What's the weird name, N'ya however you say that?"

"Who, not what, and that's a throat click in the middle. Remember how the victim spoke in his own language? He said, 'I take leave of you as N'ya!a took his leave.' The language program in the banks translated it that way, anyway; let's hope it's accurate. And in the *Oxford Dictionary of Val Chiri Gan Culture* I found a story that goes with the name, a classic that everyone would know. Kind of like Shakespeare is to us."

"Yeah? And the story is?"

"N'ya!a fell in love with one of his son's wives. Honor said one thing, lust said another. So he screwed the lady and committed suicide and took care of both."

"No way this could be suicide! And his sons are too young to be married. Old honored bullshitter told us that."

"Yeah, he sure did, didn't he? Repeated it a couple of times. He could figure out that we'd get the N'ya!a reference translated, sooner or later. But there's a son, all right, that he was hoping we'd forget about."

"The son-in-law."

"Right. Jeez, Bill, you psychic or something?"

"Go on, make fun of me, but I still think the victim had some kind of psychic powers. I mean, he predicted his own murder, didn't he?"

"But why didn't he just name the killer and save us a lot of trouble? If he was psychic, he would've known, and he said he didn't."

"Well, yeah, I guess so…but wait! He said he couldn't *say*, not that he didn't know."

Mitsu grins.

"Very good, sergeant. Now you're thinking. Look, let me tell you what I got so far. We have a man who knows he's going to be murdered. He's not just afraid of it; he's sure of it. Yet he doesn't come to us, even though he must know he's so important that we'd turn out half the force to protect him."

"Well, maybe he was afraid we wouldn't believe him."

"About this psychic message you got on the brain?" Mitsu smiles to take some sting out of her words. "I'm betting he had other reasons for knowing he was about to die. Bill, these people think in terms of honor and revenge, not laws. M.M. did something that was going to bring vengeance down on him in a big way, but he felt he couldn't reveal who that someone was."

"Like he had to protect his murderer?"

"Maybe. And he had to think about his dependents, too. The Val Chiri men take their responsibilities to the clan real seriously. Unto the seventh generation and all that jazz."

"Huh. So if he jumped the gun and offed this dude before the dude could off him, what would happen to his family?"

"That's one of the things I just looked up. If a man murders someone, all his children old enough to live outside the pouch are taken away for adoption. Any pouchlings are drowned. His wives are stripped of any and all goods they might have inherited and thrown penniless onto the street to fend for themselves. He himself is killed, of course, in some real painful way. I didn't ask for details."

"Jeez. Vengeance? You bet."

A knock on the door, and Bill jumps up, answers it, and comes back with a flat envelope and a big handful of receipts.

"Warrant came. Here's the stuff from the hotel safe."

Mitsu rips open the package and finds, just as they all had expected, the last will and testament of the Val Chiri known as Tarrgon ga Elba!a-ach, AKA the Murdered Male. She scans it over and finds what she's looking for.

"Interesting," she says. "He left the clan monies to his brother, of course, who's going to be First Man now. Then he set aside half of his personal fortune for the reward he offered and divided up the rest among everyone in his immediate family, except First Daughter."

"Hey, that's a shocker! I got the impression that he and his daughter were real close."

"Yep, bet they were." She waves the printout vaguely in Bill's direction. "This was exactly what I suspected, and I think we got our case, whether Washington lets us bring our perp in or not."

"Huh? I don't get it."

"Think about the reward, Bill. That's the hot key to press. Do you really think a clannish bunch like the Val Chiri—jeez, they base their whole lives on their position in their family—do you really think First Man would give all that cash to a stranger?" She stands up. "Scan that will into the case file while I'm gone, will you? Thanks. Are there any women officers assigned to the hotel?"

"Yeah. You need to go interview First Wife again?"

"Nope. First Daughter."

Mitsu finds the people she needs, three female officers and her translator in the corridor near the corpse. In fact, it seems that every male Val Chiri in the clan has squeezed into the narrow space to sit down on the floor around the former First Man's gurney. They say nothing, barely move, merely sit and stare at the police keeping them from performing the last rites for their leader. Mitsu uses CopComm to get replacement guards up before she takes the women officers away.

"Honored lieutenant." Brother presses the speaker-unit so hard into his larynx that it buzzes. "We must do the ceremony soon!"

"I understand that, honored voice. I'm about to wrap this thing up."

Brother goes rigid, his torso arched back, his hands clenched, his face draining to a dead and ashy gray.

"Honored voice, your brother was a far-seeing and clever man. If his daughter has inherited one gram of his courage, the thing you're so afraid of won't happen."

He sighs and lets himself relax, adjusting the speaker before he talks.

"She is a female fit to fulfill her position as First Wife. I can but hope you are correct."

First Daughter receives them in a big room with windows that give out onto a view of the San Francisco Bay, dark blue in the spring sun, and the East Bay hills, hidden behind yellow haze. Thanks to the blue tint in the glass, the polluted sky looks green. Dressed in white, her strangely smooth head emerging from a twist of scarf, she sits calmly on a human-style fiber-hide hassock. At her feet, sobbing, crouches another Val Chiri female, dressed in black.

"Second Wife," Brother explains.

"Ask First Daughter, honored voice, where her husband is."

At the question, First Daughter points with a top arm toward a closed door and speaks, slowly and calmly. Second Wife howls, then falls silent, curling round herself and clutching at her clothes with all four hands.

"He has locked himself in that room," Brother says. "He refuses to come out."

At that, Mitsu knows her theory is correct. She kneels down to look directly into First Daughter's golden eyes.

"Tell her this, honored voice. Your father was a wise man in all ways save one, and that one was the love of women. Will you not take the provision he left for you?"

When Brother speaks, First Daughter stares across the room at the far wall. For a long time after the translator falls silent, she says nothing, her mouth a thin, tight line, while the younger female slowly uncurls herself and begins to snivel and whine. Although Brother doesn't translate, Mitsu can guess that she's begging the senior wife for something. Mitsu wonders if their husband is listening, crouched like a hunted animal behind the bedroom door, or if he's killed himself. If it weren't for Washington's interference, she would order the door broken down, but as it is, she waits. At last First Daughter cuts Second Wife short with a wave of a middle arm and begins to speak. Brother translates a phrase or sentence at a time.

"Last night, my husband returned to our bed very late, at perhaps the second hour of your night. I pretended to sleep so that he would not press himself upon me. He tossed this way and that, then got up and left the sleeping room. After a few moments I too rose and went to the door. I looked through a crack and saw him hiding some object in that box there." She points to one of the wooden chests. "This morning, I found blood upon the clothes he was wearing last night. I have saved those clothes. I suspect the blood is that of my father."

"And so do I." Mitsu stands up, motioning to one of the officers. "Open it."

Second Wife howls, arching her back and throwing her head from side to side. Brother kicks her into silence and begins to berate her.

"Leave her be!" Mitsu snaps. "Could she really have turned the First Man down when he wanted to have sex with her?"

Brother shuts up. First Daughter puts a middle arm around her junior's shoulders and draws her close, a gesture of protection, as they watch the police officer open the chest. She takes a plastic bag out of her belt pouch and uses it to lift the murder weapon out.

"Looks like it's been wiped," Reilly says. "But you never know. There might be a print or two left. And what's this? A diamond. Jeez, and a big one."

"Yep," Mitsu says. "The bride-price. He took it as payment for the despoiling of Second Wife."

"And so First Daughter gets all that gold to start a new life somewhere for her and Second Wife," Mitsu says. "It's not an inheritance, so it can't be taken away from her even though she's the murderer's wife. Brother was implying that if we go along with Washington and never bring this to court, the clan will let them keep their children, too, even the pouchling. Sounds like a good bargain to me, since Washington won't let us prosecute anyway."

"Might as well give in gracefully, huh?" Bill pauses to smear his red, scabby nose with some sort of medicated jelly. "God, I'm glad we're getting out into the air."

"You've suffered for justice, pal, for sure."

"Glad someone realizes it. Oh well, virtue's its own reward, huh?"

"You bet. Let's get back to the station. I'll put in a final call to Washington on the secure line there. Our murderer's probably dead by now, whether he killed himself or the new First Man did it for him."

Since Bill's already cleared all traces of their work off the hotel comp banks, they leave the tiny office and head for the turbolifts. Even several floors below the actual living quarters, the scent of Val Chiri Gan drifts around them through the air-conditioning vents.

"One last thing I don't understand," Bill says. "That ceremony. Why do they have to hold it right away? I mean, what do they do that couldn't wait for an autopsy?"

"Eat him raw."

"What?"

"They eat their dead clan members. It's a ritual thing, or so I found out from the ROM library. Everyone in the clan gets a serving. They see it as taking a part of him into their bodies, kind of like a pouchling. That way the dead become part of the living family, and they can never be separated again. But it's not like they enjoy it or anything, so in this warm weather, they need to get it over and done with while he's still fresh."

For a minute Mitsu's afraid that Bill is going to throw up, but he gathers himself with a gulp and a sigh.

"Well, whatever's right," he says at last. "But jeez, sir, in my opinion that's carrying togetherness just a little too far."

Ch-Ch-Changes

Chaz Brenchley

all art aspires
to the condition of music

The rules are few, at Parry's. Indeed, they're barely rules at all, so much as customs observed—but they are scrupulously observed, and they can be rigorously enforced at need. Don't make that necessary. That's Rule One.

Rule Two? Don't call it a bar. Parry's quite clear about that; it's an establishment.

Don't let that stop you paying for your drinks. He's quite clear about that, too.

If you must kick up a ruckus, keep it quieter than the pilots'. They're privileged; you're not. And whatever else you do, don't approach the pilots. If one of them brings you in, that's fine: join their table, cling close, and welcome. If they beckon you over, the same applies. But always, always wait to be invited. Don't ever try to push in.

Actually, that's what most of the rules boil down to. It's the pilots' place of choice, and Parry means to keep it that way. Which means they get to do what they want, and you don't. That's it.

To be fair, that's more or less the rule all over the Margin, all along the Limb, all through human space. With them so few and the need so great, who's ever going to say no to a pilot? Whoever they are, whatever they ask? Pilots are the new black: they are always in order and may never be debated.

Actually, that last is a joke, mostly. Pilots make a disordered crew by definition, and they'll cheerfully debate with each other or with anyone, if 'debate' means argue stubbornly or viciously or relentlessly, up to the very edge of fighting. Pilots don't fight each other, and you never, ever fight with a pilot. Not in Parry's, certainly, but not actually anywhere.

Actually, maybe that's Rule One. Maybe that's all the rules there are, all over. Let pilots be, let them find their own ways to damnation.

Trust me, they'll do that. They will.

Tonight, they're being peaceable enough. Parry's all but slumbers under the dead weight of their sobriety. That's literal, more or less—pilots don't drink, don't smoke, don't drug when they're in port: they're trying to come down, to remember what it's like to live with all the limits of a body and claim it as their own, to stop at the inside of their skin—but it's also situational. Out beyond Parry's door lie the lights and noise and reckless abandonment of the Margin, every twisted thing that humans find or do for fun compressed into a mile or two of sheetwalk, into a few thousand urgent transient bodies. Pilots are all about the body, this side of n-space: they'll do most of what's available out there. And then they'll come in here, because Parry's is quiet and comfortable, a place to catch their breath and touch base with their inner selves in the company of colleagues.

They come in here a *lot*. Which is why anybody else comes too, why everybody else looks in: just to drink where pilots are and watch how pilots sit, listen to the murmur—or the yelling—of their voices and breathe a little of their rarefied air. Nothing rubs off and no one would want it to, and even so. This is still the place to be, and here they are.

Not all, of course. Not most, for human space is a skein stretched fine and far; not even most of those you might have hoped to see hereabouts, if you were that kind of fan, if hope was still a thing for you. By definition, pilots are a fly-by-night crew, here and gone, always in demand. Some like the long haul, one end of the Limb to the other; they might not show their faces in Parry's from one year's end to the next. Some are in and out, barely flitting outside this system before they're back, barely pausing before they're off again, barely worth the effort and the risk.

And n-space is another variable, as whimsical as they are. Some times, some places—if there's a difference, if you could ever confidently divide time from space and say which was which—it may be slick as oil, squeezing ships through, spitting them out; or else it can be thick as porridge, clinging, close to impassable. And some pilots are cautious by nature, taking it slow and sweating all the way, while some are devil-may-care, slapdash, heroic in the worst way. Not noticeably dead yet, but even so. Mostly those get the cargo runs; passengers would sooner wait for someone steadier. Relatively steadier.

So, yes: Parry's is quiet just now. Some of the regulars are out. Mercy Mercy and Ferrel have been gone so long, people are starting to think them lost, adrift in n-space. Irrecoverable. No surprise in Ferrel's case, but Mercy would be a real loss. Everyone loves Mercy Mercy; she's the acceptable face, the people's pilot, the single splendid example you can point to.

Could point to. Maybe. They've not been gone long enough to be certain, but the question's in the air now, whether they're ever coming back. The strangest thing, of course, is that they went together in the first place. Pilots never do that. They're too rare to risk, and if one gets into trouble the other can't get them out of it. Navigation isn't a science. It isn't even an art: it's an embedding, an act of faith written in the body, inherently individual. Impossible to repeat, almost—almost!—impossible to survive.

Which of course is why and how pilots are what they are, and why we put up with them.

THIS NIGHT—IT'S ALWAYS NIGHT ON the Margin, if "night" means "time to be out on the sheetwalk, looking for trouble," which it always, always does—there's the one settled table in Parry's, as so often, with the onlookers coming and going, staring and pretending not to stare, never quite daring to cross that gap that pilots create and Parry enforces, that narrow space between one table and the next, that unbridgeable gulf.

You want to cross that gulf, you'll need to fly. Unless you're lifted over.

This is Brone's table, by custom and practice and—well, by mere occupation. Brone the Shutterself entity, the pilot who never flies, who almost never leaves Parry's. Brone migrates in a slow shuffle between a room in the back and a table, this table, its table out here in the front where everyone can see, for values of seeing that include being baffled by layers of swaddling drab duffel. It has a head by courtesy, by inference alone, that hooded peak that's narrower than what might be its shoulders. It has a drinking tube of sorts, that emerges to suck at whatever's in its glass; some people think that's a finger. Hollow and translucent and plumbed in, but a finger none the less.

None the less: Brone is as human as any of them, these pilots that we've made by luck and guesswork, great endeavour and great loss. So many have been lost in n-space, lost to us, despite our need; none has ever—quite—lost their humanity, despite the changes bred into them, the wild experimentation, the slow gestation over generations. Despite random mutation and surgical intervention, despite mind-altering treatments and mind-altering drugs, despite it all. They're still human, if only because we say so. Because we could not bear for them to give that up, or because we could not bear to be the ones who made them or named them something other, or because we could not trust them after.

"Bodies like ships like buildings, machines for living in," says Ferenor who has never seen a building, who was bred in a bottle and hatched in orbit, cultivated for this life she leads. One of the rare successes, a design for a pilot that actually worked. Once, it worked once. All her litter-mates died or grew strange, strange as she, without the benefit of her ability. An unreproducible result; an experimental method recorded, remembered, not to be repeated. You can't call it science, if it never works again.

As usual, Brone says nothing. Does it even listen? Who can, who could possibly say? There's no standard measure for a pilot, any pilot; but whatever concept you have of what it means to be a pilot—or what it means to be human—the Shutterself entities are far and far beyond that. Far and far.

Ferenor wears her body as lightly and as fleetingly as she does her opinions—unless that's the other way around—whereas everything in Brone is slow and fixed and solid. If it knows change, that could only be on a geologic scale. Ferenor is air, limitless and uncontained, a breeze across Brone's mountain. Here and gone. Perhaps that's what it cherishes in her. Perhaps it likes them fickle, transient, departed.

Perhaps that's why it stays.

"Living is incidental." So says Ten Barry, the devolved clone. His—brother? twin? simulacrum?—who answers to the same name is for once absent from his side. They're doing their bewildering double act solo, perhaps simply to mystify twice as many people at once. One thing for sure, he won't be flying a ship alone. It takes them both: that much we know. Not much more, for some pilots are open and some have been thoroughly exposed, but the clone gestalt holds its secrets close. Are there ten? Were there ten? No one has ever seen more than two abroad, and they're believed to be the same two, though how would you, how would anyone know? And are they a single distributed individual, or a family? Or worse? And above all, of course, how does the flying happen, what's the methodology, how is it achieved?

They—or he—won't say, and there is no power and no law that might compel them. Dozens, perhaps hundreds of such laws exist in draft, all through human space; no jurisdiction has ever dared enact them. Of course it's for the greater good, we could learn so much, enhance our chances of making another generation of pilots—but what if this generation responded with a blockade, an absolute refusal to fly into that region of space? No government could survive that, however strong or secure their grip. The hold that pilots have on their privacy is so much stronger, it has never been tested. They've never even needed to threaten such a blockade. A politician's imagination is enough. More than enough. Pilots get what they want, here as everywhere. In Ten Barry's case, that means he—or they, or what you will—can be oblique, obstructive and infuriatingly unforthcoming, to their dual hearts' content.

"How incidental?" Ferenor asks.

"A ship is a machine, yes—not built for living in, no. Built to journey, to endure n-space, to come out elsewhere, with goods or passengers or war or what you will. The same is true of us: built to journey, built to survive, built to be going somewhere else. If they could make machines instead, they would do that, and do without us gladly. The living are inconvenient, and not at all to the purpose."

It's true enough, and hardly a new argument. In honesty, it's hardly an argument at all. No autopilot yet attempted has even found a way into n-space, never mind emerging otherwhere. Those that have been taken into n-space by human pilots and triggered there have never found their way out, despite the best of planning. Either the pilot has abandoned the experiment and taken control again, or else the ship has been lost entirely, to our great cost. One pilot down, each time. Very few such experiments occur. We can't afford them.

But if Ten Barry's not speaking metaphorically, at least he's told us something about his own origins. *Built to journey*, he said. If that's to say the devolved clone was created to pilot a ship, if this is someone's private and successful experiment—well, that's something we didn't know before. It might have been happenstance; many pilots are completely unprepared, unschooled, unexpected. Most, perhaps.

Perhaps that's why you rarely see Ten Barry—either Ten Barry, or any—without the other, or one other, at his side. Perhaps they act as a guard on each other's tongue, and here's this one free tonight, saying more than he meant, perhaps.

Saying it to pilots, though. There's no one else at Brone's table today, and no one close enough to overhear. Parry has a brisk way with eavesdroppers, be they human or mechanical or something other.

Pilots don't care, particularly. They're not big on origin stories from others, when they all have their own; and nor are they particularly big on posterity, that relentless search for the next generation, for more and more reliable and better pilots, better controlled. They like themselves pretty much the way they are. For sure they like the life, the privilege, the freedom.

For sure, Maellelin was never built to be a pilot. If she had been, they'd have built her to a standard measure; she wouldn't need a booster-seat just to join the pilots' table. She had the gift of it, that feeling, a sense of n-space unfolding all about her; it wasn't enough, so she had herself rebuilt. Not to scale, no. Just everything she needed, to suit her particular vision. Eyes seven times the size, and so forth. It's said that there are other changes, less clear to be seen: at the molecular level, her brain and nerves rewired. She doesn't need drugs to ease her passage through n-space, nor devices to find her way about. She only has to look. That she comes with her own ship—bespoke again, with a cockpit tailored to her size—is just a bonus.

She's promised that scientists can have her blueprints, her biotech and her body, once she's gone. If they can figure out what she was or what she had to start with, and then the nature and scope of her alterations, see what she made of herself, maybe she'll be replicable. That's if she dies within reach, within our knowledge. If she doesn't lose herself out there somewhere, beyond recall or investigation. We speak of human space as though it were coherent and within bounds, as though we were secure in our holding and in our travelling back and forth, known roads swept free of danger, but none of that is true. Not many pilots die in their beds, in port, convenient for autopsy and study.

A lot of them may not be dead at all. Adrift in n-space, beyond all understanding—who knows, who can tell?

Just how late are Ferrel and Mercy Mercy, anyway?

They're not here, that's all we know. Not here now. Maybe they'll blow in tomorrow, all smiles and ease, full of news and great occasions. A shipful of cargo and great expectations, a new route won, a new system discovered. Something.

Maybe not. Magical thinking is endemic, where pilots are concerned. Their whole process, their individual processes seem halfway to magic at least. People say that it's unlucky to wish them well: that the harder you struggle to believe they'll bring their ships in safe, the less likely that is to happen. Scientists say that. It's been measured. People try not to think about it, mostly.

Murun is here, has brought his ship in safe. To everyone's always surprise. Murun is really not what you'd look for, in a pilot.

He does not inspire confidence. Really not. The best of Murun is his companion Telfer, always at his side, calm and cooling and engaged. Telfer's the one you'd want in control, except that Telfer is no pilot. Telfer's just the rock, the counterweight, ballast or reaction mass or whatever metaphor you like: what allows Murun to work, that's Telfer. Possibly also what keeps Murun sane, if sane he be. Pilots don't usually fly with a partner—come to that, pilots don't usually have a partner—but every one's exceptional in some way, and this is Murun's.

Also he's an asshole and no one knows why Telfer stays with him, but there it is. Here they are.

Here they all are, this tableful: extraordinary anywhere, vanishingly rare all along the Limb, quite commonplace at Parry's. What people come to see, except that he'll never, never make an exhibition of them.

Parry serves drinks relentlessly, distributes smokes and other intoxicants, passes food orders through to the kitchen, answers questions from customers and servers both, watches the door, helps stray tourists find what they're actually looking for as soon as it's clear that his place is not that—and never takes his eye off the pilots' table. There's a barrier between them and the rest of the room; it's immaterial but clear to be seen and widely acknowledged. Let anyone breach that—and people will: drunk or determined, with a question to ask or an axe to grind—and Parry is there, swifter than you'd have thought possible, to steer them aside or throw them out, whichever. He's not always proportionate. Hell, he's not always appropriate. But it's his name above the door, or at least his singular initial, and he gets to make the rules and interpret them too. And enforce them, at need.

Tonight, though—well, tonight here comes a stranger. Five score eyes check him through the door, and no one recognises him. That means he's not a pilot. If he'd brought a ship to Dock, he'd be known by now: new and hence intriguing, mysterious and hence more to be gossiped about than any of the stalwarts.

Nor does he seem to recognise anyone here, even Parry behind the bar. That means he's not local, he doesn't work anywhere in Dock or anywhere on Base, because everyone knows Parry. By the look of him, he's only come here because he was told about it; and there's only one reason why he might have listened, only one reason ever for people to talk about Parry's.

But he's not heading to the bar for a drink, he's not joining the relentless not-quite-staring of the gathered crowd. No, indeed. One look around, and he knows just exactly where he's going: straight to the pilots' table, because he like everyone here knows pilots by sight alone, or else he just sees that barrier of awareness, that do-not-cross, and makes up his mind to cross it—and Parry does nothing.

No, that's not true. Parry does nothing but watch. He knows what's happening, none better; and he makes no move to interfere.

That's unprecedented. He can't have been bribed; this is his place, and what could you possibly offer him that's worth more?

Unknown territory makes uncertain ground. There's a breathlessness all over, people watching Parry watching the newcomer as he steps up, as the pilots lift their heads from that odd little conversation they're having.

They look, and see that they don't know him, and for a moment that is oh so unexpected, they don't know what to do else. Then they remember, one by one but in rapid succession, that this is Brone's table. So all their heads turn its way, relieved of responsibility, curious to see what it will do in their stead.

Unhurried as ever, Brone extends a hand—at least, two visible fingertips emerging from a fold in its swathe of blankets—and a welcome with it, gesturing towards the vacant seat opposite.

Parry never comes to take orders at the table, never—but he comes tonight, and stands at the man's shoulder with that kind of patient submissive authority that demands the attention of those on whom it waits.

He looks so ordinary, this man: there's nothing to him, no reason for any of this.

No observable reason.

Until he speaks, until he says, "I don't want a drink, I never drink in port—and I couldn't pay you anyway," which is more honest than many a proprietor would expect.

Parry takes in his stride, or rather in his stillness. Quite comfortably, he says, "The first one's on the house, always. And no one at this table drinks alcohol in port."

All of which goes to say one thing, and one thing only: and Parry might be down on eavesdroppers, but somehow everyone in the place hears that one thing, as it goes entirely and graciously unsaid.

The newcomer's a pilot after all. For all that he came in without a ship.

First Ferrel goes off with Mercy Mercy, and now this. Someone must have brought him in—but why? Any pilot can always find a ship. We have too many lying idle, when there are always passengers to ferry and cargo to shift, one end of the Limb to the other. There are a dozen here in Dock right now, their owners bidding high for any pilot's time, desperate to see their craft in service. The same is true at every station, every port of call.

Here he is, though, a pilot who didn't fly here, who must have been no more than a passenger in someone else's journey. Parry knows. Maybe Brone knows too. Maybe there's something about a pilot, something detectable, known to others of their craft. And to Parry, obviously.

Maybe he's just been talked about among themselves. Maybe he was hot gossip from the moment he arrived, and they've all been waiting to see him show up. Sooner or later, every pilot in Dock steps off the Margin and into Parry's, if only just to catch their breath before they dive back in.

He asks for honeymint, which may be the humblest request any pilot has ever made in here. Parry nods, doesn't bat an eye, but there's a murmur all around. Maybe no one's conspicuously eavesdropping, but no one's talking either, they're trying to absorb the conversation by osmosis; and he seems keen to help. His voice is extraordinary: a baritone that holds its own music, that strikes pure through every syllable and resonates all through the space, through people's heads as though it were their own proper note each time, entirely personal and entirely true.

Honeymint is good for the throat, but he really, really doesn't need it.

Except—well, is that a tremolo in his voice, or is it just a tremor? Certainly there's a tremor in his fingers, where he lays them so neatly, so carefully along the edge of the table. Here as elsewhere, every head is turned his way; here as elsewhere, every voice is hushed and waiting, leaving space for his. Maybe some of them only want to hear him speak again, and never mind the matter. Maybe. Pilots aren't usually so susceptible, but there's nothing usual happening here.

Brone gestures again, and this time maybe with an open hand, palm up. If it has palms, or hands. Nothing's certain, where there's almost nothing to be seen: a muffled movement within the fabric, perhaps another glimpse of fingers.

It's enough, seemingly. Or he was going to talk anyway, invited or otherwise. Just like he was going to approach anyway, he was going to push his way in. He has a seat, he has a drink on its way: both of those might be superfluous, might not have been needful at all. Not to the purpose. He might be all about the purpose.

He says, "My name is Almarine. I dislike to break in on you, but my need is urgent. I—I am a stranger to you, but…"

Even such a voice can lose its words, it seems, and die away, leaving a sense of absence that's both intolerable and insurmountable. No one is in a hurry to fill that vacancy, knowing how they must inevitably disappoint, however wisely they speak. Cadence should perhaps not matter so much, but sometimes—this time—yes, it truly does.

If anyone ever wants to tell you that pilots have no vanity, that they can't afford it—well. Laugh in the idiot's face. Even Almarine's silence has a mellow musicality to it, the attentive thrumming silence of a classic instrument, and not one of these wants to set their chicken-scratch voices against that, like an affront.

"You are a pilot."

Perhaps it had to be so, that Brone came forward at the last. Brone's table, after all; and Brone so seldom speaks, this wasn't so much an opportunity as a sucking vacuum. They hardly know what it sounds like, any of its cohort here; its voice is as much a shock as Almarine's, though for different reasons.

A figure so large, you'd expect it to boom hollowly, but it doesn't. There's a great deal of flesh in its voice, an unexpected wetness, a sense of marsh life where you'd think more of the high desert plains, as much of the dust and dry as you can imagine, who have never been to a Shutterself habitat.

"A pilot, yes." Almarine confirms it, and seems likely to go on, and then falls short of words again.

"Then whatever you need, in this place it is yours." And *this place* might mean Parry's establishment, or the Margin at large, or Dock or the whole station or the whole of human space: it's still a truth, plain and simple. It's not quite *carte blanche*, it's not *whatever you want*—but a pilot's need, any need, oh yes. If it's humanly possible, that will be met—and if it's not humanly possible, then it's not a need, by definition.

"I need a ship," he says—and then holds his hand up to stay them, to hold back the whole table. A little late: someone's laughing, someone's rolling their eyes, only Brone is showing no emotion at all. Brone's a rock. But Almarine goes on, "I mean, I need a ride. On someone else's ship. I can't, I can't do this alone. Not again."

And now no one's laughing, though their degrees of puzzlement or denial are probably no easier to take. Once again they leave this in Brone's hands, as though it were dependable, a rock.

It says, "What, that you will not do? Pilots fly."

That's the criterion, really, that everything turns upon. *Whatever you need,* yes—but you do have to fly. For preference you have to get where you're going, with more or less what you were given—the ship, the passengers, the cargo—in more or less working order. Within tolerances, at least, in all particulars. Pilots have come in to the wrong port with the ship and the people and the goods too strangely changed; but they flew, and they survived.

Rock bottom, if you're a pilot, you really do have to fly.

Unless you're Brone, of course. Brone's unique, which is why there can't be two.

"You don't have to fly alone," Murun says, sounding almost considerate for once. It's a matter that touches him deeply, of course; maybe that makes a difference. He curls a hand around Telfer's wrist, and smiles, and for that little moment he's almost not an asshole.

"I do," says Almarine, and it might almost be his tragedy; certainly it is his sorrow, if not its cause. "I have to be alone. I," and this is really no news, now that they've heard his speaking voice, "I sing my way through n-space. The music of the spheres is quite literal to me: from planet to planet, and from star to star. Someone else with me would…not be in tune."

Nods around the table. None of them could do that, or even understand it, but it makes perfect sense. They know a pilot who sees her path and draws it, a sequence of rapid sketches that somehow carries her and her craft along. If sketches, why not song? And if Murun needs Telfer, then of course another might need solitude.

"So," Maellelin says, "why can't you fly alone, if you have to be alone to fly?"

"I come from Reynmark's Star," he says slowly. "I grew up a planet-hopper, singing cargoes back and forth. I was happy there." More nods. Everyone knows Reynmark's, it's a constant port of call. A dozen ports of call, more habitable planets than any other system in human space, and enough traffic between them to sustain its own small navy, its own coterie of pilots.

To sustain, of course, does not mean *to keep*.

"I was offered better ships and a better life, if I would only go further. I was happy, but…the music of the planets was extraordinary; what might, what must the music of the stars be like? I could only ever hear Reynmark's Star, in-system. I thought there must be more, they must all sing in chorus; I thought I could join that chorus. I thought I had to hear it. I thought I only had to hear it, to know it. I thought it was the song the Sirens sang…"

"So?"

"So I took an offer, I took a ship to go far and far, from one end of the Limb to the other. The further I went, the greater the music, you see? I wanted to hear all the galaxy sing to me…"

"And?"

"And I heard all the galaxy sing to me, and it was the most dreadful terrible thing in my life," and they know how that feels, none better, though none of them can ever hope to hear what he's heard. Each of them in their different ways has confronted n-space, and each of them has found it appalling, each and every time.

That's the other reason why they're treated very, very well. They go through hell out there, every time they go; we have to counter that with some little taste of heaven, every time they make it back, or why would they ever go?

Conversely, they do actually have to go, to justify their status. Everyone at this table—well, except for Brone, who is a law unto itself—does that, over and over. There's not much sympathy to be found here, for a man who won't.

"Aww, did it scare you, diddums?" Murun, being an asshole, as advertised.

Almarine looks at him, and something causes Murun to fall quiet, which may be the thing least expected in this most unexpected evening.

Parry brings Almarine's drink, and he sips it, holds it in his throat, almost seems to gargle it before he swallows. Must be a singer thing.

He says, "The planets around Reynmark's Star were like, like plainchant: organised, methodical, a unity. Anyone with an ear could sing with them. The star itself was grander, symphonic, still within my compass. I thought the stars at large would be like that. I thought I could reach them. I thought I could *aspire*." Even that magnificent voice can crack, seemingly. Another sip of honeymint, another pause. "I was wrong. I could barely survive the stars."

"And yet you did. We do." Maellelin, laying down the bare base fact of it like a card that could never be trumped.

"Not me. Not again. I came too far, I heard too much…I need to go home. In other people's ships, and small jumps. However long it takes. I can still hear them, even when I'm just a passenger. Not so, not so vividly, not inside me, blood and bone, but still. I hear them. And I can only stand so much."

He stares around the table, looking for contempt and finding that—Murun, yes, but not Murun alone: this isn't asshole territory, this is earned, the achievement of weakness, of broken oaths and neglected duty—and more, a kind of weary dismissal, *if you're choosing not to be a pilot, why are you sitting at our table?* Pilots have *noblesse oblige* written into their DNA—literally, in some instances—and they're very sensitive to betrayal.

"The stars leave their scars on us all." That's Brone again, saying more tonight than he might have said in a month before this.

"Not the stars," Almarine counters, and this, now: this is what he's here for. What he's here to say. Why he needs that ride so very, very much. Three short words, in that voice, with that emphasis: they were half turned away from him already, but now they're turning back as he goes on, "The others. The voices, singing their own way between the stars. They're out there, and I hear them."

"No." That's Ten Barry, and you could say that he's invested here. "No two pilots have ever worked n-space the same way," except themselves, perhaps. If that's what happens when you clone. "We never heard of another pilot singing. We never heard of any pilot singing, until now."

"Not one of us," says Almarine, and this is what they were all listening for, what none of them wanted to hear. "Not human. Their voices, their chord-sequences, their tonality—nothing human. But singing, yes, and doing what I do, riding the music from star to star. I can't bear to hear them, but I am sure. They're everywhere, out there."

And that's the thing, there's the moment. You could call it first contact, except it's not. Just a footfall on the stair, the sound of someone else's passage. All this time, all this space, nothing but human traffic, they had almost begun to believe themselves alone; and here's this sole voice—this extraordinary voice, but never mind that—to tell them it's not so. To say there's some other culture, creature, civilisation out there. Doing what he does, but doing it routinely: training up pilots the way we train up doctors or managers or civil engineers. Or barkeeps.

Here's Parry, and if anyone actually eavesdrops here, that would be him, so it would hardly count. The world or life or the universe just changed, something just changed radically, human perspective, turning over on itself; and he's here taking orders for fresh drinks, offering snacks from the kitchen, saying, "So, will one of you be taking Almarine on, the next step, towards home?"

And they all look at each other, still swimming from the revelation; and of course it's Brone, because Brone is talkative tonight where they apparently cannot be, who says, "I will find a ship, and take Almarine home. All the way. With pauses, when he needs them."

Which is unprecedented, more than implausible; which would have broken their understanding of the very way things are, if that weren't already lying in shatters about their feet; and which none of them, not one of the pilots at the table there needs so much as a moment to understand, to acknowledge, to accept.

Because it's the human thing to do.

The Color Winter

Steven Popkes

The air smelled of whiskey, tobacco and rain.

He stood on the top level of the parking garage smoking one foul African cigarette after another and drinking from a bottle with a starry label. The rain had already soaked through his jacket. Rivulets ran down his back, his shoulders. It was not a warm rain, but a rain of mid-November: gusty, brittle, cold.

"I am Harry Linden," he shouted into the wind. "I am eighty years old. I am wet." He chuckled. "I will die of pneumonia, maybe." He laughed outright and drank from the bottle.

The laugh turned into a cough and for a long minute he couldn't get his breath. The cough faded and he drained the bottle and threw it to the street. The sound of shattering glass was lost in the rain.

The office of the Stuart Street Parking Garage was placed at the corner of Stuart Street and Berkeley Street in downtown

Boston. Two sides were made of glass to allow the owner—Harry—to watch the street, the cars entering and leaving, and the person in the ticket booth taking money.

He barely glanced in the booth at Jasper as he entered the office. The chair creaked and he looked up. "Sasha?" he asked.

"I was down here for the doctor anyway," she said. She was a big, craggy, mountain of a woman. Harry saw new valleys and fissures when she shifted her weight. A woman of twenty or so played with the hem of Sasha's dress. Her face was wide, and her eyes slanted, her fingers stubby and thick. "You should watch Jasper," Sasha continued. "Keep an eye on him. He could take you for a whole day's profits." She stared at him accusingly. "Harry Linden, you are eighty years old and you are wet clear through. You could die of pneumonia."

"Sasha." He smiled and kissed her forehead. He stroked the younger woman's head. "And Margaret. What did the doctor say?"

Margaret smiled and covered her face with her hands, peeked out between her fingers.

"Wet." Sasha shook her finger at him. "And smelling of whiskey."

He nodded and hung up his jacket in the corner. The dripping blended with the steam hiss of the radiator.

"You listen to me about Jasper. You must watch him."

Harry looked through the window towards the booth. Jasper stood still, staring at nothing, waiting for a car to come. The garage was silent but for the rain. Jasper was bald all over. His chest and upper abdomen hung on him like empty sacks, wrinkled and covered with something not quite hair, not quite feathers. If it weren't for the dish-shaped skin where his eyes should have been, he might have looked like an old bum wearing empty sacks. As it was, the ridges and wrinkles under his skin and across his body made no sense to Harry. But, Harry reasoned, *Jasper is an alien. How should you understand him*?

"Jasper will steal nothing. How is Margaret?" Margaret looked up at him at the mention of her name and smiled again. Harry and Sasha had had a daughter, Barbara. She had never married and when she was thirty-seven, she had come home pregnant and silent. Two years after Margaret was born, she died driving to work on a gray snowy morning when the Harvard Bridge collapsed into the Charles River.

As he looked at Margaret, he saw Barbara's features overlaid by Down syndrome. She had been a melancholy, practical child; a strong, self-willed woman who smiled little. Barbara was born the year Germany had invaded Poland and died the year R'rched the Rigellian crashed in Boston harbor: when things changed, he thought.

With all of that arrayed behind you, Margaret, how is it you are so happy? Harry shook his head.

Sasha shrugged. "Bronchitis. Heart murmur. It is the same or only a little worse."

"That is a small victory, anyway."

Margaret buried her face in the folds of Sasha's dress. She giggled.

Jasper had come that summer. Thus:

Harry looked up and saw him standing silently outside the glass door. He had only looked up to see if Sasha and Margaret were coming down the street to have lunch. He made a kind of squeak of alarm.

The alien did not move.

Harry was startled but not surprised. All week he had been hearing of interstellar refugees coming from some far depression or war or something else the television would not describe clearly. He had already seen a few of them on the Boston streets.

He opened the door. "How—" His voice squeaked again. He

cleared his throat and tried once more. "How do you do. Can I help you?" *You're a diplomat now, Harry?* he thought. *Butter would not melt in your mouth.*

"The name Jasper has been assigned to me. I am seeking employment," the alien said in a bass whisper. "I was told at the R'rched Center there might be some at locations such as this."

Harry shrugged. "Not here. I don't have much. Try the Rieken System lots down the street."

"Rieken System?" Jasper produced a phrase book and searched it.

Harry chuckled. "Yah. They own most of the garages around here. Except mine."

"I do not understand. I am in need of currency. My country is invaded and my…" He searched the phrase book again. "Fimily. My fimily starves."

Harry nodded. "Yes. I understand. Try the Rieken System."

"Please. You must help me."

"Goddamn it!" Harry breathed deeply. Alien, he muttered to himself. "Try the—"

"I work cheaply. I work hard and honestly. I do not sleep and need only a small place to stay, but if you do not have that, I am told I may stay at the R'rched Center. If I do not find work soon I will be deported and my…fimily will be liable for my return passage."

Harry was silent a moment, remembering the long nightmare run from Poland to America. "I haven't got much to give you."

"Much I do not need. Only a little."

He stared at Jasper guiltily. *Just what is right here?* "I— No. I must feed my own."

Sasha and Margaret came into the garage. Sasha looked over the alien to question Harry with her eyes. He shrugged.

Margaret took the alien's hand.

"Yes?" said Jasper.

"I'm Margaret," she said and gave a bubbling laugh. She rubbed her cheek against his hand. "Soft."

The alien was silent a moment. "I have been assigned—" He stopped, seemed to consider her for a long time. "I am Jasper."

At that moment, Harry changed his mind.

ALL OF THEM LIVED IN a small house in Brighton, a dingy, broken-asphalt subsection of Boston. Jasper's quarters were on the back porch, where they had put in a sink and curtains. Harry deducted a small rent from Jasper's wages and felt guilty. Jasper did not complain.

It was close to dawn, now, and Harry sat listening to the sirens and the pre-morning birds. The rain had stopped, and the city still felt hushed. Darkness made the shapes and shadows of things grow twisted and strange. A 1934 Luger he had found in the Spanish Civil War glinted an electric blue from the streetlight's glare. A pair of silver candlesticks left shadows as crooked as thumbs. Next to them was a high-domed fireman's helmet, the insignia written in Polish.

Sasha and Margaret were still in bed. Often, he prowled like this, to wander the house and listen. He looked in on Margaret, her flat face relaxed in sleep. Sasha lay still and he could not tell if she slept or not.

He heard a noise from the kitchen, a gentle tapping or scratching. Feeling his way through the shadows, he came to the back door. The noise came from there. "Damn," he muttered. He glanced at a calendar but couldn't see the date. It didn't matter. He knew the date from the sounds at the door. It was the full moon of the month: Jasper's payday. "Go away," he said. "I ain't got the money to pay you." The scratching continued. He opened the door.

Jasper stood outside, pelt or feathers or skin moonlit and silver. "Mister Linden?"

"Yah?"

"I wish to talk about my wages."

Harry nodded and moved aside to let Jasper in. Mechanically, he followed Jasper down the hall to his desk and began to bring out the checkbook.

"We do not need that tonight, Mister Linden."

Harry looked down and tried to read Jasper's face. It was still, wide and noseless, broad stretches of wrinkled skin where there should have been eyes. "Why not?"

Jasper brought out stubs of paper from within the wrinkled sacks hanging from his body. Harry couldn't quite see where and wasn't sure he wanted to know. "Here, Mister Linden."

Harry took them. They were the checks he had given Jasper. "There's three months wages here, Jasper. What did you live on?"

"I would like you to hold my wages for me. To be sent home when I die."

Harry sat down. "Die?" *I'm too damned old. I don't understand. I just don't understand.*

"Yes."

Harry waited, then sighed. "Are you going to die?"

"Yes."

"When?"

"Not less than three years from now, I think. But not more than five. Your planet poisons me."

"Then why don't you go home?"

Jasper was motionless for a moment. "I do not understand," he said finally.

"If our planet is killing you, why should you stay?"

"To make money. To send it home."

"Even if you die?"

"Of course."

Harry laughed softly. "Why not take the money home yourself?"

"When I returned there would be no money left. The return

passage would require most of it."

Harry shrugged. "You want me to keep the money?"

"Yes."

"What do I do when you die?"

"Send it here." From another indefinite place on his person, Jasper brought out a leaf of notebook paper. The page was filled with closely written characters and numbers.

Harry couldn't make any sense of it. "What is this?"

"It's an address. Take it to the R'rched Center and my money and they will send it home."

He thrust it back towards Jasper. "Let them keep your death money."

"They cannot."

"Why not?"

"They do not employ me."

"What?"

"They do not employ me."

"I don't understand." Harry shook his head.

"It is important."

Harry looked at him, then the checks. He shrugged. At least he wouldn't have to come up with Jasper's check every month. "Okay."

Jasper put the checks on the desk, turned and walked out through the kitchen.

"Don't you even say thanks?" Harry yelled after him.

Jasper disappeared through the door.

The Rieken System had sprung full blown from the mind of a nameless Harvard MBA graduate working for Gulf and Western. It owned most of the parking space in Boston and all of the really successful lots. Harry had only been able to buy the Stuart Street Garage as a fluke years before. The Rieken System, benign in its monopoly, had left him alone.

They called him that fall.

"Mister Linden?"

"Yah?" He wondered which of his creditors he was talking to this time.

"My name is Proong. Randar Proong. I represent the Rieken System."

Harry sat up. *This is it*, he thought. His mouth grew dry. His stomach clenched. *They'll squeeze me out*, part of him said. *No*, he replied. *I can sell. And cover Margaret's medical bills? You barely do that now. Maybe. I can make breathing space. Maybe I can make some real money.* Fears and hopes born in Poland and thought long dead now came back to life. "Yah?"

"I'd like to meet with you. Lunch, perhaps. Or dinner. What time is convenient?"

He held his voice low, noncommittal, nervous. "What do you want?"

"It's better to talk face to face. Dinner on Tuesday would be good for me. How does that sound?"

He felt confused, flustered, excited, demoralized. "Tuesday?"

"Sevenish? At the Copley? I could come over to the garage and pick you up."

What the hell? This isn't Poland, remember that. "Yah. Okay. Tuesday."

"See you then."

THE GARAGE SCHEDULE WENT LIKE this: Jasper opened at five AM and worked until closing—about midnight. He claimed he needed no sleep and wanted to work the hours. It meant more money he could send to his "fimily." Harry came in about noon and worked until they closed the garage and went home. Over the years before Jasper came, Sasha, Margaret and Harry's life had skewed later and later until for them evening began at midnight. Sasha regularly went to sleep at three. Harry would also sleep then when he wasn't prowling. Jasper's coming had given them back their mornings.

Their living room was a pale yellow oblong of light; lamps hung from the ceilings, the mantelpiece, stood on end tables, on small stools. Tall lamps stood next to the chairs. Sasha had a passion for light.

Sitting in a pool of brightness, Harry chewed over the conversation with Proong. It was short. It was polite. It was noncommittal. It was just exactly the kind of conversation he could imagine some minion of Gulf and Western having with a prospective victim. He had not told Sasha of the call and watched her and Jasper and Margaret with the morose satisfaction and lack of attention of the truly depressed.

Margaret slapped at Jasper playfully, clumsily tried to tickle him. This seemed to alarm Jasper and he backed quickly away spreading the wrinkled sacks on his upper body into a strange umbrella-like arrangement from under his arms. It was twice as wide as he was and iridescent as butterfly wings or the throat feathers of blackbirds. Margaret watched, laughed and clapped her hands.

"Pretty. What is it?"

Jasper relaxed and sat on the floor across from Margaret. *They make a world, the two of them*, Harry thought. Jasper leaned towards her so that she could see it easily. It shone with deep purples and blacks. "It's my..." He stopped for a long time. "My pocket. I can breathe here. Or eat as you do with your mouth."

"Eat what?"

"I do not know the word. What falls from the sky? In the color winter? When water is mostly ice."

"Snow, Jasper," Sasha said suddenly. She turned off the television. "It's called snow."

"Snow, then. We breathe it in here. All colors of it: red, green, lavender. It is what nourishes us most of all. The world poisons us without it."

Harry suddenly felt the words were aimed at him. "Snow is white here, Jasper."

"I know. I saw pictures before I left."

"What will you do with Margaret if you sell?"

I'll take better care of her, he thought. *I could get her better doctors.*

"She cannot be cured. What else can you give her?"

He shrugged and looked outside the office. The wind was blustery and cold, ripping between the Hancock Building and the garage in a long moaning howl.

"What will you do with Jasper?"

"He'll be okay. The R'rched people will take care of him."

"You took his money. His death money. Where is it?"

He squirmed. "I'll give it to him when the time comes."

"Where is it now?"

"You know where it is. It's in doctor bills for Margaret. It's in a new pair of bifocals for you, Sasha. It's in the last month's mortgage payment on the garage."

"Mister Linden?"

"What?" He half stood and turned, saw Jasper and eased slowly down. "What's the matter?"

"Nothing. It is cold in the booth. May I come in here for a few minutes?"

God. It must have been near zero outside. Rain and cold, all winter. Nothing in between.

"Yah," he said. "Aren't any cars coming anyway."

Jasper closed the door and stood silently. After a while, this made Harry nervous. "You need anything?"

"No, sir. I am warming now."

"Yah. Yah." He nodded. "You do that."

The silence fell again. Then, to Harry, the world fell soundless, anechoic and dumb. He felt pressured, embarrassed, needy—silence was only something he wanted to fill. "Jasper," he said as quick as a shout. "So, I don't know enough about you. So. Where are you really from?"

"A long way from here."

"I know *that,* for God's sake. I mean what was it like? What were you like there?"

Jasper did not move or say anything for a long moment. "I would like not to talk about that."

"How come?"

"I would like not to talk about that either. It is enough I am here. It is enough I will send them money…later. It is enough I come to a place that—" He stopped. He shuddered in a quick convulsion as a dog, or a mink might shake off water. "I would like not to talk about that. Who are you, Mister Linden?"

Harry stared at Jasper. "Can you drink?"

"Just as you. We are metabolically similar."

"No. I mean, can you drink alcohol?"

"Probably not. Do not let me stop you."

Harry pulled out the bottle in the desk and swallowed hard, then easy as the fire came into his gut. "Yah," he said finally.

"Who are you?" said the alien.

"Harry Linden. Eighty years old. Destined for pneumonia. At least, that's what Sasha tells me." He shook his head, smiled. "You know how we met?" He rushed on, not waiting for Jasper's reply. "I was a fireman in Krakow when I was a young man. Very young, you understand. Not yet twenty." He chuckled. "It was an honorable profession. Strong. Purposeful. Fearless. You must be all of these." He laughed. "So, we were sometimes weak and our bowels turned to water. Still, we knew what needed to be done and did it. There are no small victories in such a job. Every task is important. Life-threatening. Clear."

Harry swallowed again. "She was watching the fire engines. With such *concentration.* Such *attention.* It caught me. I spoke with her. Spoke with her again. Asked her to the picture show. She came with me. We did this often."

He stared out the window, listening to the wind and the vibration in the windows, listening to the wailing emptiness in the garage behind him. "Finally, her parents said, 'This fireman is not to be our son-in-law.' And they chose a tailor." He shrugged. "A good man, wealthy, with his own shop and clothing store. I knew him. Krakow was not so big to hold only strangers. And she came to me to say good-bye."

There was no garage anymore, no wind, only the light snowy day in front of the café, its sign creaking in the breeze, the snow covering them both.

"I said, 'Don't marry him. Marry me.' And she looked at me. And she *saw* what I had to give her. What the tailor had to give her. That I would go away, that the war would come between us, that she would struggle, bear a silent unhappy child alone, be grandmother to a—" He stopped, breathed deeply a moment, stared into the bottle meditatively. "Then, I only knew she saw no piece of her life with me would be easy. We would have a hard, difficult time. And she was right." He shrugged. "I looked down into the snow and made ready to say good-bye. It did not occur to me she could see that and wish to have me. 'All right,' she said to me. Just that. 'All right.' "

Harry did not move for a while, staring out the window at the blowing papers, candy wrappers, leaves. He shook himself much as Jasper had done, shrugged and drank from the bottle. "And of course I had to go and fight the Fascists in Spain after that. We were married a little while and she became pregnant. I said to myself, 'If they will fight in Spain, they will fight anywhere. Even here,' and I went away to stop them. And of course, I was captured. They took Poland before I escaped. I did not see my daughter until she was five. She did not know who I was." He turned to Jasper. "That is who I am, alien person."

Jasper stood and nodded—a motion he had learned from Harry. "I am warm, now, Mister Linden. I will go back out to the booth."

"Does any of that mean anything to you? Anything?" Harry stood at the door and stared at the alien as he entered the booth.

Jasper stopped in the booth and turned to Harry. "It means you to me, Mister Linden."

"And what the hell does that mean?" Jasper closed the booth door. "What does that mean?" Harry stood in the doorway until he grew cold but Jasper did not leave the booth or answer.

THE COPLEY WAS THE PREMIER restaurant in Copley Place, a modern pastel fortress dominating south downtown with a bland, pink malevolence. Rosewood and brass smoothed the Copley's edges, marble eased the eyes and thick carpets hushed the footsteps. It gave Harry a plush, trapped feeling, a soft claustrophobia that brought him close to hysteria. The finish on the silverware was brushed pewter and the tablecloth was a dull, rainy blue.

Randar Proong spoke softly as he suggested items from the menu. His suit matched the tablecloth, carpet and other patrons to the stitching. He smiled genially, bright teeth in a dark face. His nails were manicured.

"Try the sole. It is really quite good."

Harry felt as if he were drowning.

Proong led him unresisting through appetizers, before dinner drinks, salad, sole, dessert, to coffee.

"What do you want?" Harry felt stuffed, filled, no more alive than some lizard lying in the sun.

"The Rieken System is, of course, interested in your property." Proong chuckled slightly, looked across the restaurant. "We would like to buy it for a fair market value. More than you could make from it."

"Why?"

"There's no secret about it." Proong placed both palms together. "The market is low right now. The indigent aliens have been causing a move away from the city and property values have dropped. We feel this trend will reverse. Then, any property we purchase now we will make more profit later on. Nothing exciting."

"Yah." He nodded, intoxicated on food, wine and surroundings.

"I thought we might have a chance to chat for a bit before we begin actual negotiations." He leaned back and watched Harry, relaxed, confident.

Harry remembered that look. The Nazis in Poland had had it. So had the Fascists in Spain. The doctor who delivered Margaret had it, as did the second doctor who diagnosed Down syndrome for her, condemning her with a label.

Just what would you be selling, Harry? he asked himself. *Pain? A little heartache? So what if this empty man so easily buys you? Is that so terrible?*

"I have employees—"

"Only one," corrected Proong. "And an alien at that. We considered that an interesting move on your part. A cheap investment for the time he puts in. Especially since you don't intend to pay him."

"I will pay him." Harry straightened up.

"Of course. Later. When the time comes. I understand." Proong shrugged. "Still, there is no legal obligation for you to do so, is there? He is a legal alien. The law is quite strict on that point. But a legal alien what? Animal? Pet? No rigorous definition has yet been approved. And until it is, he has no contract, and you have no legal obligation."

"What would you do with him?" Harry stared at the tablecloth. What more did these people know?

"A policy has not yet been worked out." Proong studied his nails.

"Ah." Harry finished his wine.

"Can we begin negotiations next week?" From his coat pocket he pulled a small calendar and studied it. "About the middle of the week would be good for me."

"I must think about it," he said slowly.

"Of course." Proong nodded. The waiter passed and Proong fielded the check deftly. "Please inform me as soon as you can. Our funds move quickly, and we should work out something soon. Here is my card. Shall I call you tomorrow?"

Harry stood, nodded as they left together. Proong left him at the office of the garage not knowing what to do.

Sasha found him in the living room, sitting quietly in the blue pre-dawn light, staring out the window. On the table beside him there was a tall unopened bottle of whiskey.

"Harry?" she asked softly.

He turned to her. "Sasha?" Then, saw her. "Sasha."

She sat next to him. "What is wrong?"

He was silent a long moment, then shrugged. "I very nearly sold the garage. For a great deal of money." He shrugged again.

"To who? You would do this without asking me?" She leaned back and he saw she was hurt.

"No. I would not. But I almost did." The increasing light drew her features into perspective for him. Under the sagging flesh and partially blind eyes he still saw her as she had been on that snowy day in Krakow. "How is it you stayed with me?" he wondered aloud.

"Some question." She shifted uncomfortably.

"Yah." He nodded. "I almost sold it to the Rieken System. I didn't for no good reason." He held his hands together in his lap.

"I didn't because I was afraid if I didn't have something holding me down, I would fly away crazy. If I kept it, it should have been because Jasper trusted me, or because I would have hurt Margaret by hurting Jasper. Or some other good reason. We could have had money. I could have gotten better doctors for Margaret. I could have taken you somewhere. We could have had it easier." He shook his head and pressed his hands together until they were white. "If I didn't it must be for reasons worth that. But I didn't because I was afraid of it." She held him. "I wanted to do right. Sell or not sell for the right reasons."

After a time, he looked up at her. "How is it you stayed with me?"

She shrugged. "There was no one else I wanted."

He stood on the roof looking down on the street, across to the mirror windows of the Hancock. He had no whiskey with him and no cigarettes, but the wind was still cold and biting. At least there was no rain. He had no real thoughts, just a long gaze and a series of incoherent musings. At some point, the wind died down. He did not notice.

He started at a touch on his face, of feathers and water. He looked up and saw snow coming down in fine, faint flakes. From down below he heard, "Snow! Snow!" He went to the other side of the roof and looked down. Margaret clapped her hands clumsily and jumped up and down. Jasper danced beside her, his body extended into a net of dragonfly's wings, moving them like bellows and singing in a deep bass croon.

They did not see him and he watched as they tasted the snow.

Your First

C.L. Anderson

"We can rebuild him. Make him better, stronger, faster…"

"What are you, nuts? He was a total pain. Worse: weaker and slower."

"Well, it was a thought. So, what are we going to do with the parts?"

"I don't know. Some of them should be good for the new Skydancer project. We're still short, like, nineteen solid automata for that one."

"Still, it's a shame. He was our first."

"And we all know you never forget your first. But we've done a lot better since."

"I'm not so sure we have. I mean, the bio-quantum interface…"

"Was what made him such a pain in the ass. You never knew what he was going to do next… What?"

"Nothing."

"You are not going to blame his instability on me again."

"You were the one hooked in when we laid down his initial parameters."

"Because you were still getting over your breakup with Whatshisname."

"Dave."

"Dave. If you'd had the helmet on, we'd have had a tin Heathcliff with a bio-quantum brain and we'd've never gotten him out of brood-mode."

"So instead we got the real-boy wannabe. Is there an official name for a Pinocchio complex?"

"Impostor syndrome. It's when you're afraid everyone will find out you're a fake."

"That sounds like First... I still don't understand how he got smashed up like this. I mean, his boosters were perfectly fine yesterday."

"You don't suppose he went flying in the lightning storm, do you?"

"Don't be ridiculous. Who would have ordered him to do that?"

"JK33 maybe?"

"Now you're getting paranoid. JK33's got all the failsafes."

"33's also got the alpha box with full capability to give orders to the other automata, and he never liked First."

"So 33 did what? Killed him out of jealousy?"

"I'm just saying it's a possibility. I never believed those three laws of robotics would hold once the 'bots got into widespread use anyway. And you've got to admit, 33's been acting kinda buggy lately. Almost as buggy as First."

"This is how First got his Pinocchio complex. You're the one who wants them all to be real boys."

"What? Oh, please. I just want them to work right."

"It's your definition of 'right' that worries me sometimes."

"Look, just forget it. We'll recycle First."

"Good. So where is 33?"

"He flew out this morning. Remember, we needed the new parts in from the yard. I sent him. He should be back in an hour.

Before the next thunderstorm."

"Okay. Listen, since you've got JK33 updated we can use him in the live flight sequences."

"I didn't update 33."

"Yes, you did, it's here in the log."

"I'm telling you, I didn't. Crap. Check the camera log."

"On it, but who the hell would lie about you updating 33? Oh…"

"My."

"God."

"FIRST!"

Gray to Black

Brenda W. Clough

She didn't see the fruit beside the bed. Fumbling sleepily for her slippers after a festive Friday night, Laurel put her bare foot on it. It squashed in a cool spurt of juice, dead ripe. The complex fruity aroma, sweet as summer, fumed up into her nose and filled the sunny bedroom. "Ned? Can you eat your damn nectarines and granola in the kitchen?"

Ned leaned out the bathroom door, half his chin white with shaving gel. "Wasn't me, babe. Maybe the cat."

"Right. Like Missy can open the fridge."

Her old tabby sat on the open windowsill by the bed, peering out at the street. Sirens wailed distantly and honking voices blared over loudspeakers. Laurel yawned, pushing back her blonde hair. The wonderful sugary smell made her too sleepy to investigate. Today was laundry day, so she'd remake the bed anyway. She wiped her sticky foot off on the sheet, almost ready to flop back onto the pillow. But the doorbell pealed discordantly.

"You wanna get that, babe?"

Laurel shuffled barefoot and sticky to the door, Missy scampering ahead of her. Coffee, that's what she needed—her standard three daily cups of java. She pulled open the apartment door and realized she was still sprawled on the unmade bed asleep. This was a scene from a movie! One of her favorites—*ET*. She recognized the white plastic sheeting that carpeted the hallway and stair, and the dozens of guys in white spacey suits. Down beyond the lobby mailboxes the plastic tunnel thing was attached to the building exit, and she could hear the scary whooshy air pump on the soundtrack.

She smiled. "Which one of you is the cute FBI guy?"

Somebody flung a plastic sheet over Missy. "Roll it, roll it! Okay, into the cage, quick!"

The cat's howl of fury made Laurel blink awake for a moment. "Hey!"

"Oh Jesus."

"Is that the cyst?"

"She's barefoot! Jesus."

"It *is* the cyst! This is going to be bad—get the CDC guy, stat!"

"What's going on?" Through their thick plastic face plates she could see them staring at her. At her foot. "I'm not really a slob," she explained. "I was going to wash the sheets anyway."

WHAT LAUREL HATED MOST ABOUT quarantine was the way the doors made her ears pop. Negative pressure, they said—her rooms were deliberately lower in pressure than the rest of the isolation ward, so that air rushed in and never out. The idea made her feel choky and claustrophobic. She had demanded a window—there was one in the wall, tightly sealed over, so it wasn't like she was being outrageous or anything. A month of escalating demands and nasty emails from her sister Jessie had finally got it unblocked, so that she could peer through the treble thickness of reinforced glass and plastic at the sky.

She sat at the window for hours, stroking her belly and watching the autumn wind thresh and pluck at the sad little pine trees near the sea. The sea. The lovely warm water that would cradle her heavy body and wash away the hospital stink of disinfectant.

She had listened to the explanations that first day, but hadn't understood them very well. Hookworms she had heard about, about how you stepped on them and then they got inside you and crawled up to your stomach—or was that tapeworms?—and lived there. She had explained that it wasn't worms but a fruit, one of Ned's nectarines, but she might as well have talked to the wall.

She had caught up with all the coverage on the Internet. They had picked up her sheets with tongs, and pried up the carpet, and taken all the bedroom furniture away. Everyone in the neighborhood—fifty garden apartment blocks worth of people—had been quarantined. Every square inch of wall and brick and floor was sterilized, and still that wasn't enough. Their own place, 1201 24th Street, had been dismantled brick by brick, stud by stud, and incinerated.

The news shows went crazy about it. Laurel thought it was disgusting, the way they zoomed in on the details of how the ashes were going to be encased in molten glass and stored under a mountain in Nevada. She and Ned had chosen that bedroom set at Ikea! It was weird to remember how happy they had been that day.

She had not asked what had happened to Missy. One look at Ned's big stupid face that first day, blank with horror under the smear of shaving cream, and she'd known he wasn't going to be there for her either. She couldn't imagine now what she'd seen in him. And the way he had exclaimed, "You mean—aliens? Like the ones Sigourney Weaver fought?" The idea of being with Ned now was vaguely stomach-turning—probably morning sickness.

Instead she'd phoned Jessie right away, before they took her cell phone. And her sister had come through. Jessie was the smart one in the family: the one who knew how to build pages and host web forums and marshal public opinion about the rights of living things. She had zoomed in, strafing like a fighter plane, dressed in a navy-blue business skirt suit, waving her lawyer credentials and yelling, "You! Gestapo! We have a Bill of Rights in this country, you know!"

Jessie had gotten her the laptop, and the webcam, and the window, and the other doctors, the ones on *her* side. More importantly, she had gone to Bloomingdale's and bought Laurel the most adorable blue striped Donna Karan tankinis, four sets, sizes ten through sixteen, so that everyone could see and share in Laurel's development.

"I don't like to think of it as an invasion," Laurel had announced with pride for the camera. "It's more like a pregnancy." She had been the most widely watched live webcast in the history of the world, even more than for Michael Jackson's funeral!

But she had been careful to stand at a good angle, not straight on to the cam. When she stood foursquare and looked at herself in the mirror, she could see the difference. A regular pregnant woman looked like she had a basketball inside, round and low. Laurel was getting bigger sort of high and askew, more to the right than the left. The doctors said it was because the liver is on the right.

Laurel was careful not to look at a lot of things, as a matter of fact.

Jessie made sure that the website was overwhelmingly positive. It was a pleasure to go over and click on the links about the sanctity of life. Jessie said, the way the laws were written about abortion and patient rights and endangered species, they could barely touch Laurel with a ten-foot pole. All they could legally do was observe her.

Once the forum even had a long screed from a Catholic priest: "Laurel Franzini: Immaculate Conception?!?" Too bad it turned out that the priest was fake as a three-dollar bill, incarcerated in a mental home. The Catholic bishops had made Jessie take that post down.

Only once had Laurel surfed over to the other site, the one run by the Centers for Disease Control. Of course it wasn't linked to hers. That had been nasty: scrolling past icky pictures of the flukes that lived inside fish's heads in California, or tobacco hornworms encrusted with wasp larvae, or a kitten bloated with worms. (Why had she never asked about Missy? She'd had that cat for twelve years. Someday soon, she would.) With uneasy fascination she read about twirling trout and sleeping sickness. Parasitic infestations could force snails to alter their behavior, change gender, commit suicide even.

And right there alongside those hornworms was a picture of herself, in the blue tankini! It had been small consolation that the blue went great with her fair coloring. She immediately clicked over to the *USA Today* page to read about the upcoming Bruce Willis movie.

Of course there were about a million and a half medical things they wanted to do to her. Jessie had been really proactive about that, supervising every procedure and keeping an eye on the egg-heads to keep them from going hog-wild.

"She's a human being," Jessie had told Katie Couric on TV. "Just because she has a medical condition doesn't mean she's lost her rights as an American citizen!"

But, short of dissection, there were still a million and a half things. Samples, peeing into jars, feeling and measuring her growing belly, little tubes of blood, looking into machines, sitting in machines, being attached to machines with wires, all day, every day. It was just something you had to put up with.

"We're trying to help you, Laurel," the doctors said. "We're hoping to save your life."

"I feel fine," Laurel replied. More and more she was inclined to disbelieve them, simply from the way their voices came out of speakers on the wall instead of from their mouths. Surely all this fanatic isolation was silly? She couldn't even touch Jessie. Her sister had to wear the same big white suit and the thick gloves and helmet as everybody.

"I'm tired of quarantine," Laurel said. "When is it going to be over? My neighbors are all out. When's my turn?"

Jess patted her shoulder, her hand in the white glove as clumsy as an oar. "Let them just take another series of MRIs, okay, hon?" Through the speakers on the wall her voice sounded like a distant quack.

Laurel knew she was whining—did she use to whine? But she couldn't help it. "Last time it was 'see if the radium treatments took effect,' and the time before that it was 'after the full course of antibiotics.'"

"What's the rush, Laurie? You have everything you need right here."

Laurel tried to explain. "I've spent the whole summer indoors. I want to go out. I want to swim at the beach, before it's too cold. You know I hate cold swimming."

Even through the speaker she could hear the change in Jessie's voice. "Laurie. You've never liked swimming. Ever. The humidity makes your hair frizz out. Or the beach—you remember when you were four, the tantrum you had about the sand getting into your shoes…"

Something weird felt like it crawled all down her spine when she saw the way the white helmets turned so that the doctors could look at each other, and the way Jessie met their gaze too.

"Reading all those things about wasps and caterpillars makes you paranoid," Jessie said.

"I am not a victim! I am an empowered person, with civil rights, just like you said, Jessie. You can't keep me in here forever."

Jessie hugged her around the shoulders, but the embrace crackled like plastic wrap. "Hon, trust me—your big sis is looking out for you, okay? Did you get your coffee this morning?"

"I don't like coffee."

"Oh! Well then, you be a good girl and have your MRI."

They did this every single day, almost—shoved her like a pizza on a spatula into this oven thing. There was a panic button to hold while the magnets somehow took pictures of her organs and brain. She had gotten so big now it was pretty cramped inside. She had to lie perfectly still for what felt like hours, and with all this weight on her front it made the small of her back hurt. She felt like a sock puppet, a lab rat. And all because she'd stepped on an alien cyst that had fallen in through the window!

Suddenly she knew she couldn't stand it any more. She used to be okay with small, closed spaces, but not now. How much longer were they going to push her around? Weeks and weeks of this crap—she had to get out. Out! She hit the panic button, and bells began to clang. They whipped her stretcher out of the chamber, twittering with questions, and she was able to sit up. She snatched up a pair of scissors from the instrument cart and stabbed the points into the nearest thick white sleeve.

"Aaah! Laurie! No!"

"Jeez, help her!"

"Holy shit!"

Astonished, Laurel found that she was hacking and stabbing at Jessie. Well, of course it was the fault of all this thick white protective gear, that made even your own sister look like a monster. The other doctors grabbed her arm, forcing her back, but their shouts and cries were distant and unimportant, out of synch with the dim movements of their lips. It sounded like Jessie was crying, having hysterics muffled inside her helmet, but they were all talking at once and the speaker crackled and spat with the overload. They pushed her back into a chair and left her by the MRI machine, clustering around Jessie, shepherding her out through the whooshing door so that they could take off the encumbering suits and help her.

Laurel sat sulkily in the chair, her head bowed and her hands clasped over her huge lopsided belly. They were in such a fuss, they'd forgotten that the suits transmitted to the wall speaker.

She could hear everything even though they were outside.

"You're all right, Jessica. Look, the suit wasn't breached."

"Thank God they were just bandage scissors!"

"She just cut the first layer, you see? You're all right. You haven't been exposed."

All the doctors sounded alike, but Laurel could recognize Jess's convulsive weeping. "Oh Jesus! What was she doing? Oh God, Laurie was attacking me! Laurie!"

"Ms. Franzini, try to calm down, please. We've told you, you've seen, how the invader is growing in Laurel's system."

A vulgar blatting noise, as Jessie blew her nose. "You have to save her. Please! You said you'd save her."

"Ms. Franzini, we can't. We cannot get the alien out without killing her. You remember what happened to the cat. The life form has insinuated itself into her circulatory system, the lymph nodes—"

Another, more authoritative voice. "Ms. Franzini, it's worse even than that. Yes, here's another tissue. Get her a glass of water, somebody… These are today's brain scans, Ms. Franzini. You see that blue strand, between the hemispheres and up into the corpus callosum? It's possible that… How can I put this? That she's not your sister anymore."

"Oh Jesus! Laurie would never have hurt me, never. Not Laurie!"

"Ms. Franzini—Jessica—do you understand? There are many shades between gray and black, but there comes a point when the color is definitely black. We've disagreed about when that point is crossed. It was good and right of you to fight for your sister. But I hope this convinces you now, to drop your court case. You cannot think only of Laurel now. You have to consider the rest of the human race. We are being invaded. Laurie is more than your sister now. She is Normandy, Jessica. Iwo Jima. A beach-head."

At the mention of names she didn't recognize Laurel quit listening. Gray, indeed! She rolled her eyes and sighed. Of all the silly hysterical panics. None of these people had any common sense. It wasn't an invader. It was a baby, sweet as summer, heavy as a fruit. And ready to pop any day now, ripe and ready to melt. She stroked the awkward angular dome of her front. If only she could get down to that beach and float, weightless, then she'd feel better. Warm salt water—all her troubles would dissolve!

She looked over at the instrument cart. One of those spatula things might help pry the flashing away from her window. She picked up the sturdiest one and tucked it into her blouse above the big asymmetrical bulge.

Slick

Sylvia Kelso

When I first saw it, I thought something had died.

And in *my* waterhole. At least, my favorite waterhole, the best one on the place, and the place has been ours since Granddad's time.

Then I thought, pollution. Those Neanderthal pig-shooters have been down here again, lighting fires and dropping beer cans at their backsides and slopping the waterhole full of oil.

Because it looked like an oil slick. A raggedy, ten-foot-wide oil slick, not quite above the water, not quite under it. Dull yellow, bobbly, undulating, sort of. Like a mat of old wattle flowers. Or the half-submerged rafts of yellow gloop you see, out near the islands, when the coral spawns.

It's not really a waterhole, the way most people use the word. It's an anabranch, one of the secondary courses that the river fills when it floods. But once the flood ebbs, the water stays there, caught between the shallow places, a long, long, meandering ribbon shining through the grass and the tall piebald trunks of the blackbutt trees, smooth white above, scaly dark below. Rising over the knobbly piers of root that split the cattle-tracks, leaning out over the pitted mud, reaching down, down, into the coffee-crystal water, smooth, still, shimmery, among the flotillas of waterlily-pads.

Nobody knows how deep it is. Deep enough to make cattle swim when they cross, deep enough never to show the bottom. Like I say, in white man's memory, it's never run dry.

So when I saw the slick, I rode down for a look. The mare was twitchy, but the mare is always twitchy along the river. I don't know if it's the way the dead pandanus fronds rattle when she steps on them, or the smell of those cursed pigs. But the waterhole's a good mile from the river channel, and I've always loved the place. So quiet, except when we come through mustering. Otherwise, there's just the crows and a magpie or two, and the silence of the river country. And that long, sea-sound draw of wind through miles of trees.

It was a job to get near the water-rim. The mare kept jibbing and roots seemed to be everywhere. Nests of them, long, dark, crisscrossing roots stubborn as pythons, all over the lower bank, that had washed out into a regular cliff. I could see the thing over the top. Dusty yellow, floating, undulating. Like a slick of really heavy industrial oil.

The mare put on a turn at the roots' edge, so I didn't actually get much of a look. Enough to think it wasn't really oil, and wonder what on earth it might be, and with a jerk in the stomach, that maybe whatever-it-was was decayed, rotten, dead—

And by the time I wrestled the mare back, it was gone.

For a while that really puzzled me. But we'd come back from a different angle, and the sun was on the water, so it could all have been a trick of the light. Because now there was nothing at all. Just the waterhole, shimmering, that liquid amber sheen of undisturbed standing water. And the roots going down into it, and a waterlily, holding up one stained-glass blue flower.

Imagination, I thought. Stupid, I thought. And went off in a hurry to block the cattle that had just come scooting down my bank, and forgot the idea that for one moment, under the clotted pollen yellow, there might have been something more.

An arm. A face.

THAT MIGHT HAVE BEEN ALL there was to it—how many times has that been all there was to it? Except about a month later, we came back. Mustering stragglers, and I ended up with the river country. Riding through, checking for fresh tracks, listening for crows, that'll tell you where the cattle are. Hearing the wind, and the quiet. Because the country was surprisingly empty. I hadn't found a beast, when I stopped by the waterhole for my dinner camp.

It was October by then, starting to build up for an early Wet. Hot. Not the burning inland heat, but wet heat, sweaty, sultry, thick as porridge, with the big, early storm clouds packed up before midday, snow-pale and silver, hanging southward over me, making the river country seem quieter, and more hushed, and more—ominous—than it already was.

So when we made the waterhole I was glad to let the horse wade, at a sandy place, and dip up a fairly clean quartpot-full while he drank. I had an old brown gelding that day, that the river country never worried a jot. I tied him in the shade at the top of the high bank, put a fire together, and boiled the quart for tea. And then, the way we always did if we had no cattle, stretched out by him in the shade for half an hour's sleep.

Not that I usually do sleep. But I did that day, because it was in my ears when I woke up.

A horse's snort. Not that easy clear-the-flies snort, but the nostril-crack they make when they're alone, and surprised. Or afraid.

I sat up fast. That should have made him jump. He never even twitched. He'd swung round beside me and his neck was straight up, head horizontal, the way horses look when they've absolutely panicked, and his ears were tight forward, and he was stiff all over. Staring.

At the waterhole.

I was on the ground in the grass. Thin old khaki-pale grass, but enough to hinder my view. I went to jump up and stopped in case it sent the horse right off. I knelt up instead and squinted through the stems, over the last smoke wisps, down the bank. Dust and grass-stubs, all pale Dry-time colors, then the black and white trees and the coffee-colored mirror of water between.

There was nothing that I could have expected. Nothing floating. No yellow stuff. Nothing on the bank. No sound.

No sound at all. The wind had stopped. The air was practically sitting on me, thick, and still, and heavy with storm, the light had gone all shadowless with one of the big clouds over the sun, and usually that's when birds sing by daylight. But there wasn't a sound.

Nothing but the horse, still carrying on like he'd seen a ghost.

And the ripples, the last of the huge, slow ripples, coming to shore in the waterhole.

I CAN'T REMEMBER WHAT I told myself. A fish? A croc? They're supposed to come up along the river, though I've never seen a mud-slide myself. Something dropped by a bird? A pelican must've dived? And flown off again?

None of that should have worried the horse.

I REMEMBER I SADDLED UP, not exactly in a hurry, but not wasting time, either. There was something—strange—about the silence, the light, something more than river country and a day working up to storm. But when the ripples stopped the horse had just dropped his head and gone back to normal, so I told myself it was more imagination. Nothing to worry about.

But I didn't forget it either. When the first storm came through and we checked the fences on every blessed river crossing, I went down in the old Toyota four-wheel drive. Cranky and shaky and short of a passenger-side window, but it would be better, I told myself, than a horse.

Which it wasn't. Late afternoon, headed home, I drove over the bottom crossing, at the foot of the waterhole, and put a new underwater snag into the sump.

The truck had to come out of the creek, of course. If more rain came, no point in losing the lot. But it couldn't be driven any further. And we didn't use two-ways. I had a whole lot of choice: leave the truck and walk home, in the dark, or sit tight, and wait for somebody to come out, next day.

They knew where I had gone. And it was coming on to rain. Which meant the full moon wouldn't light me home, and I'd get wet as well.

I had an apple left from dinner, and a tarp in the back, along with the axe, and matches, and tea in the old tucker-box. I said a few sulfurous words, then took it all up on the highest spot along the top bank, and started settling in for the night.

The storm came through just before dark. Not much wind. A slow-moving front, so it seemed to go on for ages, great, wide sheets of lightning, white as searchlights, and then the thunder. Ker-thump. Ker...thump. Not the nasty high crackle of a dry storm or an actual strike. This was the rich, solid bass note you get with decent rain.

I had dug a drain and tied the tarp down well. I sat dry while the last wood faded down into coals, and listened to it all. The rustle, drum, patter of rain on the tarp, the husssh of rain on leaves, the steady purr of rain on bare ground and worn-out grass. The slow, fading thunder-peals. The trickle and tap, the splat and plink as the last drops came to ground.

Then I wrapped the old corn-sacks round me for token blankets, and lay down to sleep.

I DON'T KNOW WHAT TIME I woke. The rain-noise had all stopped, I remember that. And the moon was out. Full and clear, in a cloudless sky. The whole side of the waterhole was lit up, black and silver, like they say in paintings, chiaroscuro. Tree-shadows in separate leaf-clots, the way our thin-leaved timber grows, and a snatch of branch between, black and silver netting-work, patterned on the ground. Wisps of hair-and-silver shadow. Grass. Soft splotches, where water had lain long enough to turn to mud. And the waterhole, beyond the grass-stems, a silver and charcoal patterned plain. Bright as the moon, and that was glowing like platinum, almost over my head.

But it was not the moon that woke me up.

It was—I don't know how to describe it. It was music, I know that. You can tell music from random noise. Song? I suppose so. It was no nightbird I could pick, and I can tell a frog-mouth from a mopoke owl. Let alone that heart-stopping screeee a curlew makes. Like a damn lost soul, people say, when they wake up with their hearts in their mouths and their hair on end. Like a banshee, that calls without warning, mourning, waking the dead.

This was not a bird. It was high, and lilting, sort of, and if it had been human I couldn't have said if the singer was woman or man. But it had more parts than one, and patterns, and I couldn't understand them, but I knew the patterns had sense. They were made of words.

All that doesn't say anything about—the real thing. How beautiful it was, how absolutely pure and unearthly, like the voice of moonlight. How liquid, running like distilled water, trills, arpeggios, cascades of it, smooth, sure, unbroken.

And so sad.

Imagine all the water in the world, all the world there has ever been. And it has a memory. It remembers everything it was, from the first beginning. Fog. Mist. Cloud. Raindrop. Snow. Running water. Rivulet, stream, river, the sea's untouched foundation. Living things.

Cells. Amoebas, embryos. Water plants, sea plants, land plants, grass, stem, leaf, tree, all the juice and sap that makes them live. Coral polyps, oysters, fish, whales. Ants, insects, monkeys, elephants. Human beings.

Conceived, and growing, being born, living, gathering the water into them, giving it patterns, giving it shapes. Growing old, fading, decaying. And the water running out, to begin again, another life, another shape, over and over. Remembering it all.

Because water is life, and water is eternal. But everything that's born is going to die.

The tears were already running when I woke. Sliding sideways down my temple, then over my cheeks when I sat up. Not needing to speak, to hold my hands out. The tears were saying it for me. Water answering water. Called by water, its own element, its memory, its grief.

Calling water back.

The noises reached me first. Ripples in the waterhole, not the slap a fish makes, but a slow, turning slushshhh. Slap, tap, against the margin roots. Trickle, splash. Water falling downward out of air, back into itself. The way it does when a swimmer breaks the surface. Rises from the level, shedding, dripping, comes to land. Stands up.

And then the pattern, splat, tick, splat, of remaining droplets on grass and leaf. Light and silvery as the moonlight. Moonlight moving, liquid, laborious, a mass of moon-shadow and highlight, up the bank.

It was slow-moving. Effortful. The struggle up between the roots, the snap of broken sticks, the ruffle of dragged-down grass, the labored breath. And moonlight is not sunlight, it lights but never truly illuminates. I never did see the details. Just dark and silver moving, coming where I called it. The breaths, slow and whistling, the flop, flop of difficult, unaccustomed feet.

It was dark under my roof. That blurred the arrival, when moonlight slid behind it, leaving just a silhouette. Two arms, two legs, a down-bowed head. A mass of body. Moon-faded, bobbly masses slung across a shoulder, trailing over ribs. I put my hands out, and it bowed to come under the lintel and collapsed, gasping and panting, next to me.

My hands gave me the first truth: it was flesh and blood. Alive, responsive, flexible, warm, under the surface-chill, the cold slick of skin still wet from the water. Firm, cold-tautened skin, slippery and smooth over solid muscle as an Olympic athlete just out of the pool.

Just at first, it might almost have been a woman's body. Not the skin texture, or the bulk of muscle, but the contours, the proportions, the weight of flesh rather than bone in the shoulders, the fineness of ribs and waist… But I've never held a woman naked, so maybe I imagined it. After all, male swimmers are smoother muscled than runners or wrestlers, anyhow. And when the hands drew me close, they were too big for a woman's. Long, smooth hands, with very long fingers, yes, but the wrists and palms you would never take for anything but male.

Or the body. A swimmer's body, with the strong swell of pectorals, cool and smooth as living marble, and the male nipples, the ridged belly muscles, the flat taper of the torso, that no woman has, and the heavy girdle of muscle over the hips. You can see it on those old statues. Or on pictures of champion divers or triathletes. Men who really swim.

And it was definitely a man below that, with the long smooth thigh muscles, still slippery and chilled from the water, rippling against me. All of him was smooth, cold and firm but slippery as water-smoothed marble, his chest, his flanks, his shoulders, with the heavy bunch and flex of muscle down the back, the ridged loins, the tight curves of his backside, even the long, long, delicately boned, bruised feet. The hands, smooth and eager, slipping round me, following as I undid clothes, touching, exploring, arms, neck, breasts, belly, the eager, opening mouth. And the hot, smooth column of the phallus rising, curving a little, all but leaping into my hands.

Touching, eager to be touched in turn, more than willing to be touched all over. Except for his hair.

If it was hair. It began on his head, yes, and went down over his back, I know that much, and it fell down over his ribs sometimes, and his flanks, like a great heavy tress. I thought of it as hair, and I think it must have been the yellow stuff I saw in the water. I felt the weight of it, like wrist-thick dreadlocks, when one fell across my neck or arm. Dreadlocks is what I thought, but maybe… We see things as what we know.

All I know is, the first time it fell, I tried to touch that too. He let out a hiss as if I'd burnt him and grabbed my hand away. Not hurting, but fast and strong enough to get it over: Not that. Not there.

No words. There were never any words, from either of us. But he talked to me, all the time we lay there. Sang to me, in that liquid music, water's voice. Calling, flowing, telling me, It has happened, you have heard me, for this night, this hour, this second, I am not alone. I am alive, you are alive, water waking, meeting. You are here.

While we made love, in the moon's dark on the dusty corn-sacks, the way dolphins ought to do it in the moving sea. Arms linked, bellies, bodies pressed together, one flesh leaping, curving, singing, joy met and plunging into union. Flesh, blood, being, all in their own element, shared.

Here in the hospital, nobody knows me. I made absolutely certain of that. I've been planning this ever since I woke that morning. With the first light showing the trees, gray and faint as pencil-lines, and the leaves blurry in their sheaths of dew. And the little trail of mist, white as breath, just masking the water, that was absolutely still, absolutely empty, with the sheen of old, cooled steel.

And nothing beside me, except the smell of sex and sweat from the cornsacks and the great wet patch under them, on the ground around them, where we had lain.

It was under the tarp. Where it ought to have been dry. So I made sure I pulled the tarp down, and folded it, and doused the sacks in the waterhole, and folded them too. Before I made another fire and sat down to boil tea for breakfast, and wait for the noise of an engine and the moving hood of the new Toyota among the trees, with one of my brothers driving up.

I never went back to the waterhole, any more than I looked for a sign that morning. I knew it had all been said. I didn't expect anything else, and there wasn't. Not a ripple, a snatch of song, a glimpse of yellow, floating—hair.

And I never told the family anything. Except, about a fortnight afterwards, when we all went to the Amateur Races, I said I thought, for the Wet, maybe I'd stay over, perhaps get a job, in town.

Then it was easy enough to move to the coast, another town, another job, change clothes and fashion with them, start wearing hippie things, loose and floppy, up in the tourist resorts. When you come into town already pregnant, so long as you have a story, there's really nothing to hide.

I did work at saving money. I haven't worked—I knew I wouldn't be able to work—the last two months. Not that it's been a hard pregnancy, as these things go, but I wanted to be sure.

The family think I'm just wandering about a while. I write to them, or at least to Mum. Talk about people I meet, things I do, send photos. With me carefully not in them, or behind someone else. If anything's been difficult, it's not having Mum here, to moan at about all the things that must be usual. The swollen feet, the backaches, the having to pee every five minutes. The sudden urge to go out and eat waterlily roots, in the middle of the night.

I never had an ultrasound, though. It's the only thing that's really worried me. She might have had all sorts of defects. But it was just too risky. If they'd noticed. Not that something had been wrong, but that something was different.

The labor was easy too, the way I knew it would be. I could feel that, the way, since that night, I've felt everything. As if it was water, moving through me, speaking without words, in the blood.

The doctor's just been in. There was a bit of a fuss after she was delivered, they had to take her to the ICU to make sure she breathed properly. But he says I can have her this morning. He raised his eyebrows a bit when I said I wanted an immediate discharge, but after all, I'm healthy. She's healthy. And they always need the beds.

I know exactly what we'll do afterwards. Out of here, down to another coast-town, get a job. Somewhere near the beach, where a creek or a river comes in. Where we can stay for a couple of years, until she's old enough—

Until she can swim.

Somewhere, perhaps, that I can take her out on a boat, between the islands. To see the dull yellow rafts floating, dipping in the swell, undulating, when the coral spawns.

Somewhere she can make her mind up. Which way she wants to go.

I won't think past that. I know what I have to give her. A mother, a place to grow up, kid things, grandparents later, maybe, depending how things go. All the things you can have, when you're one of us. I know what's expected of me. There were never any words, but I know. It's what we were there for. Water to water, life to life. However he got there, whether he was trapped there, he's going on now. I don't know if she remembers, but he will. Water to water. Going on, the way she will, after I'm gone. Into a new shape. Living again.

Of course I know what it could have been. Living in the bush, I know about sex, you can't help it. And anybody half-smart knows about men. It could have been that, yes. One quick, slick fuck, no promises, all they want, and off they go.

Except I still remember that first minute, when it was flesh and blood I touched, but it might as easily have been a woman in my hands. And I wonder, was he really a he? Was it just for the moment? For whatever he is, does being man or woman matter? What would have come out of the waterhole, if the one who heard the singing was a man?

Not so practical, really. Because I do know the other stuff. I read a book about it, down at a resort once. Reproduction of a species. Selfish genes. Just as slick, getting the chromosomes carried over. Nothing more.

But I heard the singing. I can remember the sadness. And the way it sounded, when I held my hands out, and he took them. That wasn't selfishness. That was joy.

I STILL WANT TO HAVE her with me now, to see her and hold her. Give her the first real drink. Make sure she's—

Really here.

In this world, the daylight world. She must be perfect, just like us, or there would already have been the most enormous upset. That fuss about breathing must have been the only hitch. She must already have—adjusted—properly.

She can't breathe, the way I'm almost sure he did, through

whatever it was that wasn't hair.

The doctor's back again. Carrying her himself, really quite gushy. She looks just like any other newborn, screwed-up face, eyes shut like a kitten, that cute little mouth. Her head's quite bald, but he says that's pretty normal. And she breathes through her mouth, and snorts a bit, the way kittens or puppies do. And sucks like a limpet. He says that's normal too.

He was leaning over the bed end when he said it, laughing at the faces I made. "No," he said, "she's fine, absolutely fine. Picked up the oxygen in a minute. Slick as the way she arrived. Everything else is perfect—well, some unseparated digits, you'll have seen those. Second and third toes, both sets. Looks a little odd, perhaps, but it's not unusual. Heritable, actually. It won't affect her gait, and if she does get self-conscious, later, it can be fixed. The surgery's purely cosmetic, though it's better done before she's two." He laughed a bit more before he walked away. "Myself, I'd stick with nature. If she asks, you can always say that once upon a time a fairy godmother left her a special gift. So if she wants, she could be an Olympic swimmer: and she will go like a piranha in the water. It really helps to have webbed feet."

When he said that I must have squeezed her because she stopped sucking and opened her eyes. I know newborns aren't supposed to focus, but she saw me. I could feel it. And I saw her eyes as well.

They reckon you can't guess the color this soon either, but I know. They're a bit muddy yet, but underneath it'll be a deep, filtered-coffee brown, and when she's older, they'll pick up that little shimmer from the mica-silt. The color of the waterhole, when the through-stream's still running, after a really big flood.

I nodded at the doctor and said, "Yeah. Maybe she will."

Ask Arlen

Maya Kaathryn Bohnhoff

Plummeting through the pre-dawn sky, all Qtzl could think of was that his family would never know what had happened to him. He would burn his epitaph across an alien sky alone, while the only eyes that would see him—alien eyes—would mark him as a meteor.

It didn't happen quite that way. He managed to bypass his malfunctioning navigational array, regain control of the craft before it began to disintegrate in the atmosphere of the planet, and fire up his braking field. It made his descent more spectacular, but slowed the Ship. He downed it in a labyrinthine maze of mountains and sat quaking, but alive, wondering what he ought to do next.

"Qtzl," Ship said. "You are alive."

"Indeed. Thank you."

"Your vital signs are quite strong, though your respiration is a bit elevated. May I recommend that we attempt communication with any nearby comrades?"

"Do that." Qtzl glanced around, discomfited by the sound of hissing from somewhere to the stern of the small craft.

"Communication impossible. Order disregarded."

Qtzl brought his eyes back to the spherical console display. "Impossible? Why did you recommend we attempt it, then?"

"Protocol," Ship said, and managed to sound reproachful. "May I recommend that you get out and reconnoiter?"

"No, thank you. I'd rather not find out, for the sake of protocol, that reconnoitering is as impossible as communication."

"The planet's atmosphere is breathable," Ship informed him, reproach thickening. "I repeat: I recommend that you get out and reconnoiter."

Qtzl did that, if for no other reason than that the continued hissing from astern made him nervous. Outside, he could see that the damage was severe. The bow planes used for atmospheric maneuvering were sheared off and the landing cradle had failed, dumping the craft onto its braking-field generator. The communications array was smashed beyond recognition and steam oozed from a seam behind the cabin.

"Damage report," he ordered, trying to sound authoritative rather than frightened. "Source of steam."

"Environment controls disabled…coolant chamber breached."

Qtzl took a step backwards. "Are you likely to explode?"

"Likely? That is a judgment call. Likelihood of explosion, twenty to one against."

"Possibility of repair?"

"Repair necessary to continued functioning."

Qtzl tried to swallow around the dry patch in his throat. "No, no. I mean, what's the possibility that I could repair you?"

"You installed my navigational array," Ship said.

Qtzl colored all the way to the tip of his crest. "Point taken," he said and trudged off in search of shelter, cursing his mechanical ineptitude. This was like a grade-B ixltl—foolhardy adolescent stranded alone on an alien and possibly hostile world, no way of contacting his loved ones. Alone against—

"Ship, life form readings, please."

"You are surrounded by an abundance of small life forms, Qtzl."

"How small?"

"Very small. The largest is approximately eight ixiqs long and four ixiqs in height."

"Intelligent?"

"Intelligence is a relative concept. Could you be more specific?"

"Are they people?"

"No people are present."

Qtzl sighed, ruffling his neck frill. Someday perhaps Ship consoles would be less dogmatic. "I need shelter. Could you—I mean, please locate shelter."

Ship was silent for a moment, then said, "There is an artificial structure 100 itixiqs to the east."

Qtzl's blood froze. "Artificial?"

"A domicile. It is vacant...presently."

Qtzl was both excited and fearful as he approached the domicile. It was perched near the top of a wooded slope, hemmed in by what he assumed were trees; only the second story's high, peaked roof nudged above the many branches.

He entered through a door screened by flowering plant life. The building was, as Ship had said, vacant, but not empty. It was full of furnishings—some comfortingly and eerily familiar, others whose uses Qtzl could only guess.

He was at once unnerved and delighted. A person lived here! An alien person whose dimensions were not unlike his own. He wondered how soon the alien would return. He opened his mouth to ask Ship, but realized Ship would only say—with impossible condescension—that it was not omniscient. That fact bothered Qtzl deeply just now.

His senses told him that no food had recently been prepared here and there was a fine layer of dust on the furnishings which spoke of disuse. Perhaps this was someone's sabbatical refuge. His explorations revealed much of interest. There were but two small sleep chambers (or so he took them to be) with one padded pallet apiece. Both were flat; Qtzl couldn't imagine sleeping on them. He was boggled by the number of belongings this alien had accrued.

He was also boggled by what he took to be representations of the planet's natives. Although there were images of a number of fur-bearing animals—chiefly hanging within frames on the walls—by far the preponderance of pictures were of a bipedal, bilaterally symmetrical being that wore fur only on or around its head and which possessed two eyes, a small mouth, and a pointy, erect nose. They were neither terrifyingly ugly nor mesmerizingly beautiful, despite what the popular media suggested to the contrary. But they were undeniably alien. Except for the eyes, Qtzl found the faces mystifying; without a neck frill and crest, how could he ever hope to read their emotions? Creator willing, he would never have to try.

During his meal of synthesized rations, Ship informed him that it had been doing some calculations. "Repair is possible," it told him, and proceeded to rattle off a list of necessary materials. "Needed metals, minerals, and chemical compounds are present in this planet's mantle. They are also present in the artifacts found in this domicile, which indicates that the natives mine and refine them. This society would appear to be fairly advanced in metallurgy and chemistry. It should not be impossible to effect my repair."

"Will I be able to do it?"

"I will offer instruction and guidance," said Ship, and Qtzl imagined smugness in the tone.

"How do I go about obtaining the materials?"

"I have no idea."

KERWIN FREES WAS A UFO chaser. He was a card-carrying member of MUFON. He was also a card-carrying member of CSICOP (which he referred to lovingly as "the psy-cops"), and saw no contradiction in the dual membership. He was both skeptic and true-believer but, at the moment, the true-believer was dominant, for Kerwin Frees had just seen a UFO land in the deep, piney woods beyond the south shore of Lake Tahoe.

He had not been chasing UFOs when he witnessed the long trail of light arcing from the heavens. He had been lying on the hood of his Saturn stargazing, drowning his senses in the immensity of the universe and a beer, figuring that next month when the tourists and fair-weather Tahoe-ites began to arrive, he would go to Montana where there'd been a rash of sightings.

He was immediately galvanized, beer forgotten. He had just enough time to lift his field glasses and track the fiery object's fall. Most people would have taken it for a meteor. Kerwin Frees did not make that mistake. The trajectory was all wrong, suggesting at least a partially controlled descent; its trail flattened out before disappearing behind a wooded ridge. It was not a jet—no jet had ever plummeted from that distance. It was not a space shuttle—he knew this because he had the shuttle schedule (hacked out of a NASA computer) memorized.

Kerwin Frees poured out the remains of his beer, tossed the can into the recycle bin in his trunk, and shut himself into his car with his CB radio.

QTZL SLEPT CURLED IN A large cup-shaped chair. He did not sleep easily or well and was up before daybreak exploring his borrowed lodgings and pondering his predicament. He had the Ship's Field Remote Unit scan the foodstuffs in the alien's larder, and while it was thus occupied, he found what looked vaguely like a computer in a cozy, cluttered chamber. The FRU confirmed the find. It was a computer of sorts, and was connected to some sort of network. Munching on some dry, crumbly white squares Ship had deemed edible, Qtzl watched the FRU put the alien artifact through its paces.

"The machine incorporates no intelligence," Ship told him after exciting the boxy alien unit into a series of bleeps and chitters. "It models reality in simple binary languages which are relatively nimble, but not exceptionally powerful… The network to which it is connected," Ship added after a pause, "is, however, rather extensive. If you will allow me the time, Qtzl, I can explore the pathways. Perhaps I can determine a means of procuring the materials necessary for the repair of my transport module."

Qtzl allowed the time, using it to his own purposes. Sometime in the middle of a fitful nap, he wakened to Ship's strident desire to share its findings.

"This society functions on a free market system not unlike our own. I have located sources for the materials you need, and can arrange to have them delivered to this place."

"How?"

"Quite simply by placing orders into the computers of the various sellers. I already have experimented with such a tactic. The computers, lacking intelligence, do not question my addition of spurious orders."

"But…how will we pay for it?"

"We have nothing with which to pay for it," said Ship patiently.

"But that's stealing," Qtzl objected. "I won't steal."

"Then you will not get home."

"Stealing is reprehensible."

"We seem to have a moral dilemma."

Qtzl rolled his neck frill and waved his arms in a gesture he hoped looked more impassioned than frantic. "Options! I need options."

"If you had some sort of legal tender, you could purchase the materials, and I could then place the orders legitimately."

"Good! What tender?"

"Apparently, this society functions with a multi-leveled equivalency system. Precious metals are the actual units of value; however, one does not use them directly in bartering."

Qtzl's momentary relief flagged. "You mean, I can't just go dig up some ores and do business?"

"Apparently not. The second tier of exchange involves chits called 'currency' which occur in a multitude of denominations and which are symbolic of the actual units of value. There is then a third level of exchange called 'credit' which exists solely as electronic information and which is symbolic, in its turn, of the currency. As nearly as I am able to determine, most business is conducted without any physical exchange of real property. All transactions are controlled by computers…which makes their lack of sophistication beneficial," it added after a moment.

Qtzl pondered this, then decided it behooved him to ask, "In order to purchase our materials, what must I have?"

"You must have an accumulation of this symbolic data in an institution known as a 'bank.'"

There was no Tlvian equivalent for the word, so Ship simply said it in the language of the builders of the network. "Bank." It was a perfectly ugly word, Qtzl thought, sounding approximately like someone choking on vetshmil.

"And how," he asked, "does one acquire these symbolic units of value?"

"One works. When one works, one's employer deposits these symbolic units of value into the aforementioned 'bank.' The problem, of course, is that each employed individual is known to the system by a unique code which includes a name and a number."

Qtzl had not thought it possible for Ship to sound perplexed or uncertain. He revised that estimation now, and was not happy about it.

✦

METEORITE. THAT WAS WHAT THE police, the late night news, and the next morning's newspaper labeled it. The only people who suspected it was anything else were fringers—crazies who used citizen band and the Web alike to report everything from abductions to Elvis sightings. It wasn't long before a simple arc of light had been transmuted into a dozen or more close encounters of various kinds, including detailed (and wildly different) descriptions of the aliens.

Kerwin Frees was an experienced hand at this. He knew how to read between the lines, how to suck an atom of truth out of many gross tons of fiction. He took careful notes of each description of the earthfall, paying special attention to where the correspondent claimed to be at the time of the sighting. With any luck, he would be able to use the information to fix the landing site.

"WHAT ARE THESE?" QTZL ASKED, staring at the screenful of scribbles Ship presented to him.

"These are job listings. People seeking employees let their needs be known by posting them on this network. It is fascinating, Qtzl," Ship added, sounding almost enthusiastic. "These people are quite literate. They run the machines. The machines do not run them. Nowhere have I found a machine that is a decision-maker; they are merely implementers."

Qtzl was too lost in his own miseries to care about the state of machine intelligence on this alien world. "I can't read them," he said glumly. "It might as well be the scratchings of zik-ziks."

"I can read them," said Ship. "What sort of job would you like?"

"I can't apply for any job. I can't appear physically. After all, I hardly look like a native, do I?"

"No, you do not. Therefore, it will be necessary to obtain a position which does not require your personal attendance."

"Oh, certainly. And how am I to undergo the Sizing-Up without making a personal appearance?"

"I am not certain that this society observes that ritual." Ship was silent for a moment, then came back with a series of job listings highlighted on the computer screen. "Here, for example, are a number of entries which simply say, 'send résumé to' what I assume are surface coordinates. Several even allow electronic submissions."

Qtzl felt a stirring of interest. "So, assuming we find a position for which I'm qualified—then we tender my attributes electronically?"

"Precisely."

Qtzl ruffled his neck frill in agreement. "Then let's find me a position that requires no personal appearances and which will pay well enough to cover the necessary purchases in a reasonable length of time."

Ship went to work immediately, which put it out of communication with Qtzl for an inordinate amount of time. Bored and fidgety, he resumed his exploration of the alien abode. He was afraid to go outside—even with Ship monitoring his every move—so he settled for a further tour of his absent host's belongings. In a small adjunct to the sleep chamber, he found some interesting garments which, for lack of anything better to do, he tried on. Standing before a reflective glass, Qtzl was admiring how the color of the robe he wore set off the turquoise of his skin when Ship beeped him. Hiking up the long skirts, he hurried into the computer room.

"I have compiled a selection of positions for which résumés are requested and which do not rule you out by qualification," Ship told him. "It is a short list."

It was indeed a short list. A company located somewhere called Elk Grove needed something called an 'accountant.' When Ship explained the duties of the task, Qtzl was boggled yet again—how could anyone keep track of imaginary units of value?

"Digits," Ship said (smugly, Qtzl thought), "are digits no matter where in the galaxy one goes. We will send a résumé there."

Ship had also found an engineering position and several programming slots with a large company that seemed to be doing research in space travel. "You are an above average speaker of machine language at home."

"But I don't know the languages their computers speak, Ship."

"I do, and what I know, I can teach you."

"Why bother?" Qtzl asked, feeling useless. "You take the job. I'll just...putter. Maybe explore the area." He conjured an image of himself as the intrepid explorer, charting alien territory.

Ship quickly dismantled it. "Qtzl, it would be extremely unwise for you to leave this domicile without my Field Remote. You simply would not survive. There are large, wild lifeforms in the surrounding woodlands."

"You said there were only small lifeforms in the surrounding woodlands."

"I have revised my assessment. There are large lifeforms. Four-legged. And they move in packs of three to ten individuals. Some roam quite close to this domicile."

Qtzl gave up the idea of exploring, intrepidly or otherwise.

Ship fabricated and sent a sterling résumé based on a combination of Qtzl's expertise (a rather limited set) and its own. A week passed without positive response. All of the prospective employers insisted on interviews; three told Ship it was over-qualified.

"This is more difficult than I anticipated," Ship admitted.

Qtzl fanned his neck frill in frustration. "We have," he noted, "a limited amount of food left."

"However," Ship continued, as if Qtzl hadn't spoken, "I have found another employment opportunity. This one requests a résumé, a photo, and published clips from anywhere in the United States."

"United states...?"

"A group of sovereign or semi-sovereign provinces which function as part of a federation founded upon the principles—"

"What's a 'photo?'"

Ship idled momentarily. "A two-dimensional representation of a person rendered on paper in a chromatic medium."

"Published 'clips'...is that like aired writings?" Qtzl's interest was piqued. He'd exhibited a flair for both prose and lyric during his school days. In fact, he'd won a number of essay contests and had aired a few pieces of short fiction and philosophy. Not that anyone had noticed...

Ship emitted the mechanical equivalent of a sigh. "The advertisement is from a city newspaper. A large one, judging from the estimation of its readership. They need a 'columnist'—that is, one who writes prose of philosophical bent and gives advice to the readers."

Qtzl twitched his crest. "I am filled with philosophy, but advice? About what?"

"It does not say," said Ship.

"I need a...'photo,' you called it."

"Very good, Qtzl. Yes, 'photo.' You need one. And some examples of your prose."

"You have that in your database."

"Indeed. Shall I select a cross-section of your philosophical meanders?"

As Ship's AI system was not programmed for wry humor, Qtzl was sure he must have imagined the barb. "Do that," he directed, feeling somewhat more buoyant. "I'll find a 'photo' somewhere. They're all over the backs of these...'books.'" During his rambling exploration, he had found a volume with a representation of an Earth personage in shades of gray. He located it now, and carefully excised it from the book's glossy wrapping, using a foraged utility blade. By the time he had finished, Ship had produced several pieces of his finest commentary, and had come across sample advice columns in the newspaper's online archives.

"It is called 'Ask Angela,'" said Ship. "In it, a reader asks a question and Angela provides the answer."

"What sort of question?"

"For example, this female complains that after the birth of their first young, her mate has ceased to accord her the attention due her. She is uncertain what to do to recapture his interest."

"And what advice does Angela give?"

"She tells the female to decrease her weight and revitalize her… assets. This is an approximation, of course. This will, according to Angela, put something called 'pizzazz' back into the relationship."

"That's terrible advice! How can decreasing her body weight possibly increase her powers of attraction? A female is supposed to gain weight when she produces young. It's the natural indication of her elevated status. Doesn't this society have a Mating Codex? This female should sue for Breach of Attraction!"

"I am uncertain how this society handles their domestic matters. Perhaps the bearing of young is not as highly regarded here as it is at home."

"Nonsense. The society will not survive long that devalues its young." Qtzl stood and began to pace. "I shall not only tender my 'published clips,'" he decided, "I shall give a real answer to this question. Ship, read me the entire column."

Ship did, and Qtzl gave his own opinion about mates with wandering attention and the merits of a matron's physique. He recommended legal action only as a last resort, suggesting that some remedial classes in couplehood might bolster the mate's flagging attention span.

Scanning the photo of the Earth person for transmission, Ship said, "And what is the name of your alter-ego, Qtzl? I do not think Qtzl Fhuuii is a common name here."

"Well, I think it should sound something like that other one, er, 'Ask Angela.'"

"'Ask' is a verb meaning to inquire. Angela is a name suggesting the columnist is a saintly being from the next world sent back to this plane to intercede on behalf of others."

Qtzl was impressed. "All that in three syllables! Is there a word in this economical language for a saintly being from another world who's stranded on this one?"

"Alien. Also known colloquially as an 'ET.'"

"Well then. That's it. 'Ask Alien.'"

"I do not think we wish to call attention to your…non-local origins."

Qtzl's feelings were hurt. "Well, then you suggest something."

Accordingly, Ship reviewed databases of common names beginning with the letter 'A' and came up with 'Arlene.' Close to 'alien,' but not close enough to draw suspicion.

Ship dispatched the packet to the newspaper and Qtzl began an expectant wait. While he waited, he returned to the transport module to assess the damage and began the painful process of learning the natives' difficult language. "All gutturals," he complained. "It's enough to give a person a sore throat."

By the end of another week, Qtzl had managed to read a book or two. It was challenging; even Ship was at a loss over certain words and concepts, and Qtzl began to suspect that he had stepped into a very strange world indeed, much like his favorite childhood story of Qalss in Tuiifooshand.

A decaday and myriad résumés later, Qtzl had read a variety of books—mostly of a type called 'science fiction.' It was not without its counterpart on his own world—every people, he suspected, dreamed of other peoples on other worlds. He also learned how to play computer games and developed a taste for something called 'cheese puffs,' which was one thing his borrowed cupboards seemed to contain in abundance.

And then came the call. Not a call, precisely, for the only address Ship had left the newspaper was an electronic one. They wanted Qtzl—or rather, they wanted someone named…

"Arlen?"

"They apparently thought 'Arlene' was what they refer to as a 'typo.' I am not certain why they came to that conclusion. They want to know your last name and phone number. They wish to speak to you directly."

"I has anticipationed them," said Qtzl in what he imagined to be perfect American. "I has been studying them lingo."

Ship was silent for a moment, then said, "Perhaps I shall tell them you are away and will call them back in several days. I believe that should be enough time to remedy your lamentable lack of language skills."

Three days later Qtzl spoke to the newspaper's managing editor. He was nervous, most especially when the man asked, "Where're you from? Originally, I mean."

"Uh," ad-libbed Qtzl, "why do you ask?"

"Oh, your accent. I can't quite place it. French, is it?"

French. Qtzl glanced feverishly at Ship's remote self, stationed, as always, by the computer. The screen flashed to life and began to display information. French: Native of an autonomous provincial unit called France which lies across a large body of salty water from these shores.

"Ah, yes. Er, French, well..."

"No, wait...Canadian, isn't it? Quebecois?"

The computer screen cleared and displayed instructions.

"No, um, Winnipeg actually."

"Ah. That explains why your name doesn't sound quite French. 'Quet-zell'—am I pronouncing that right?"

"Ket-zell," Qtzl corrected him, eyes still on the computer. "It's, er, Belgian. I'm—ah—third generation Canadian." He rolled his eyes. How would he ever keep all this straight?

"Why," he asked Ship later, "didn't we just say 'yes' to French or Quebecois?"

"Because then I would have been required to tutor you in French. Teaching you American has consumed enough of my processing time."

Qtzl did not let Ship's cool derision deflate him. He had passed.

He had pretended to be an Earth person—Human, they called themselves—and passed.

"Now," Ship continued, "we'll need a bank account in which your new employer can deposit your wages. We will also need a 'credit' account on which to charge your purchases. I shall take care of these details."

"And I," said Qtzl, "will bring home the xuti."

In the next several days the letters arrived over the network to print neatly on the borrowed computer's output device. Qtzl was to select the ones he found most interesting (though his new employer did offer suggestions), answer them and send them back with replies attached. A simpler job, Qtzl could not have imagined. Despite his first impression, the humans were not nearly so alien as he had thought, although it was clear their society possessed its share of peculiarities.

Dear Arlen,

A while back, I sent my friend—I'll call her "Sue"—a chain-letter. I've always thought of Sue as a good friend, but she broke the chain! In two months she has yet to send the letter to the people targeted by her list! I'm not superstitious or anything, so I'm not afraid I'll have bad luck because Sue broke the chain, but I'm really irked that she'd be so irresponsible. I don't know which makes me madder, her laziness or her lack of loyalty to me as a friend.*

*My sister says I should nag** her about this. Should I? My husband says I should break off our friendship before anything bad happens. What do you think?*

Steamed in Amarillo

*Ship's memo: *Please see attached notes on the term "chain mail" or "chain letter." I construe from these materials that chain mail is associated both with extremes in fortune and with protection from* *harm—from ill fortune, one must assume. Evidently, sending the chain mail along to the 'target' intact engages protective function, while severing the chain disables it, thus calling down a curse on the hapless recipient.*

***For your information, a "nag" is a colloquial term for a hoofed quadruped of doubtful quality, usually referred to as a "horse," scientific term, equus.*

Dear Steamed,

It sounds as if chain mail is quite dangerous. I'm surprised it is legal. I am equally surprised that you would send such dangerous materials to someone you consider a close friend. You are obviously a foolhardy human being, and I think you owe your friend, Sue, an apology. On the other hand, she would seem to owe you some remuneration for the broken chain.

By the way, I think you should consider sending letters made of some less inimical material—I am told paper is a suitable medium.

I would also recommend against turning Sue into a horse. It sounds as if that process might be difficult to undo and would only compound your folly.

"YOUR EMPLOYER CALLED."

Qtzl looked up from the book he was reading—one of a series about the inhabitants of a planet named Mars which, if the story could be believed, was this planet's next orbit neighbor.

"And?"

"He likes the column. He referred to it as 'kitschy.'"

"What's that?"

"I am not certain. I could find no reference to it in the dictionaries at my disposal. It is most certainly positive. He also wishes to know if you wish to use the photograph we sent or mail him another. He indicates that a photo used for publication needs to be of a higher quality than the one we sent. He requires a scanned image of the original 'black and white glossy.'"

"What is an 'original black and white glossy?'"

"The photo we sent was evidently a second or third generation print. We need to find an original photograph."

"But I liked that one. I liked the way the person's fur grew all around its face. It looked almost the same upside down as it did right-side up."

"Mr. Barnett says he must have an original photograph either mailed or scanned and downloaded. I suggest we find such a photograph."

Qtzl searched. He searched the bookshelves, the desk drawers, the closets. When that failed to turn up any sort of 'black and white glossy,' he turned to a tall cabinet in a corner of the computer room. It was not a pleasant task; the cabinet was overflowing with sheets of cellulose, paper and semi-transparent flimsies all crammed into brightly colored covers of a thicker material. After sustaining a number of small, painful cuts to his digits, Qtzl found a red folder that bore the title "Cover Shots." This turned out to be just what he was looking for.

"Look!" he told Ship, holding the folder open for the remote to see. "This is the most extraordinary bit of luck! Not only are there photos here, but they are very like the one of the human whose picture is on some of the books I've been reading."

Ship looked. "Qtzl, the photo in your left hand is the original of the picture we have already sent."

Qtzl held up one of the photos. "Are you sure? Perhaps it's merely ethnocentricity on our part. You know the old saying—'all aliens look alike.'"

"First, Qtzl, being a machine intelligence, I am not prone to ethnocentricity. Second, my optics are far more sensitive than your own. This is not only the same person, it is the identical photograph."

Qtzl was amazed. The Deity had favored him with yet another miracle. "Relief! I was wondering how we were to explain to Mr. Barnett that I now looked like someone else."

"I am given to understand," Ship said, "that inhabitants of this planet change their physical appearance quite liberally by surgical means. Moreover, some writers use photographs that do not accurately represent them to their readers. It is possible that this photograph does not portray this…Stanley Schell. Put the photograph on the desk, Qtzl, and allow me to digitize the image."

"Why didn't you let me take the call from Mr. Barnett?" Qtzl asked as the FRU glided to hover above the picture.

"You were sunning yourself on the roof."

"You could have called me in."

"No need. I was perfectly capable of handling the situation. I explained that I am your secretary, Fru Shipley. The photo is sent. Your first column will appear in the Sunday issue. Credits have already been deposited to your account. At the current rate of pay I estimate it will take approximately eight month's wages to purchase and process the materials necessary for my repair."

"Eight months!"

"We must also purchase provisions, Qtzl. You are not a hunter. Therefore, we will need to shop at the local food depository."

"And how are we supposed to do that? I've read *National Geographic*. I've seen 'Godzilla versus Gamera' and 'War of the Worlds'; I look like a giant lizard and you look like a miniature Martian."

"They deliver," said Ship. "Our first groceries will arrive this afternoon at exactly three hours, post meridian. I suggest we stay out of sight. Now, should you not return to reading your mail? A number of people are seeking your advice today."

✦

Dear Arlen,

I feel a little funny writing to a column about this, but I don't have anyone else to turn to. After our annual New Year's Eve party my husband's sister and her husband were the last to leave. As we were saying our good-byes at the door, my brother-in-law (I'll call him Fred) slipped up behind me and goosed my buns**! I'm torn—should I tell my husband? Part of me wants to, but this little voice in my head insists it will ruin his relationship with Fred and hurt his sister very badly.*

Speechless in Tulsa

*Ship's note: *A goose is a large aquatic fowl which makes a sound not unlike one of your sneezes and whose natural gait is a waddle.*

***Since Speechless is not explicit about what variety of buns to which the brother-in-law applied the goose, we can assume only that they were a baked foodstuff made of flour, milk and eggs (perhaps goose eggs?).*

Dear Speechless,

I think you should most certainly tell your husband about the incident. He may well wonder why there is goose down in his baked goods. Telling the truth may be embarrassing, but it will save you from having to fabricate a lie.

As to your brother-in-law—shame on him! I believe you should confront him and allow him to make restitution for his peculiar behavior. I would suggest the least he could do would be to bake your family some fresh buns!

By the way, I have been reading a lot about human psychology and it sounds to me as if you might have something called multiple personality disorder. Nothing to be alarmed about, I'm sure—in fact, it sounds as if it might be quite entertaining to have several personalities at your disposal—but I would recommend that you make an appointment to see a psychiatrist before the little voice in your head advises you to do something dangerous.

"The groceries have arrived."

Qtzl was slow to emerge from the Stan Schell novel he was engrossed in. He made a noncommittal noise in the back of his throat and turned the page.

"Your taste in literature seems to have lodged in a rut," Ship observed. "Is that not another Stan Schell novel?"

"I like the way he deals with alien races. Quite enlightened for someone who's never met any."

"He is a science fiction writer," said Ship, as if that alone was supposed to deter Qtzl from reading his work. "That is an 'escapist literary form about unlikely characters from implausible futures thrown into impossible situations.'"

"Such as being stranded on an alien world?"

Ship persisted. "He is not considered to be one of the 'greats.' He is, I believe they say, firmly mid-list."

"And what do the 'greats' write about?"

"War, sex, death...bullfights."

"Ffsstt," said Qtzl, "I shall go get the groceries." He padded downstairs, the soft, orange material of the leggings he was wearing puddling comfortably around his feet. The delivery boy had left the box of groceries in its usual place under the back awning. All Qtzl had to do was lean out of the door and get it. He peered through the long, transparent panes. He slid back the door, stepped out and picked up the box, pausing for just a moment to close his eyes and breathe in the sweet, tangy air.

He loved that smell. There wasn't anything on his world quite like it. Ship had determined that it originated from the sap of the trees that towered around the house. He had decided that when he left, a box of those spiky seed pods they dropped everywhere would come with him.

The snap of a twig and a chuff of sound brought Qtzl to sudden focus on the world around him. There, just beyond the deck where he stood, right up against the side of the house, a group of native quadrupeds stood and stared at him. Their black-lipped mouths were full of the flowering blooms that had appeared all around the alien domicile and though they seemed frozen with surprise, their jaws never ceased moving.

"Sh-sh-sh," hissed Qtzl, box clutched in his quaking arms, crest flat to his head. "Sh-sh-ship!"

Ship took an eternity to respond. Meanwhile, Qtzl shook harder; his crest was all but clamped to his head; more blossoms disappeared into the all-devouring mouths of the alien lifeforms. At last, the FRU's blessed hum could be heard behind him.

"Yes, Qtzl?"

"Are…are these carnivores?"

"No. Herbivores."

His crest relaxed. "Are they…people?"

"No, Qtzl. They are called 'deer'. A peculiar lifeform variously celebrated and despised. My research indicates horticulturists hunt them because of their dietary cravings."

Crest merely quivering now, Qtzl carried his box into the house with as much dignity as he could muster.

"Qtzl," Ship said when he had stowed the groceries and returned to his book, "they want to syndicate you."

His crest flattened again. "They what?"

"We have been approached by a national newspaper syndicate. They wish to purchase your column for distribution to all of their publications. This is a good thing, Qtzl. This will hasten my repair."

Qtzl glanced at the pile of letters he was scheduled to read that day. The one on top, like many others he received these days, was not asking for advice, but thanking him for advice already given. National syndication. "Will I be famous, Ship?"

"I believe so."

Qtzl wrinkled his nose and whistled softly through the flattened slits. How strange if he should gain on this alien world what had so far eluded him completely at home. His fondest dreams to the contrary, none took his philosophical meanderings seriously, nor read his poetry in klatch shops, nor hummed his songs as they went about their business. Not even members of his immediate family would take his advice. "Life," he murmured, "is full of strange turns."

KERWIN FREES HAD NARROWED HIS search to a small valley between two low ridges. It was rural—even for the Tahoe area—but he was hopeful that among the clusters of summer homes and isolated retreats someone had seen something.

He had mapped a course that took him on a rough circuit of the area, going door-to-door. Not many doors opened. This time of year, most of the summer homes were awaiting their occupants, while the ski lodges had just bid their owners good-bye. Of the few people he spoke to, only two had actually seen the blazing trail of light. One, out for a late night walk, had seen it reflected in the water of a large pond; the other, an insomniac, had glimpsed it as it passed over a skylight. A handful more claimed to have been awakened by something—some noise or tremor or explosion—and had assumed it to be thunder or a stray jet.

Still, he was able to determine approximately where the 'meteorite' had skimmed the treetops. It was pushing twilight when he pulled his car into a little cul-de-sac called Perelandra Circle—an ironic and downright un-Tahoe-ish name. There was one cabin in the cul-de-sac.

As he pulled into the drive, he was startled by movement on the roof. He glanced up, but caught only a flash of turquoise above the ridgepole. If it was a raccoon, they'd taken to dressing up for their nocturnal forays. There was no car in the drive, but a light was on inside. It was extinguished even as he approached the front door. He knocked, he rang, he knocked again. He tried to peer through a front window. He thought he saw movement in the darkened room, but he couldn't be sure.

Probably a kid, he thought, or a woman, left alone and waiting for parent or partner to come back from the store. "Hey!" he called. "I just want to ask a couple of questions about a meteorite fall we had a while back. I'm a…an astronomy student and I was hoping I might find it. It'd really help my grades."

There was a long silence, then, a voice just on the other side of the front door said, "Meteorite?"

"Yes. It was April 16th. At about 1 AM."

"It fell near here?"

"Very near. Possibly in that little valley behind your house. Did you see it?"

"No. I'm sorry. I did not see it. I was…asleep."

Kerwin Frees muzzled his frustration and asked, "Did you hear anything then? I talked to several people in the area who said something woke them—like thunder or a jet going over."

Now the silence was profound. Then, Kerwin Frees imagined he heard murmuring on the opposite side of the door. "Do you think you might open the door? It's kind of hard to communicate like this. I'm not dangerous."

"Sorry, I'm afraid I can't do that."

"I understand. So did you? Hear anything?"

"I heard nothing. We had not taken occupancy of the house just yet."

Frees frowned. "A minute ago, you said you were asleep. Now you say you weren't in the area?"

"We were, as you say, 'in the area.'" It was a different voice—much more confident. "We were not in the house at that time. We were camping across the valley."

"You still might have heard something."

"We did not."

It was a strange interview, Kerwin Frees thought later, as he drove home in the dark. A very strange interview. He let his imagination run with it; he had stumbled across a hostage situation, or one side of a love triangle, or someone who had broken into the house and was using it without the owner's knowledge.

The more he thought about it, the more this last idea stuck with Kerwin Frees. He decided he would call the sheriff's department in the morning and suggest that the house might bear watching. Could just be kids using the place as a party spot, or it could be someone a lot more sinister. He wasn't prone to poking his nose into other folks' affairs, and he didn't feature himself as a good Samaritan, but he might be able to keep some poor schmuck from walking into a very sticky situation.

STAN SCHELL WAS TIRED. IN fact, he was exhausted. It was day ten of a two-month book tour and he sat in a titanic Barnes and Noble in Sacramento wishing he was browsing for books instead of sitting behind his signing table praying the cluster of newcomers by the front door had come to see him. Still, he was grateful to be here; the other stops he'd made so far had been in small town specialty stores that had barely enough room in them for the signing table, let alone the two or three people who might show up to have him sign a book.

Working on his second latte from a neighboring bistro, he caught himself pondering who had first noticed that books and espresso go together like bagels and cream cheese, and realized he was hopelessly bored. And depressed. And exposed. He was between two sale tables, in conspicuous view. He'd signed a few books—might even sign a few more—but mostly he'd sat under the flickering glances of browsers, trying not to read their thoughts. Sometimes people would stop, pick up a book and indulge in pleasantries, such as informing him that they didn't read science fiction in a tone of voice that suggested they didn't understand why anyone would.

At the bottom of the latte, he decided he'd had it with trying to look interested and interesting. He pulled a newspaper from his briefcase and pretended to be looking at the ad for his signing. Then he gave up all pretense and turned the page. An audible sigh escaped him—and went completely unnoticed by the flock of shoppers around the sale tables. The section he held—the section the promotions manager had given him because his ad was in it—was inhabited by gossip columns, allegedly witty and urbane commentaries, and advice to the lovelorn.

Stan glanced surreptitiously around. He seemed to have become such a fixture over the last two hours that people had ceased to notice him. He turned his eyes back to the paper. His mind was desperate for something to do. He read 'Dear Abby.' Then he read 'Miss Manners.' Then he turned the page and met himself face to face.

He was simultaneously nonplussed and pleased. Evidently the paper had run an article on the hometown boy as well as the paid ad. His eyes brought into focus the two words that appeared next to his face on the page. Ask Arlen. His gaze dropped to the text below. Dear Arlen, it said, I feel funny writing to a column about this…

"Excuse me, but could you sign my books, please?"

"Huh?" Mouth still hanging open, eyes possibly bugged out, Stan looked up into the face of a fan. She smiled shyly and proffered two of his novels for him to sign—a paperback and the hardback that would go out of print in a month, barring divine intervention. He dropped the mystery back into the briefcase and scrambled for his pen. "That's what I'm here for," he said and smiled.

The girl cocked her head and looked at him as he imagined Alice must have once looked at the White Rabbit. "You're the guy that writes that advice column, aren't you? Ask Arlen?"

He stared blankly at the flyleaf of the hardback, once again meeting his own black and white gaze. "Looks that way," he said and signed his name.

When he visited the offices of *The Bee*, Ted Barnett's face lit up in recognition. "Well, if it isn't my star columnist."

"No," said Stan, "it's not," and proceeded to confuse the hell out of him.

At the end of an hour interview, he knew that Ted Barnett did not read science fiction and that his star columnist was punctual, easygoing, undemanding, and transacted all business over the Internet. He'd never missed a deadline. He had a unique slant on life (something Stan had already gleaned from a perusal of the column) and was from Canada.

Stan also knew the columnist's email address. He was surprised to find he'd known it before he entered Barnett's office—it was the local in-box of his summer house in South Shore Tahoe. It rather looked as if he was going to have to take a trip upstate. He did not request that his photo be removed from the column, nor did he, to Barnett's obvious relief, insist that the column be suspended. He could not have said why he did not do those things, although he suspected unhealthy curiosity and a fascination with the bizarre (which had contributed to his delinquency as a writer) were somehow involved.

"It seems," said Ship, "that our descent did not go unnoticed."

"Should we be concerned?" asked Qtzl around a mouthful of cheese puffs. "The human thought we were a natural occurrence."

"One he is particularly interested in. If he locates the exact earthfall of this 'occurrence,' he will find…me. He is already very close."

Qtzl's crest pulled itself tightly against his head. He felt a strong urge to hiss. "What can we do?"

"Very little, Qtzl. We cannot move me."

"You're well camouflaged."

"To your eyes perhaps. Who knows how well camouflaged a human will find me?"

Kerwin Frees was not a wealthy man by any stretch of even an impoverished imagination. He kept a bit in savings for the all-too-frequent rainy day and had a few investments. He lived frugally on a teacher's salary during the school season so he could afford to chase UFOs the rest of the year. Now he dipped into savings to do something that would most assuredly cause his colleagues to doubt his sanity. He rented a helicopter to fly over the sixty or so acres he'd targeted as the most likely place for the UFO to have come to earth. To make the sort of showy splash it had in the midnight sky, it would have to have been of a size that couldn't fail to disturb even the densest forest. He started the pilot at one end of the target valley and asked him to take a zigzag course down the length of it, flying as low as was safe, practical and legal.

The pilot, for his part, was close-mouthed and taciturn, not even asking his client what they were doing, until they were making their third dogleg over the forested slopes, Frees peering intensely into the greenery below, camera clutched in his hands. "Exactly what is it we're looking for?"

"I'm not sure…exactly." That was the truth. Did he keep his eyes peeled for a flash of sunlight on metal? For a burnt swathe of forest? For a few flattened trees? Yes, all of the above. "Something unusual."

"Unusual as in what…Sasquatch?"

"What? Oh. Oh, no. Nothing like that. I'm an astronomy buff.

A meteorite fell out here a while back. It'd be great if I could find it."

"Wouldn't that have been on the news?"

"It was."

"Huh. Missed it, I guess. Not that I pay much attention to things like that. Ball lightning—now that's something I'm interested in." The pilot, suddenly garrulous, proceeded to regale him with a series of ball lightning stories, and Frees, guiltily interested, listened to them.

Somewhere in the middle of the third or fourth tale—one in which the pilot suspected the lightning of owning some form of primordial intelligence—Frees suddenly lost the thread of narration. His eyes had found something unusual: flattened treetops pointed as eloquently as any arrow to a long scar in the bare earth to their east. The scar ended in a dense thicket of brush. He took a flurry of photographs.

"What?" asked the pilot. "You see something?"

"Something. Could you get us closer to that…that scar in the ground down there? There—just beyond those broken trees."

The pilot whistled. "See what you mean." He heeled the 'copter over and headed back around for second, lower pass.

"I don't suppose," said Frees, snapping madly away with his old Pentax, "that you could land us down there?"

"No-o-o way. Nobody could land down there. Except maybe your meteorite."

Frees nodded and glanced around the area for landmarks. He found one of particular interest—the cabin on Perelandra Circle, which was, he calculated, mere hundreds of yards from the crash site. If there were people in that house, they couldn't have avoided seeing the off-world visitor plummet to earth.

THE HOUSE DID NOT LOOK lived-in. There were no vehicles

around it. No smoke curled out of the chimney, though the air was beginning to cool slightly with the onset of evening. Stan contemplated his approach. He could sit here until his eyes froze open, feeling like a poor man's Spenser, or he could get up and boldly go where no one else had any right being.

He did not know martial arts. He did not carry a gun, mace, or pepper spray. He was a poor excuse for a red-blooded American homeowner. Despite these minuses, he started up his car, pulled off the shoulder of the badly paved road and drove brazenly into his driveway. No one ran out shooting. He heard no slamming of windows or doors.

He took a deep breath, then got out of the car, patting his pocket to make sure his cell phone was still there. At the first sign of trouble, he would call the police. He should have called them before, he supposed, but what was he supposed to say? "Hello, officer, I'd like to report that someone pretending to be me is writing an advice column from my summer cabin." Oh, yeah—that sounded believable.

He slammed the door of his car, then opened it and slammed it a second time. Then he approached the house, while having a loud conversation with himself. The front door was unlocked. He hesitated again, thought about the police again, then opened the door. "Hello?" he called. Silence. "HalloOoo!"

The place was clean—had even been dusted—though the cleaning service wasn't due to go over the place for several weeks. He made his way through the living room toward his office, where he knew he would find evidence of habitation. A glance told him it was the center of the interloper's activities. The computer was on and apparently downloading something. Even as he watched, it finished up and returned to the main email window. Curious, he opened the message icon that had appeared at the end of the download.

"Here's your new batch of goodies, Arlen. There're some real doozies in here," said the message, and was signed, "Alec." Probably an editorial assistant. Still more curious, Stan opened the download and read,

Dear Arlen,

I was lunching the other day with an important client, when suddenly in the middle of the meal, she got out a mirror and a dental pick and began cleaning her teeth right there at the table! I almost came unglued. Try to imagine a sophisticated-looking woman in a Christian Dior suit sitting in a five-star restaurant giving herself a root-planing!

I am in a complete dither—this woman represents our most important account, but now I'm afraid to be seen with her for fear I'll find out she's got some other private chores she likes to do in public. I find it hard to believe she's never been thrown out of a restaurant for this. What should I do?

Stymied on Staten Island

Fascinating. It really was a doozy. In a sudden fit of unnamable urges, Stan sat at the keyboard, opened a word processor file, and wrote:

Dear Stymied,

Since you're eating in five-star restaurants, I must assume you must have a little cash to throw around. Next time you're out to lunch with your client, slip the maitre d' a twenty and ask him to toss the woman out on her ear at the first sign of dental hygiene. Alternatively, you might consider stationing a couple of friends at a nearby table with instructions to squeal "E-ee-w! Gross!" the moment she goes for the floss.

He was absurdly pleased with the response. Pithy, he thought. Doing an advice column could be a kick. That did not answer the question of how someone else had come to be writing an advice column in his name…or rather, his face.

He was on the verge of searching the room in answer to that question when he heard the back door open and close. A peculiar humming tickled his ears. Hair rising all over his body (his chin felt as if it were in contact with a hedgehog), Stan slipped from the chair into the closet four feet behind it. Once there, he tried to peer through the louvers but found he couldn't see a thing. He settled for listening.

What he heard was a bizarre series of clicks, whistles, hums, chirps and hoots that were answered by a similar barrage of sounds. He thought he could almost make out words, but couldn't imagine what language he was listening to. It sounded made-up, but then the only made-up language Stan had ever heard was Klingon, so he hardly counted himself as an expert on the subject.

The sounds became suddenly more forceful and then, Stan heard his answer to the letter read back in strangely accented English. The reading was followed by a particularly loud hoot. "This misses the point entirely! For someone to display her teeth so prominently in a public place—well, it's a miracle a fight didn't break out. How irresponsible!"

"There is a point, Ketzel, and I believe it is you who has missed it," said a second voice in perfectly unaccented English.

"How so? Clearly—" (Stan could hear the manic depressing of keys on his keyboard.) "Clearly, to suggest this action is merely rude is to minimize—"

"Ketzel, who entered that reply? This file has just been downloaded."

There was a pregnant pause.

"More to the point," continued the unaccented voice, "where is the person who entered that reply?"

There was a flurry of movement. One of them had left the room. Stan held his breath. A few moments later, the flurry was repeated in reverse.

"There is a ground vehicle before the house! Someone was

here."

"Excellent logic, Ketzel. Although, I should say the vehicle's presence suggests someone is still here."

"Would you, er, scan, please?"

There was a muted twittering sound and Stan's hair saluted again. Instinct drove him to the floor of the closet to hide in a jumble of ski jackets, bleacher blankets and two large teddy bears he had purchased, but never given to his niece. It was from this motley refuge that he saw the closet door swing open and peered up into the face of a giant, frilled lizard. Hovering near its shoulder was a sleek, silvery object that bore an uncomfortable resemblance to the probes used by Martians in the movie "War of the Worlds." The lizard's monstrous, orange eyes swept the closet, coming to rest on the assorted debris on the floor.

Stan, numbed to speechlessness, prepared to surrender. The lizard's mouth opened and perfectly intelligible English words came out.

"I don't see anyone."

"Ketzel," said the sleek, silver probe, "observe." A gleaming tendril issued from the probe and aimed itself at the tip of Stan's nose.

The lizard's eyes focused. "Oh," it said.

"E-ee-ee-ee!" said Stan, and fainted.

"It's him. There are some differences between the 3D and the 2D, but it's him."

"I would have to agree. I suppose it was remiss of me not to suspect he would have to return to this domicile at some point. It is nearing the time of year when many of the inhabitants of this particular society go on vacation."

"Vacation?"

"Similar to what you were doing when we became…lost."

Stan assumed he was dreaming. The only viable alternative was that, sometime in the recent past, a short-order cook in Tahoe City had hidden his stash of recreational drugs in a jar of chili powder.

"He poses a singular problem. What do we do with him until we can leave?"

Do with him?

"We don't have anywhere near the resources we need to leave... do we?"

"No, we do not. The engine refit is nearly complete, but the long-range navigational array is still a shambles, and the port gimbals suffered severe damage when we skidded sideways among the rocks. Really, Ketzel, we are fortunate there is anything left of the forward steering mechanism at all."

Stan was dismayed to realize he was listening to a real conversation taking place somewhere behind him. He opened his eyes. He was stretched out on the sofa in his office staring into the glass panels of the tambour door of a bookshelf. Reflected clearly in the panels was one helluva tall reptile and the sleek little probe Stan had seen in an earlier psychotic episode. He closed his eyes then opened them again. The reflections were still there.

Abandon logic, all ye who enter here, Stan told himself, and studied his uninvited guests as they continued to ponder his fate.

"Perhaps if we just keep him here, quietly, no one will notice."

It was probably not really a reptile, Stan thought, but merely looked like one. Maybe he was some sort of intelligent dinosaur—the kind Bob Bakker would just love to find on his front porch some cool summer evening.

Hello, I'm homeothermic.

It did resemble Bakker's drawings of dilophosaurs...except, of course, that it was wearing his sister Genevieve's fuchsia sundress. Absurdity rose in his throat, nearly choking him.

"The vehicle before the house may draw notice," said the Martian probe. "And it is probable that someone will mark his absence. He may well have informed someone else of his intention to come here."

"I did." Stan sat up and turned to look at the...whatever. "I told my agent, your editor, and several close friends that I was coming to Tahoe to see who's been using my address—and my face—to publish an advice column."

There was a heavy silence, then the dilophosaur shuffled to face him. "Hello," it said and its rubbery mouth curled into an approximation of a smile. "I'm Ketzel." It glanced sideways at the probe floating silently beside it. "I'm from—well, very far away—and I'm lost and I need to get home again."

"And you left your ruby slippers at home, right?" *Good response if this is a hoax. Please let it be a hoax.*

The reptilian head canted sideways. "Excuse me?"

"He makes a reference," said the probe, "to a popular movie—ixltl, to you—in which the lost heroine gets home through the agency of a pair of ruby slippers she has inherited from a deceased crone. Yes, Mr. Schell, that is essentially correct. We have crash-landed on your world and our only means of getting home is damaged, though not beyond repair. We have hopes of earning enough capital to purchase the materials necessary to restore it."

Stan blinked. "You're kidding."

The probe floated over to the sofa, pausing to hover right before Stan's startled eyes. "You suspect a hoax, and this is understandable. Please notice that I am not suspended by any wires."

Stan waved a trembling hand around the probe. It was as good as its word. "Okay. I see that."

"Ship," said the lizard. "Show him where you crash-landed. That will prove we're not a hoax, won't it?"

It was a spaceship. By God, it was a spaceship! Kerwin Frees's hands shook as he let the foliage fall back into place. He took a step back from the mound of uprooted shrubbery. It had crash-landed here and had been carefully concealed. And there were signs that it was under repair.

By whom?

He glanced up the hill toward the little cabin on Perelandra Circle. By someone in that house?

He turned back to the ship, his camera bouncing against his chest. Evidence. That was what he needed. He pulled a couple of arms-full of greenery away from the vessel and began shooting. He was between shots, looking for a different vantage point when he heard someone approaching from uphill.

As often as he had allowed himself to imagine an encounter of the third kind, as often as he had invented his response, he had never imagined he might panic. But he did. He stumbled to the bow of the ship and threw himself into a ramble of underbrush, just barely able to twist into a position from which he could see the stern before he was forced to freeze.

A man appeared first—a bearded man in a forest green shirt and jeans. Frees had no time to be disappointed before 'it' came into view—a reptilian alien lifeform decked in bright fuchsia. It was a sundress, he realized, a woman's sundress. That fact had barely jolted him when he noticed the sleek metallic object floating between the two other figures.

The reptile, speaking, began pulling camouflage away from the vessel's nether end. Words floated back to Frees's ears—English words. "See?... This… Ship…believe us?"

Another voice spoke. The reptile's mouth wasn't moving, nor was the man's. The voice came from the floating 'droid' which now bobbed about the stern. A moment later, it began moving forward toward Frees's hiding place. His throat felt as if a peach pit was stuck in it.

"As you can see," the floater intoned in perfect English, "the bow planes have suffered the most damage. We are currently attempting to procure the materials necessary to repair them."

"Will you really be able to do that?" asked the human, and Frees's eyes were drawn to his face. It was a familiar face. He was certain that if his brain wasn't caught in some insidious form of paralysis, he'd be able to put a name to it.

"Ship is fully capable of self-repair," said the reptile. "We only need the materials. That's why we…availed ourselves of your cabin."

The man nodded. "And my face." He sighed. "Okay. I believe you. Good God, do I have any choice?" He turned to look at the reptile. "How can I help?"

The reptile's mouth widened without revealing teeth, had it any. "Don't show the whistle on us, please."

"Blow the whistle," said the droid.

"Whatever. Please don't do it. Let us continue with our ruse. We'll be out of your chair soon, I promise."

"Out of your hair," said the droid.

"Whatever. We'll be out of it. What do you say?"

The man glanced back and forth between the two aliens. "Can I go inside the ship?"

KERWIN FREES WAS GASPING BY the time he made it back up to the road. He was closer to the house than he'd meant to be, but the aliens and their human cohort were still downhill in the ship. He started to turn toward his concealed car, but caught sight of the vehicle sitting in the driveway of the cabin. He hesitated only a moment before hurrying to investigate it. It was a small Japanese sedan, fairly new. He slipped in through the passenger door and went speedily through the glove box in search of—ah! Registration.

Stan Schell. Now he knew where he'd seen the guy before, on the back cover of several science fiction novels in his massive collection, and in a number of widely-separated newspapers. Science fiction writer and advice columnist, what a combination.

The revelation gave him pause. He glanced around the property. No other vehicles—no camera crews. Nobody. Okay, not a movie, then. Could it be a hoax? A publicity stunt of some sort? He had no way of knowing, but he had ways of finding out.

THE SHIP WAS REAL. AT least insofar as Stan could tell. Not that he had much experience with these things except on paper, but the craft was not a Roswell Special—there wasn't an ounce of tin-foil in it, nor one stick of balsa wood. It was made of metal and something that was like plastic or fiberglass. It was big, too—nearly as big as a semi—and complicated-looking.

Inside, they showed him which systems were working, pointed out where repairs needed to be made, let him sit at the controls. He kept trying to be skeptical, to pass it all off as an elaborate hoax, but he could think of no one he knew who would or could orchestrate such a hoax.

He found another reason to disbelieve the hoax angle. Ted Barnett had assured him that the advice column with his face on it had been appearing and gathering loyal readers for months. It had evidently become a household word in homes where no Stan Schell novel had ever been read. Meanwhile Stan (I-don't-read-that-section) Schell had gone unawares. Where was the joke in that? Maybe it was a conspiracy intended to see how long it would take a writer to discover his identity was being plagiarized. Maybe it was a test case to see if an identity *could* be plagiarized. Maybe…

Maybe these were aliens.

"Pardon?"

The lizard looked at him through its gigantic orange eyes, its hands (or whatever) folded before its chest in a prayerful gesture. In his sister's sundress. His laughter, already uncontrollable, segued into a fit of hiccups.

"Ship! There's something wrong with Stan Schell!"

Oh, there certainly was. Either he was going not-so-quietly mad, or he was receiving the most extravagant gift the Universe could offer a writer of science fiction.

"He is laughing," said the probe. "And he is experiencing something called hiccups. Not a life-threatening situation. There are several suggested cures. We might try startling him."

The lizard was silent for a moment, then said, "I believe we already have."

BACK AT THE HOUSE, STAN and the aliens had tea and cheese puffs. Then, "Arlen" composed answers to his letters. He kept the answer Stan had made to the first of these—out of respect, he said, for their host.

Oddly, Stan wanted nothing more than to sleep. Overwhelmed, he supposed, and he surprised himself by actually being able to sleep. He curled up on his bed and slumbered deeply until his cell phone woke him.

It was his agent.

"Well?" he asked "Did you find anything?"

Only two aliens and a wrecked space shuttle. Nothing to get excited about. "Yeah. Someone's been using the cottage as a...base of operations. It's not...quite what I thought it was, though. Look, I'll have to explain it to you later. It's...complicated."

"Well, so's this. I just got a call from *The Tonight Show.*"

"The... You're kidding. I thought they weren't interested in me."

"They aren't. They're interested in 'Arlen.' A Mr. Barnett let them in on the connection between the column and Stan Schell and suddenly you're famous—SF writer moonlights as advisor of the lovelorn. They want you to come on the show and read some of the letters you've gotten—and, of course, the 'charmingly odd-ball' answers."

"But I don't have any answers!"

"And they want you to field questions from the audience and just generally, well, be Arlen for them."

"But I'm not Arlen! I'm Stan Schell! I write science fiction. I'll talk to them about that all night, if they want."

"That's just it, Stan they don't want. Maybe we should just turn your trespassers over to them."

For a moment Stan contemplated that—going onto *The Tonight Show* and telling them all about today. Maybe even showing pictures. There was a camera in the front hall closet.

As soon as he had the thought, he discarded it. Doing that would result in one of several horrific scenarios: (1) No one would believe him; he would be labeled a crackpot; and his career would come to an abrupt halt. (2) No one would believe him but a legion of UFO chasers; he would become a poster child for 'abductees' and hit the talk show circuit while his writing languished. (3) Everyone would believe him, including the government; he would end up in a witness protection program or, worse, he and the aliens would become 'guests' of the U.S. government.

"Look, just tell them I don't want to do it."

"Are you nuts? This could be—"

"Excruciatingly embarrassing, that's what it could be. I'm a science fiction writer, dammit. A good one. Just keep getting me gigs as a science fiction writer."

"There aren't that many gigs for science fiction writers, Stan. At least not ones at your level. This could get you exposure."

"Exposure? I'd rather run naked through Central Park."

"Think about it, okay?"

"Yeah, right."

✦

"What is *The Tonight Show?*" the lizard asked the moment Stan poked his head tentatively into the office.

"Why do you ask?"

"I have gotten an email about it. I have been asked to appear on this *The Tonight Show* to discuss the column and 'share some excerpts,' but I have no idea what this means."

Explain a nighttime variety show to an alien. Interesting assignment. Stan supposed he could mis-explain it, but he knew that the FRU would be able to disabuse Qtzl of any false impressions. He explained as best he could, and was surprised at Qtzl's immediate comprehension.

"Yes, yes! We have this at home, too. People speak and sing and dance and show their prowess at game or thought. Yes, I know this. But at home, these…shows are broadcast widely. Many thousands of people can experience them. Is it so here?"

Stan nodded. "*The Tonight Show* is probably the most exposure a person can get in one hour. It's been known to make or break careers."

Qtzl's neck frill, which had risen to the occasion, sank back to his shoulders. "But, Stan, I cannot appear on your show. If I do, everyone will see me. Then what would happen?"

Stan had no answer to that. In his books, aliens were feared, loathed, embraced whole-heartedly, worshipped. He realized he had no idea how real human beings would react to real aliens. "I don't know," he admitted.

"Could you do the show?"

"How could I do it? I don't write the column."

"Well, you did write one reply. It was perhaps not as well thought out as it could have been, you missed a few issues… But that doesn't matter, I could coach you. I could be in contact with you all the time you were on the show. I could put my words in your mouth."

"How?"

The FRU chose that moment to float silently into the room.

"That's how," said Qtzl.

"Damn," said Stan.

"OKAY, OKAY, OKAY," SAID THE young man in the third row. "I got one for you. There's this girl in the group I hang with who's real cute, but has this really disgusting habit, okay? Whenever we do fast food, she orders a hot dog, okay? And she takes a bite out of one end and then—this is gross—she turns the hot dog around so that I'm staring right at the bite and takes a bite off the other end. What can I do about that?"

"Not sit across from her?" Stan suggested. The audience laughed and Stan felt a warm glow spread across his cheeks. *Cool.*

In his ear, Ship chirped in annoyance. "Please, Stan, let Qtzl take care of this."

"Don't be obtuse, young man," said Stan after pausing to field Qtzl's thoughts. "This...female...is obviously attracted to you and is inviting you to partake of a Food Ritual with her. In any culture this is a first level mating rite, to which there is only one response. You must lean across the table and take a nice, big bite out of the proffered end of the food item. Unless, of course, you do not find the female attractive. Do you find the female attractive?"

"Well, yeah..."

"Then you simply must bite the dog, young man. The only other acceptable response is to get up and leave the eating area. But this would leave the female with the impression that you find her repulsive and don't wish to share her food. In fact, you may have already skewed your chances with the young woman." ("That's screwed, Qtzl," said Ship patiently.)

The audience loved it. Every off-the-wall second of it. A week later, Ship's port bow gimbals were on their way to recovery and 'Arlen' had been asked to appear on *The Late Night Show*.

KERWIN FREES STARED AT THE row of photographs bobbing festively from a line hung across his tiny kitchen/darkroom and flogged his brain through a tangle of seemingly unconnected facts. Fact 1: An alien spaceship had crash-landed in the Sierra Nevada. (The evidence of that hung right before his eyes.) Fact 2: The aliens were staying in Stan Schell's Tahoe summer cabin. (Was the tangential fact that the man was a science fiction writer merely a cosmic coincidence?) Fact 3: Stan Schell knew the aliens were using his house. (Witness the series of photos, taken yesterday through Schell's front window, of human and reptilian alien sharing cheese puffs in front of the TV.)

Then there was the information Frees had stumbled across while trying to glean information about Schell from his newspaper editor. It made an already incredible scenario absolutely bizarre: An alien ship crashes. Shortly thereafter, Ask Arlen, a demonstrably weird advice column, appears in a Sacramento newspaper. Shortly after that, it goes into syndication. About this time, Stan Schell appears in Ted Barnett's office asking after the author of the column that bears his picture. He reveals that the email address to which Barnett delivers his readers' letters is his own. Schell goes to Tahoe, purportedly to confront the face-stealing columnist. He discovers, instead, that there are aliens hiding in his summer cabin—something Frees had to assume was what he'd witnessed upon his discovery of the crash site. Schell immediately calls Barnett and "confesses" that he is the source of the column after all.

Okay. What did it all mean? That aliens had come to earth to write advice columns for human beings? Even Kerwin Frees's imagination balked at that. Were we that pathetic, or was this some sort of very peculiar plan for world domination? And what was he supposed to do with the information? He had been sitting on it for nearly a month, pretending to be gathering more, all the while wallowing in this insipid state of confusion.

He shook his head. Having achieved the dream of every UFO chaser the world around, he had no idea what to do next. The police were out. They wouldn't believe him. His UFO chasing buddies were also out. While he used them as sources of information (all of which he took with liberal amounts of salt), he wasn't sure what they'd do with a real, honest-to-God alien. He realized he was afraid to find out.

Yet, the aliens would not be here forever. When their vessel was repaired, they would be gone, and he would have missed the opportunity of a lifetime. His options seemed to have dwindled to one. He moved to his computer, opened his email exchange and carefully composed a message.

STAN SCHELL WAS WRITING UP a storm. Whatever else this experience provided, he knew it would end up on the shelves of bookstores everywhere. Better still, it would leave the stores and find its way into homes nationwide. He had no doubt some people would actually read it. Since his face had appeared in newspapers and on TV screens nationwide, Stan's modest sales had become decidedly immodest. His book covers were being redone—"Stan 'Ask Arlen' Schell," they would say. The only human beings who had reason to know he had not always been Arlen had a vested interest in keeping the column alive.

To the first talk show host who speculated as to why a science fiction writer would pseudonymously write a wacky syndicated column for the socially challenged, he owed the widely-bruited tale that he had been afraid people wouldn't accept advice from a writer of fantastic fiction. He had nodded amiably, too, when that same host suggested his mindset was a little bizarre. "A little alien?" he'd asked when the host seemed to be searching for a word. The audience chuckled. He loved that sound.

"Do you think anyone really takes your advice?" last night's host had asked him.

Dear God, I hope not, he'd thought, opened his mouth and parroted Qtzl's "Well, I should hope so. I mean, look at the (twullip, said Qtzl)...uh, crap these other columnists dish out. ("English, Qtzl," admonished Ship.) To take their advice is to perpetuate undesirable behavior by failing to respond to it in an appropriate manner."

"Like neglecting to take a bite out of your girlfriend's hot dog."

The audience tittered.

Stan flushed, simultaneously embarrassed and pleased. "Exactly. How many nascent relationships have been chortled by such inattention to ritual?" ("Throttled, Qtzl," said Ship.)

The tittering escalated.

"We should commission a study," said the host and cut away to a commercial on laughter and applause.

Clearly, people didn't know how to take Stan or his alter-ego. Was he a con man—a clever writer with his own money-making shtick—or was he a sort of a rain man, a walking malapropism, a social misfit who had somehow parlayed his cock-eyed world view into celebrity? He was fairly certain no one had arrived at the truth—that he was a struggling writer being fed lines by an alien.

Interviewers hovered between the smugness of a shared joke and the credulity born of uncertainty. Some were afraid to poke fun at him for fear, his agent told him, that he'd reveal himself to be a sufferer of Asperger's Syndrome or some other condition it would be socially indefensible to joke about. It hardly mattered. Qtzl didn't seem to understand when he was being made fun of and Stan, though sometimes on the verge of bolting from stage or studio, would simply deliver his prompter's solemn responses into whatever situation he found himself. The result was always laughter, which translated into book sales, fame, fortune, and talk of him hosting his own talk show. The fact that his books tended to be rather serious in tone only added to the mystery.

There was nothing of Arlen in Stan's novels (which were now all back in print and selling briskly, thank you), which led to his emergence as a character of great complexity.

Then the fact of his electronic link to an offstage source came to light. "Legal counsel," he'd told the host of a much-watched day time talk show. "I have to be very careful what I reveal about the people whose letters I've responded to. If I were to give away their location—even the town they live in—or their real names, which they sometimes confide in me...well..."

The explanation had not been acceptable to everyone. Before long it was being trumpeted by the tabloids that there was a man (or woman) behind the scenes. Someone was feeding Stan Schell his lines. Speculation blossomed, naturally, and gave birth to a ludicrous array of ideas, the dominant ones being that (1) he was fronting for someone who was equal parts rain man and elephant man—a tragic, fragile soul who did not dare appear; and (2) his offstage prompter was a person of such fame and fortune that to reveal themselves would bring unwanted attention, even ruin. Candidates for this included the Queen of England, the President of the United States, a terminally dignified news anchor, and an ultra-right wing radio personality with MPD.

All this spawned something Stan had always thought was an oxymoron—unwanted attention. Six months after he had first appeared on *The Tonight Show*, mentally humming "This Could Be the Start of Something Big," he was beginning to whine about his "lack of privacy and personal control." He'd heard any number of Hollywood celebrities make that plaint and had thought them unrealistic weenies. Deeply immersed in his personal drama, his own weeniness escaped him.

One afternoon, Stan Schell took control of his life in the only way he could. He shaved off his beard, leaving only a professorial goatee. He was congratulating himself and patting his face dry when the FRU shuttled into the bathroom behind him.

"Stan," it said, "we have a problem."

"Out of cheese puffs?"

"No, Stan. This is rather more serious."

He turned to look at the FRU, vaguely disturbed, as always, that no expression could be read in the gleaming manta shell. "Not the Ship."

"Someone has advanced the idea that you are a front for an alien presence on Earth."

Stan burst out laughing. "Who'd believe such a ridiculous story? The person who made that up—"

"But, Stan, he did not make it up, as you well know."

"He?" Stan felt his pulse leap. "He who?"

Ship proceeded to tell him about the college student who had appeared one evening trying to get information about the crash of a meteorite. "I have no doubt that he witnessed our landfall."

Stan shook his head. "Ship, think about it. Who's going to believe a whacko tale like that?"

"Tabloids, Stan. UFO chasers. There is more. We have received a threatening email. This person has said he will expose the location of this cabin to tabloid reporters if you do not—as he put it—come clean."

"I can't 'come clean,' Ship. Not without giving you and Qtzl up to..." He realized he had no idea what he'd be giving them up to. "How soon can you leave?"

"I estimate three more days of constant work on my part."

"Did this guy leave a return address?"

"Yes."

"Then we'll have to try to stall him. I'll...invite him up here—Thursday. That will give you your three days."

Ship hovered silently for a moment. "What will you do, Stan Schell, when we are gone?"

"Me? I don't know. Retire. Try to make it on science fiction alone. I can't continue to be Arlen."

"Why not?" asked Ship.

"I don't think the way he does. I'm not alien."

"In your books you purport to write from the alien's point of view. Is that not what writing science fiction is all about—being able to put oneself in an alien setting of some sort? To be able to report what one sees through alien eyes? You once claimed you were a 'damn good science fiction writer.' How can that be if your imagination fails to let you be alien?"

Damn. Out-argued by a machine. An alien machine.

Stan wandered into the library and pulled one of his books from the shelf. *Stepping Over Shadows* the cover said—a story of aliens transported against their will to a strange new world called Earth. He perched on the corner of his desk and read the passage describing the alien protagonist's first encounter with human beings. He skipped pages and read a paragraph or two about the alien's voyage aboard the Earth ship. It was good, he thought. He had captured the alien's fear and bemusement in the face of human alienness. And that had been written long before he'd met a real alien.

His computer screen still displayed the threatening email. He read it, then sat down and sent a message to Kerfrees@shore.net. Then he called Ted Barnett at *The Bee*.

Kerwin Frees's heart turned over in his chest as he read the email. He was going to meet the aliens. He sat back in his disreputable over-stuffed chair and stared at the pine knots in his ceiling.

Stan Schell's message had posed one particularly disturbing question: *What do you want?* What did he want? Fame, fortune, notoriety? Or did he just want to be right? Did he just want to know that there was life Elsewhere—intelligent life, life we could shake hands with, communicate with, grow to like, even befriend as Stan Schell (damn him/bless him) had befriended his alien refugees. In three days he would know (hell, he already knew) that he was right. The question in his mind was: did he need the whole damn world to know he was right?

STAN HEARD THE BACK DOOR open and close. Qtzl came in, wearing a bright yellow sundress with orange tulips on it.

"I have come to say good-bye, Stan," the alien said, and Stan read honest emotion in the odd eyes. "Ship has run a diagnostic and says we are able to leave here. I can return to my family—my world." He paused and tilted his head from side to side several times as if he might shake the appropriate words loose. "I will miss having fame and fortune. It was something I never could achieve on my world."

"I know what you mean."

"Yes. I suppose you do."

"But just imagine, Qtzl, what will happen when you return after all this time and tell everyone where you've been, and how you had to brave alien danger to get home? You'll be a celebrity then, I'll bet. Everyone will want to know your story. Everyone."

"If they believe me. I have been known to…exaggerate."

"You have Ship. Would Ship lie?"

The reptilian face brightened. "No machine intelligence has never been known to even exaggerate. But…may I take some Earth artifacts back with me anyway—a set of your novels, perhaps?"

Stan nodded, feeling a lump begin to grow in his throat.

"And this garment." He fingered the hem of the sundress which came to just above his oddly jointed knees. "May I take this, too?"

"Sure. Sis won't miss it. Take those pine cones you've been hoarding, too, won't you? I sure don't know what to do with them."

Qtzl's crest bounced up and down in pleasure. "Thanks, Stan.

And now I must go. Ship is requesting my presence."

Stan checked his watch. "Yeah. Frees will be here any minute. You'd better get going."

They paused long enough for Stan to take a photograph of Qtzl in the yellow sundress. It seemed the appropriate way to remember him. Then the big lizard went to where Ship lay completely right side up on its landing struts, there to load his pine cones, books, and other Earth artifacts.

Stan waited. Not long. Kerwin Frees showed up punctually at his front door.

"Where are they?" He'd barely stepped across the threshold when the words were out of his mouth.

"They're leaving."

"They're—? You conned me!"

"You didn't leave me much choice. I couldn't expose them."

Frees gave him a panicked glare and bolted out the back of the cabin. Stan followed him down the hill to where Ship was overseeing Qtzl's clearing away of the last bit of brush. It looked somewhat the worse for wear, its once gleaming sides burnt and battered. But it had assured Stan it was serviceably sound and quite capable of getting Qtzl home.

Frees had frozen at the stern when Qtzl, still wearing the yellow sundress, turned and waved cheerily. "Oh, hello! You must be Kerwin Frees. I'm Qtzl Fhuuii. Come to see us off, have you? How nice. Isn't that nice of Kerwin Frees, Stan Schell?"

"Very nice."

Frees's voice was so desperate it nearly squeaked. "You can't leave! Don't you understand how important this is to Earth?"

"We realize how important it is to you." Stan moved to stand in front of the younger man, making him have to dodge a bit to keep his eyes on Qtzl and the FRU. "Would you really have spilled this to your UFO-logist buddies—to the tabloids?"

Ship uttered the closest thing Stan could imagine to a mechanical sigh. "I believe he did, Stan Schell."

Stan glanced up the hill toward the cabin. A small knot of people had appeared at the top of the trail, bristling with cameras and microphones. Someone shouted, and the knot loosened and began to tumble down the hill. Stan turned back to the spacecraft. "Good-bye, Qtzl. Good-bye, Ship. I think I can honestly say I'll miss you." He smiled. "Don't forget to write."

Qtzl's frill bounced, and his crest stood up smartly. "I shall write, Stan Schell. You'll see. Check your email often."

"I didn't do this," said Frees, pointing uphill.

"Uh-huh."

Qtzl and the FRU disappeared into the Ship.

Frees danced around, putting himself between Stan and the reporters. "I didn't do this."

Ship uttered a soft, keening song, like a zephyr through the pines then, moments later, lifted itself majestically into the air. Any sound it might have made was drowned in the trampling of flora under the feet of the approaching journalists. Ship hovered above the treetops—posing, Stan thought, wryly—then tilted its bow skyward and disappeared in a long streak of light.

Just like in the movies. Stan tilted his head to one side. He wondered if the video currently being shot would be blurred and grainy—like the ones in those ever-popular sightings shows.

A babble of voices swamped his thoughts. Microphones thrust into his face. On the other side of them, over a tangle of arms, Frees stared back at him, face sweating.

"What just happened?"

"What did we just see?"

"What was that?"

"Can you explain what just happened, Mr. Frees?" Stan asked.

Kerwin Frees's mouth opened and closed like a beached trout's. "It was a spacecraft," finally emerged. Frees's eyes lost their glazed look. He grabbed a microphone. "It was an alien spacecraft that crash-landed here months ago and was mistaken for a meteorite. There were two alien beings aboard, which this man—" He stabbed a finger at Stan. "—hid in his summer cabin. He used the aliens to parlay a successful career for himself as an advice columnist."

It sounded so inane, Stan almost lost himself to hysterical laughter, but the reporters jostled him, shoving their many microphones into his face.

"What do you say, Mr. Schell?" an eagle-eyed young woman peered at him from behind a red windsock.

"And you're from?"

"*The Skeptical Examiner.* We got a call saying that an alien spacecraft was sitting in this ravine. Was that what I just saw taking off?"

"Well, I hate to rain on your parade, but the so-called spacecraft is local. The rest of it—special effects. Hollywood." He smiled at the woman. "I'm sure that makes perfect sense to you."

Frees shrieked. "That's insane! You all saw the aliens! You all saw the ship!"

"Special effects," Stan repeated.

"What about the column Ask Arlen?" asked Frees. "You didn't even know it existed until you saw it was being run with your picture. You tracked the writer here, to your summer cabin. And you found aliens."

Stan feigned shock. "Are you suggesting that aliens were writing an advice column?"

The reporters laughed; Frees reddened. "You know the truth."

"I know that nobody here would believe a story like that. I certainly wouldn't, and I write science fiction. So, my line is: no comment. Now, if you'll all excuse me, I have an advice column to get out."

He pushed past the reporters, ignoring their cries for his attention, and made his way back up the hill. Frees, stranded below, managed to keep all but a few from following him.

Ted Barnett met him halfway up the hill. "What was that all about?"

Stan shook his head. "I couldn't even begin to explain."

"Was that an alien spacecraft?"

"Wasn't that what I said it was?"

"Yes."

"And did you believe me?"

"I'm here, aren't I? I leaked the information, didn't I?"

"That begs the question. Do you believe that was an alien spacecraft?"

Barnett hesitated. "I'm not sure. I hate to sound like a rank materialist, but the more important question to me is: are you really Arlen? Or was it somebody else?" His eyes grazed the clouds overhead.

"Why don't you reserve judgment until you get my next column?"

Barnett nodded. "Okay. How does this Frees character figure into this?"

Stan glanced down the hill to where the UFO chaser was still drowning in journalistic undertow. "He concocted a story about aliens writing the column—about me hiding these aliens in my summer cabin. He was harassing me."

"And this is your way of getting even."

"Maybe. Or maybe it's my way of getting the aliens out of here safely. Or maybe it's my way of getting more free publicity."

He left Barnett and went back up to the cabin, where he closed and locked the door in the faces of a couple of tabloid reporters. The act gave him a perverse and childish sense of satisfaction. From his office window he watched Kerwin Frees swimming uphill against a current of microphones and cameras. At the bottom of the hill, a handful of people were going over the crash site in minute detail.

Stan frowned. He hadn't thought of that—hadn't considered what kind of evidential residue Ship might have left behind. He called the police and reported that he was being over-run with trespassers. Then, musingly, still not certain what he had just gained and lost and gained, Stan Schell sat down at his computer to answer the day's letters and meditate upon the alien point of view.

HUMANITY

Steelcollar Worker

Vonda N. McIntyre

The enormous fuzzy balloon bounced from Jannine's fingertips, rose in an eerie, slow curve, and touched its destination. The viddydub forces took over, sucking the squashed ball into place with a loud, satisfied slurp.

"Work always reminds me of that Charlie Chan movie," Jannine said.

Neko, farther along on the substrate, pitched an identical elemental balloon into the helical structure. She had an elegant, overhand throw; she had played ball before she left school, but she was too small to get a scholarship.

"What Charlie Chan movie?" she asked. "Not that I go out of my way to see Charlie Chan movies."

"The one where he's dancing with the globe?" Jannine checked the blueprint hovering nearby, freed an element from the substrate, and moved it into place.

"Do you maybe mean Charlie Chaplin?" Neko said. "*The Great Dictator*?"

"Chaplin, right." Jannine picked up a third element, tossed it, caught it again, danced on one toe.

Neko tossed an element through the helix. A perfect curve ball, it arced, touched, settled, like a basketball into quicksand. Its fuzzy outlines blurred as it melted into the main structure, still a discrete entity, but pouring its outer layers into the common pool.

"I don't think you'd go too far as a dictator," Neko said.

"I don't want to be the dictator. I want to be the guy who pretends to be the dictator."

She leaped again, twisting as she left the ground. But the system wouldn't let her spin. It caught her and stopped her with hard invisible fingers. She found herself on the ground, with no sensation of falling between leap and sprawl.

"Are you all right? I wish you wouldn't *do* that. Jeez, it makes me nauseous just to watch you."

Jannine picked herself up. Smiling, she glanced toward Neko, but Neko's blurry face showed no expression.

"I'm okay," Jannine said to reassure her co-worker. Neko couldn't see her expression any more than Jannine could see Neko's. "Someday the system will handle a spin. How'll I know if I don't try?"

Neko picked up one more of the furry elemental balls and dropped it into place. The elementals scattered at her feet, bumping and quivering, sticking briefly to the substrate or bouncing off. Once in a while, two melded into dumbbell-shapes, then parted again.

"The system will handle a spin when you grow a ball-joint in your wrist," Neko said, exasperated. "You *could* read the documentation when there's an upgrade."

"Oh, when all else fails, read the instructions." Jannine laughed. "I don't have time to read the instructions." She wished the company would let her take the manual home, but that was against the rules. You were only allowed to read the manual in the company library.

Jannine and Neko walked down the helix, positioning the elementals, now and again prying one out and replacing it.

A herd of elementals quivered toward Jannine, like bowling balls under a gray blanket. Several escaped and flew off into the sky.

"Warm fuzzies today," Neko said.

"Yeah." Jannine went to the system and asked for cooling. The elementals calmed, settled to the ground, and re-absorbed their covering blanket. Once in a while, an elemental emitted a smear.

The helix extended out of sight in both directions. Jannine and Neko had been working on this section for a week. Jannine loved watching the helix evolve under her hands. The details of substrate, helix, and elementals changed so fast that a human could alter the helix better than a robot, even better than enzymes.

A flicker in Jannine's vision: the helix and the substrate and Neko vanished.

Jannine found herself in the real world. The couch held her among water-filled cushions, cradling her body.

Quitting time.

The screen of her helmet reflected her face, an image as unreal and distorted against the smoky plastic as Neko's face had been, back inside the system. The screen's color faded. The audio fuzz cut out.

The clamor and bustle of the factory surrounded her: the electronic whine of the system, the subsonic drumming of coolant pumps, the voices and shapes of her co-workers as they got out of their couches and tidied up for the day shift.

With her free left hand, Jannine opened the padded collar that secured her helmet. She raised the mechanism from her head. The noise level rose.

She shivered. The factory was always chilly. Her awareness of her body faded when she worked. She never felt cold till she came out of her workspace and back into real life. On the substrate, the temperature hovered just above absolute zero. Down there, she always felt warm. Up here, where the laboring pumps only incidentally lowered the temperature a few degrees, she always felt cold.

She unbuckled the cuff around her right wrist and freed her hand from the magnetic control.

Wiggling her fingers, clenching her fist, shaking her arm, she slid out of the couch. All around her, her co-workers stood and stretched and groaned in the cold. She unplugged her helmet and wiped it down and stowed it. She wished she owned one, a helmet she could impress her own settings in and paint with her own design.

Neko crossed the aisle and joined her.

"Brownie points tonight," Neko said.

She moved smoothly, easily, with none of the stiffness everyone else was feeling. She moved like her nickname, Neko, cat.

"A bonus, huh?" Jannine said. "Great. We make a good team."

They'd fallen into the habit of chatting for a few minutes after work while they waited for the crush at the exit to ease.

But instead of replying, Neko stared at Jannine's control couch, at the manipulator that reduced the motions of Jannine's hand to movements in the angstrom range.

"Did you notice what it is we're making?" Neko said.

Up on her toes, Jannine shifted her weight from one foot to the other, bouncing in place, trying to get warm. The day shift people came into the factory, moving between the hulking shapes of the couches.

"Yeah, I guess," Jannine said. "I wasn't paying attention. Just following the blueprint. Some vaccine, same as usual."

"Let's go." Neko strode away, her hands shoved in her pockets. She moved as gracefully as she did down on the substrate, where gravity could be tuned and made a variable.

Jannine hurried after her. She waved across the factory at Evan, the day-shift worker who co-habited her couch. But this morning, she didn't wait to talk.

She followed Neko through the security checkout. They were nearly the last ones out, but waiting had saved them standing in the crowd. Jannine's life gave her plenty of lines to stand in.

Jannine thought the security system was stupid, a waste of time. No one on the production floor had access to anything that they could carry away. Except the helmets. You'd have to be awfully stupid to try to walk out with a helmet, however tempting it would be to take one for your own.

Jannine shoved her i.d. into the slot. She waited. The computer checked her and passed her and rolled her i.d. back. At the same time it emitted a slip of paper, thrusting it out like a slow insolent tongue. It beeped to draw her attention.

Ignore it, she told herself. She wanted to, but Neko had seen it. If Jannine left the note, Neko would wonder why, or, worse, retrieve it for her and give it to her and expect Jannine to tell her what it was. Neko might even read it herself. Jannine grabbed it, glanced at it, and shoved it into her pocket.

"What's up?" Neko asked.

Jannine shrugged. "Nothing. Busybody stuff. 'Eat your vegetables.'"

"Sorry." Neko's voice turned cool. "Didn't mean to be nosy." She turned and walked out of the factory and into the new day.

Damn! Jannine thought. She wanted to try to explain, but couldn't think of the right words.

She hurried to catch up, blinking and squinting in the bright sunlight. When she'd arrived at work at midnight, rain had slicked the streets. Now the air and the sky were clean and clear.

"Want to get a beer? I'm buying."

For a second she was afraid Neko would turn her down, keep on walking into the morning, and never talk to her again. Neko strode on, shoulders hunched and hands shoved in her pockets.

Then she stopped and turned and waited.

"Yeah. Sure."

Finding a place that served beer at eight o'clock in the morning was no big deal near the factory. A lot of the workers, like Jannine, came off the substrate with nerves tight, muscles tense. In reality, she'd spent the last eight hours lying almost perfectly still. But she'd felt like she was in action all the time. Her work felt like motion, like physical labor. Somewhere, somehow, she had to blow off the tension. Beer helped. If she drank no more than a couple, she'd be able to pass the alert at midnight, no problem.

She slid her hand into her pocket and crumpled up the note. A couple of beers would let her stop worrying about that, too.

"Jannine!"

"Huh? What?"

Neko shook her head. "You haven't heard a word I've said." She pushed open the tavern door. Jannine followed her out of the sunlight and into the warm, loud gloom. They submerged in the dark, the talk, the music.

Neko slipped through the crowd toward the bar. Jannine, head and shoulders taller than her friend, had to press and sidle past people.

Jannine joined Neko by the wall, put her i.d. into the order slot, grabbed a couple of glasses, and drew two beers. The tavern charged her and returned her i.d. Neko retrieved it for her and traded it to her for one of the beers.

"Thanks!" Neko shouted above the racket. Four or five people were even trying to dance, there in the middle of the room where hardly anyone could move.

Jannine looked around for a table. Stupid even to hope for one. After work she preferred standing or walking to sitting, but Neko obviously wanted to talk. They weren't supposed to talk about work outside the factory.

Somebody jostled her, nearly spilling her beer.

"Hey," she said, "spill the cheap stuff, okay?"

"Hey yourself, watch it."

She recognized the guy: two couches over and one down. Jannine didn't know his name. Heading back to the order wall, he emptied his glass in a gulp. She felt envious. He could drink like that all morning. She'd watched him do it more than once. He always passed the alert when midnight rolled around.

"Neko!" She caught Neko's gaze and gestured. Neko nodded and followed her.

Jannine pushed her way farther inside, holding her glass high. She passed the bouncer. She knew one was there, out of sight in the small balcony above eye level. She'd come in here four or five times before noticing any of the people who kept an eye on the place. The balcony, upholstered in the same hose-down dark fabric as the walls, blended into the dimness, unobtrusive. The bouncer let the artificials take care of everything but trouble.

Jannine reached the hallway.

"Wait—" Neko said as Jannine slid her i.d. into the credit slot of a private room.

The door ate the i.d. and opened.

"What for?" Jannine crossed between the equipment and set her glass down on the small table in the corner. "Hardly spilled a drop," she said.

Neko hesitated on the threshold.

"Come on, it's paid for," Jannine said.

Neko shrugged and entered. "Yeah, okay. This is kind of extravagant, but thanks." She shut the door, cutting out the din, somebody yelling at somebody else, a fight about to start. After work, your body was geared up for action, and your brain was too tired to hold it back.

Jannine drank a long swallow of her beer, then made herself stop and sip it slowly. She was hungry. She ordered from the picture menu on the back wall.

"Want anything?"

"Sure, okay." Neko sounded distracted. She pushed a couple of pictures, barely glancing at them, then sat at the table and leaned on her elbows.

Jannine swung up on the stationary bicycle and started to pedal. It felt good to get rid of the physical energy she had been holding in all night. Sweat broke out on her forehead, under her arms.

"Did you see what we were making?" Neko said again.

"If I'd stopped to think about it, we wouldn't have done such a long stretch and we wouldn't have gotten any brownie points." Jannine tried not to sound defensive. "Besides, I was worried about the warm fuzzies."

"It wasn't natural," Neko said. She drained her glass, put it down, and raked her fingers through her shoulder-length black hair.

Jannine laughed, relieved. "I noticed *that*," she said. "I thought you meant something important. Jeez. Nothing we build is natural. If it was natural, we wouldn't need to build it."

"But we weren't using the regular base pairs. We were using analogs."

"Yeah. So?" Jannine wondered if Neko, too, had been set up to test her. "I build what they tell me. It isn't my job to design it."

Continuing to pedal the bike, she wiped sweat from her face with the clean towel hanging from the handlebars.

"It must be something dangerous," Neko said stubbornly. "Something they don't want out in the world. Yet. So they make it with synthetic nucleics. So it can't reproduce."

"It isn't dangerous to *us*," Jannine said, confused by Neko's distress. They were building a set of instructions. Neko knew that. Being scared of it made as much sense as being scared of a music tape.

"I don't mean *now*, I don't mean yet. But later on when they use it. Whatever it's coding for could be dangerous to us the same way it could be dangerous to anybody."

"I think you're being silly. They always start sterile, till they're sure about the product."

An artificial stupid pushed through the hatch in the bottom of the door, rolled inside, slid their food onto the table, and backtracked. The hatch latched with a soft *snick*.

Jannine swung off the exercise bike and wiped her face again.

She took the lids off the plates and pushed Neko's dinner, or breakfast, toward her.

"Do you mind if I have another drink?"

"Go ahead." It was polite of Neko to ask, since Jannine's i.d. was in the slot. But she should've known she could have whatever she wanted.

Jannine broke open the top of the chicken pie she'd ordered. Steam puffed out, fragrant with sage. When she had a night job, she liked to eat breakfast before her shift, in the evening, and dinner after, in the morning.

"How can you work out and then eat?"

Jannine shrugged. "I don't have a problem with it. I'm going to eat and then work out, too."

Neko preferred dinner at night and breakfast in the morning. She had a couple of croissants and an omelet spotted with dark bits of sautéed garlic.

"No hot date today?" Jannine asked.

Neko drank half her second beer and pushed her food around on her plate.

"I'm not really hungry," she said. "I guess I'll go on home."

"I thought you wanted to talk. That's why I got the room."

"I wanted to talk about the helix, and all you want to say about it is 'No big deal.' So, okay. So maybe we're building them a nerve toxin or some new bug."

"What do they need with a new bug? There's plenty of old bugs."

"Right. So it's no big deal. So forget it."

"Maybe we're building some new medicine."

"I *said* forget it." Neko pushed the plate away and stood up.

"If it was anything bad they'd classify it, and we'd never work on it. I don't even have a security clearance, do you?"

Neko didn't reply.

"*Do* you?"

"No. Of course not. I mean..." Neko looked embarrassed. "I

guess I used to but I'm sure it's expired by now."

"Why did you have a security clearance?"

"If I could tell you that I wouldn't've had to have it!" Neko said. "I've got to go." She downed the last of her second beer and hurried out of the room, slamming the door behind her.

Jannine watched her through the room's transparent walls till she disappeared. She was surprised by Neko's weird reaction.

"Sorry," she said to the walls. "Didn't mean to be nosy."

She ate her dinner, more because she'd already paid for it than because she still felt hungry. For the same reason, she lifted weights for a while and pedaled on the bike till her hour ran out. She got down, retrieved her i.d. before she got charged for more time, and left the private room for the ASes to clean.

The tavern was still crowded, but quieter. She made her way through it without bumping into anyone.

Outside, the sky had clouded up. It looked like more rain. Jannine trudged toward home. At her last job, her co-workers had created a complicated system of intramural sports. There was always a team to join, or a team that needed a substitute. Any warm body would help. They welcomed a warm body who was a halfway decent player. At this job, though, her co-workers went straight to the tavern or straight home, or did something with some group that didn't include Jannine.

Maybe it's getting time to move on, she thought. But she didn't want to move on.

Morning rush was over; the streets were quiet for daytime. In the middle of the night, when she came to work, delivery trucks created a third rush hour.

The mist grew heavier. The droplets drifted downward. The rain began. It collected in her hair. Damp tendrils curled around her face.

Her apartment was nothing special: a one-bedroom, the bedroom tiny and dark and cold. It always smelled musty. Not quite mold. Not quite mildew. But almost. Jannine looked at her unmade bed. She imagined crawling between the cold, wrinkled sheets.

"Shit," she muttered, and returned to the living room. She turned on the entertainment console and flipped through a hundred channels on the tv, fifty channels per minute, leaving them all two-d. Nothing interesting. She should've rented a movie. She could call something out of the cable, but it took too long to work through the preview catalogue, even on fast forward. All those clips of pretty scenery or car chases or people making love never told her what the movies were about. Usually the clips were the best part anyway. She left the remote on scan and tossed it onto the couch. The tv flipped past one channel, another.

Jannine went to take a shower. As she sorted through the pockets of her sweat-damp clothing, she closed her fingers around the note.

"Shit," she said again.

She smoothed the crumpled paper, staring at it, afraid to find out what the black marks said. Maybe it was too damaged to be read.

She dug the reader out of the closet, shoved the note into it, and listened.

"This evening, please report to room fifteen twenty-six instead of your usual position. Regular hourly wage will apply—"

Jannine shut off the reader, pulled the note out, and flung it into the sorter.

She'd avoided this test twice already, once by pretending she never received the note and once by calling in sick. She couldn't afford another sick day. Maybe tomorrow she could pretend she'd forgotten about the instructions. Once she hooked into her helmet, maybe they wouldn't bother her. She was a good worker, always above average. Not too far above average.

Jannine wondered what she had done, why she had to take a test.

She should've started looking for a new job as soon as she got the first note. But she liked working on the substrate. It was fun. She was good at it. It paid well. And despite Neko's worries, the company mostly produced crop fortifiers and medicines.

If she got away with forgetting the message—she didn't believe she would, but if she did—she'd have a week or so to look for new work before her employers realized they were put out with her. Maybe then at least they'd fire her without making her take the damn test.

Leaving her clothes strewn on the floor, Jannine climbed into bed, pulled the cold covers around her, and lay shivering, waiting for sleep.

At midnight, Jannine arrived at work and pretended it was an ordinary day. She checked in and played through the alert without paying any attention to it. When she passed, it congratulated her for a personal high score. Seeing how far up the ladder she'd run the testing game, she cursed under her breath. She hated to stand out. It always caused more trouble than it was worth. If she'd been less tired, less distracted, she would've paid attention and kept her results in the safe and easy and unremarkable middle ranges.

That's what I get for lying awake all night, she thought.

She reached out to cancel the game and use her second try. She'd never canceled a game before. That, too, drew the attention of the higher-ups.

"Good score."

Jannine started. "What—?"

An exec, in a suit, stood at her shoulder. She couldn't remember ever seeing an exec on the production level. Sometimes they watched from the balcony that looked out over the work floor, but hardly ever during the graveyard shift.

"Good score," he said again. "I knew you could go higher than you usually do. You got my note?"

He smiled, and Jannine's spirits sank.

"Yeah, well, thanks," she said, not really answering his question. "I better get to work."

"You *did* get my note?"

She saw that this time she wasn't going to get away with pretending she didn't know what he was talking about. He could probably whip out security videos that showed her taking the note, glancing at it, shoving it in her pocket. From three angles.

"I completely forgot," she said. "Is it important? My teammate's already waiting for me."

"We brought in a temp. Come along. We mustn't put this off again."

Jannine was scared. A temp was serious business, expensive.

Reluctantly, she followed the exec out of the alert room. They passed through sound effects and bright electronic lights. Jannine's co-workers played the games, proving they were fit to do their jobs for one more day.

Nearly late, Neko hurried toward her favorite alert console. She saw Jannine and the exec. She stopped, startled, looking as scared as Jannine felt. Behind the exec, out of his sight, Jannine shrugged elaborately and rolled her eyes toward the ceiling. She tried to communicate: No big deal, see you later. She wished she could make herself believe it. Her hands felt cold and her stomach was upset.

The exec's i.d. opened a door that Jannine had never been through, that she'd never seen anyone use. The exec entered the elevator.

"Come on," he said, smiling again. "Everything okay?"

"Where are we going?"

He pointed upward. That was no help. The building was twenty stories high. Jannine had never been above the production level.

She entered the elevator. The doors closed behind her. She stood there, waiting, looking at the exec. She didn't know what else to do. The upward motion made her feel even queasier. Her ears popped. The elevator stopped. The doors opened behind her.

"Here we are." The exec gestured for her to turn and precede him out.

He took her down a carpeted hall. She hardly noticed her surroundings. Photos hung on the wall. Fields and forests, she guessed, but out of focus, weird pastel colors. Some upper class fad.

The exec opened another door.

A dozen people sat at blank computer terminals, waiting. One machine remained free.

"Right there," the exec said. "Get settled, and we can start."

Jannine didn't recognize anyone in the room.

Everyone else is new, she thought. They're applying to work on the substrate, and there's a new test to get the job. What did I do to make them think *I* should have to take it? Somebody must have noticed something. Now I'm screwed.

The job test she'd taken a few months ago was all physical. It was still hard to believe she'd found such a job, with such a test. She hadn't known how to figure out a safe middle score, so she'd come out near the top of the group. She had always been athletic. Not enough to go pro. She'd tried that, and failed.

She approached the computer terminal warily. She stared at it, disheartened. Its only interface was a keyboard.

"I don't type," she said. She spoke louder than she meant to, startling several of the others, startling herself. A nervous laugh tittered through the room. Jannine turned toward the exec. "I told them, when I applied, that I don't type!"

"That's all right," he said. "You won't need to. Just tee or eff."

She sat down. She began to shiver, distress and dismay taking over her body with a deep, clenching quiver.

The chair was hard, unyielding, uncomfortable. Jannine wished for her reclining couch, for the familiar grip, the helmet and collar and imaginary reality.

The screen blinked on. She flinched. She ground her teeth, fighting tears of rage and frustration. Her throat ached and her eyes stung.

"Any questions about the instructions?" the exec asked.

No one spoke.

"You may begin."

The screen dissolved and reformed.

I should have been looking for another job a month ago, Jannine thought angrily, desperately. I knew it, and I didn't do it. What a fool.

She stared at the keyboard. It blurred before her. She blinked furiously.

"Just tee or eff." One of those. She searched out the T, and the F. She pressed the T. On the screen, the blinking cursor moved downward, leaving a mark behind.

She pressed the T twice more, then varied the pattern, tentatively, with the F. The blinking light reached the bottom of the screen and stayed there. The patch of writing behind it jumped upward, bringing a new blank box beneath the blinking square. She pressed the keys, faster and faster, playing a two-note dirge. Her hands shook.

She touched the wrong key. Nothing happened. The system didn't warn her, didn't set her down as it would on the substrate, made no noise, made no mark. Jannine put one forefinger on the T and the other on the F and played them back and forth. All she wanted to do was finish and go back to work. If they'd let her.

The screen froze. Jannine tried to scroll farther down. Nothing happened.

She shot a quick glance at the exec, wondering how soon he would find out she'd crashed his system.

He was already looking at her. Jannine turned away, pretending she'd never raised her head, pretending their gazes had never met.

But she'd seen him stand up. She'd seen his baffled expression.

Paralyzed at the terminal, she waited for him to find her out.

"Are you all right?"

"Yes," she said.

"You finished very quickly," he said.

She glanced up sharply. Finished?

The test ought to go on and on till the time ran out, like a game, like the alert, games you couldn't win. You were supposed to rack up higher and higher scores, you were supposed to pretend it was fun, but you were judged every time against the highest score you'd ever made.

The screen had stopped because she'd reached the end of the test.

The *end.*

Amazing.

The exec looked at the screen over her shoulder, reached down, pressed a key. The screen blinked and reformed. Jannine recognized the pattern of the beginning of the test, and she thought, Oh, god, no, not *another* one.

"You're allowed to go through and check your answers," the exec said. "Plenty of time before the next section. Don't you want to do that?"

One of the other test-takers, still working through the questions, made a sharp "Shh!" sound, but never looked up.

"No," Jannine said. "I'm done. I don't want to go through it again. Can I leave now?"

"I really think you should work on this some more. It's for your own good."

"I don't want to!" Jannine shouted. "Don't you understand me?"

"Hey." The test-taker who'd shhed her sat up, glared, saw the exec, shut up, and hunched down over the test.

The others continued to work, without a glance at Jannine or at the exec.

"I understand *what* you're saying," the exec said. "I don't understand why. You do fine on the alert, so it isn't test anxiety, but your score on this is terrible."

Jannine felt spied on. He'd been watching her answers as she chose them.

Angrily, she rose. She was taller than the exec, and bigger.

"I'll tell you why," she said. "Why is because I don't want to take your stupid test." She knew he was about to tell her she'd failed, she couldn't work here anymore, she was fired. "I quit!"

She pushed past him, heading for the door. She was halfway down the hall before he recovered from the shock and came after her. She'd hoped he'd just write her off, let her go and be done with her. She hoped he'd spare her more humiliation.

"Wait!"

He was mad, now, too, and wanting to take it out on her. She could hear it in his voice.

"You're a valuable employee," he said. "We think you have a lot of potential."

He baffled her. "Can I go back to work?"

"What's wrong with you?" His voice rose. "What do you have against being promoted?"

So that was what this was all about. A management test. Not a test to keep working on the substrate.

"Who asked you?" she said, furious. "Who *asked* you to promote me?"

He stopped short, confused.

"You can take the test again."

"Why can't you just leave me alone?"

"Will you talk to me about this?" The exec rocked back on his heels and folded his arms and looked at her. "Do you…do you need help with something?"

Jannine hated the pity in his face, the pity that would turn to contempt.

"I quit! I said I quit and I mean I quit!" She fled into the elevator. When the doors closed, she was shaking.

The elevator halted at the production level. The doors opened.

Instead of the quiet, cold workspace, each person in a couch, no noise but the pumps and the high-pitched hum of the electric fields, Jannine walked into midmorning break. Everybody milled around, drinking coffee and eating junk food, stretching and moving.

She crossed the floor without stopping. She hoped no one would notice where she'd been, or notice she was leaving. The best she could hope for now was to get away clean.

"Jannine!"

Jannine's shoulders slumped. If she'd just disappeared, she never would've had to tell Neko what had happened. But she couldn't keep walking, not when Neko called to her.

"Where have you been? Where are you going?" Neko hurried to her side. "Are you okay? Was it the alert? You never fail the alert! How late did you stay out this morning, anyway?" She grinned. "I'm sorry I was so grumpy. Are you done with counseling? Can you come back to work?" She lowered her voice, whispering, confidential. "The temp is really good. I think he wants to work here. Permanently. He's even got his own equipment. Are you in trouble?"

Jannine wanted to explain, but she had no idea how. She wanted desperately to get out of here.

"I quit," she said.

"You—what?" Neko stared at her, stricken, then awed. "You quit! Because of what I said? Is that why you had to go to counseling? How did they find out? Jannine… Oh, you're so brave!"

"Brave?" Jannine said, baffled.

"I ought to walk right out the door with you!"

"No," Jannine said. "No, you shouldn't, that'd be dumb." Neko thought she was leaving because of the company's products. That was okay, because Jannine couldn't explain why she'd quit. It was too complicated and too embarrassing. But she couldn't let Neko quit, too. Not if she was going to quit because of what she thought they might be building. Not if she was going to quit to be in solidarity with Jannine. That would make everything, even their friendship, a lie.

"Do you mean it?" Neko said. "That's such a relief! You won't be mad? Did they know I—? I can't quit, Jannine, I'm awfully sorry. I can't afford it, I need this job..."

Jannine felt betrayed. That made no sense. She didn't want Neko to quit. Hell, she didn't want to quit, herself. She would've felt awful, she would've felt guilty, if Neko had tried to leave with her, and she would've tried to talk her out of going. No: she *would* have talked her out of going, no matter what she had to tell her. No matter how much she had to tell her.

The lights blinked: end of break. Everyone had to get back to work. The temp would be in Jannine's couch.

"It doesn't matter," Jannine said. "I have to leave."

"I'll walk you to the door."

"Why?" No one was supposed to leave the floor during work hours. "You'll be late. You'll lose points."

"I don't care!"

At the checkout, the barrier gave Jannine her i.d. It refused to hand over Neko's. Neko hesitated. She could come through the barrier. But she'd have a hard time getting back to the floor: security, explanations, maybe even counseling. A lot of lost points.

"It doesn't matter," Jannine said, disappointed despite herself. "Stay here."

"Well...okay, if you're sure..."

Jannine went through the barrier. It closed again behind her.

"We'll get together," Neko said. "For a drink. Sometime. Okay?"

Without turning back, Jannine raised her hand in a final wave.

The exit opened. She walked out onto the rain-wet street, into the darkness.

✦✦✦

A Mighty Fortress

Brenda W. Clough

His cell was exactly ten paces in each direction. If you could call it a cell: the force-field walls were clear, nearly invisible except when the distant primary Caruso heaved above the horizon to gild the curve above his head. At this latitude Friday, the lesser sun, never rose into view. He might be utterly at liberty, lord of illimitable space, standing on the high place and surveying Ugolino, his planet and kingdom. But then he returned to his pacing again.

He lacked only some way of keeping count of his pacing. With subtlest cruelty his captors had denied him writing implements. A Catholic would use a rosary. He had seen a rosary once, clenched in an old woman's hand. The woman must have been old—he remembered the dirt engraved in the wrinkles of the knuckles, and the black crescents under the broken nails—but her face had been invisible, hidden under the other corpses.

Again he took control of his straying thoughts. He stepped out with resolution, raising his voice in song: "For all the saints, who from their labors rest! Who thee, by faith, before the world confessed…" The old hymns of his boyhood, verse after ingrained verse in eight or ten or thirteen beat lines, were as good as any abacus. The futile prowlings of a caged beast were transmuted to worship in the eyes of his viewers. Besides, he knew he had a tin ear. Being forced to listen to him sing the same antique songs, day after day after tuneless day, must be torture for his captors.

It was one of the first rules of generalship: always keep the troops busy. Now, with the body safely occupied with pacing, and the resonant songs to distract the spies, his mind could work. At every tenth step he could look down over the edge, a thousand meters to where the atmosphere thickened into breathable pinkish soup. Still poisonous of course, at 20% methane.

That was the cunning of his prison. If by strength or wit he should breach the energy wall, he'd suffocate in the gossamer atmosphere as he plunged down the vertical cliff to his death. Should he survive the climb down to the surface, he could breathe methane. And if by chance the supply buggy was nearby on its automated round, it was no refuge. He had observed the buggy closely over the past months. What else was there to watch? He had noted its route as it slowly trundled along, foreshortening, and then too close to see as it came up to the base of his mesa, and then slowly retreating on its fixed course. The vehicle was nothing but wheels and the hoist machinery. The cargoes on the open bed were sorted onto individual pallets and sealed against the ammonia sleet. For a long time there had been ten pallets, then eight, and six, and now only three. Somewhere on this hellish planet there were others like himself.

They must be weak, and the difficulties were insuperable to the weak. But he was strong. Not only in himself, but in friends. Supporters and partisans had died defending him; after his capture, petitions and hunger strikes had been organized to force his release. At last it had come, as it always must, to force. The army would liberate him: soon, soon. Unless he could escape first. That would be politically preferable—to lead his troops in triumph through the defeated capital, rather than to be rescued passively like Sleeping Beauty from her tower.

But Wors was reliable. Closer than any brother—certainly of better faith than that snake Lidi. Wors had laid contingency plans, spider-webs of fine complexity. But he knew his part well, because Wors had repeated it often. "They will not, they cannot deny a prisoner the consolations of religion," Wors had insisted. "When you receive something, my general, with the Easter lily on it—a medal, a card, a tract—then be ready. Watch for rescue!"

"I shall rise again, and they shall not know me," he had replied, deadpan. The entire meeting—it had been the Joint Chiefs of Staff, as hard a crew as any Supreme Leader could wish for—they had laughed and laughed, clapping each other on the back and slapping their knees in mirth. God, those had been good times. Nobody had believed then that things could come to this.

For a moment he was in the here-and-now again, pacing his eyrie prison. But he focused, lifting his voice in song again: "O Zion haste, thy mission high fulfilling…" Then he turned his thoughts to how rescue must come.

All he needed was a pressure suit. In the suit he could brave the hydromethane atmosphere. He could descend to ground level by clinging to the hoist cable. It ran over a simple pulley recessed into the cliff top. It might even be that his weight alone would suffice to lower him down. If not, he could descend hand over hand. He'd have to time this break carefully. Just as the supply buggy neared the base of the mesa: that was the moment. The spy cameras and sound pick-ups were high above his reach beyond the struts that supported the field generator. But the signal took ten minutes to get to enemy headquarters. Ten more minutes for a signal to come back, and perhaps five good minutes in between of the inevitable hysteria and indecision that was typical of the enemy's lower echelons. He'd have twenty-five minutes to swarm down the cable and override the buggy's programming. He would drive west to the prison base, the only settlement on Ugolino, gambling on reaching it before the air reservoirs in his suit ran out. And there he would commandeer a ship, and return to Prospero in triumph.

Wors would know this. Everyone would. His captivity was being broadcast. He knew it. Thousands, perhaps millions were watching to see how the Supreme Leader, their master, bore adversity. They should see no crack in his armor. And Wors, intelligent fellow, would somehow smuggle a pressure suit onto his pallet. Disguised as clothing, perhaps. It would arrive today!

And today, therefore, called for his most iron control of self and countenance. When the pallet was extruded through the energy wall he must unpack it just as usual. He must not betray by so much as the twitch of an eyelid that the suit had arrived. He must cling to the routine, pacing, singing, until the next supply buggy was close enough.

When he thought about it like that, it seemed an impossible task. Those forty-eight hours would seem as long—longer!—than his entire imprisonment. Not that the Supreme Leader could be jailed for long…

Even over his untuneful song he could hear it, the whiz and hum of the hoist. In his reverie he must have failed to spot the supply buggy's approach. Careful, very careful he was not to speed up his pace or skip a word. "O day of God draw nigh in beauty and in power…" The watchers should not see the Supreme Leader betray himself. The pallet inched up over the stony edge. With a final whine it flipped downwards and scooted forward through the energy wall. Even then he didn't react. He finished the last verse of the hymn first. Then he turned, majestically, and knelt to rip the plastic sheathing away.

He fanned away the lingering stench of ammonia. Where would the pressure suit be? Laid flat under the water jugs? Rolled small and crammed in beside the food concentrates? Slowly he unpacked the pallet, missing nothing. This would not surprise his captors. A prisoner learned to savor every tiny new thing. The arrival of supplies was always the highlight of each forty-eight-hour period.

His hands quivered in spite of himself as he lifted out the last packet of crackers. Nothing. Nothing! What could be wrong? Could it be that Wors had failed him? Impossible! Methodically he repacked the pallet again, loading all the supplies back so as to unpack them once more with even greater attention. He could not miss a pressure suit. It would not be possible to compress it small enough, say, to be disguised as crackers. Perhaps in a bread bag, or between the shirts…

With a terrible shock he realized that he had packed and unpacked his provisions a dozen times or more. The packet of crackers sagged from over-handling, nothing but a bag of crumbs in his shaking hands. He threw it down with an oath and stamped on it.

It was a brief and familiar comfort to feel it explode under his heel. It came to him that he had smashed other cracker bags like this before, other items even.

"My God, how long?" he groaned aloud. How long had he been going mad here in solitary confinement?

It had been months! For a while he had kept tally of the forty-eight-hour supply cycles—he could see the hatch marks he had pressed with his thumbnail into the plastic of his basin. But it was entirely possible his captors had tricked him, confusing him by changing the interval between supply deliveries. And then the obsessive packing and repacking had further confused his count.

"Wors, you traitor," he muttered. "You swine…"

But wait. Wors was dead. He remembered clearly now, the tingling buzz of the gun in his hand as he had emptied the charge into Wors's body. And yes! The delicious thrill up his leg from his booted foot, as he had stamped on Wors's head and crushed the skull in!

All this time he had been singing, singing. Now he heard the grand words rolling out of his mouth: "Awake O sleeper, rise from death!" He had to laugh. It was guff, the most blatant nonsense, all this watery spirituality. A ruler could have no truck with such stuff. Or could the very hymns be a trap as well? Endlessly repeating praise and worship, was he being subverted by their message? Those holy-boleys from his childhood had yearned to get their hooks into the Supreme Leader of Prospero! How they would blush when they learned the hymns were only a signal to Wors, the signal that he was prepared for the rescue attempt. Except that Wors was dead.

It was all illusion—but an illusion with a purpose. Anything to keep his mental resources hoarded, until rescue came. The army was conquering Prospero again, grinding these insects of rebels into paste. He had to endure only a little longer!

But was Wors dead? If he was, could it be that his victorious troops were also lost? Perhaps there was nobody coming to his rescue. Prospero could be enslaved at this moment, groaning under the tyranny of his enemies. Perhaps he would die here, chained to this rock.

A day would come when no buggy would arrive. When he was forgotten—was he? Was anyone really watching, or was he alone, forgotten? If his people had despaired and gone over to some other leader, they would need him no longer. He could starve. Or the power cells could fail. No maintenance crew, no visitor at all, had ever come here since he was immured. Without power he would freeze and suffocate in the dark.

He had condemned political prisoners here himself in his day, to that very fate. That bastard Senti, for one. The traitor. He hoped Senti had died whimpering, gnawing on the rocks. Or… singing, perhaps? "Glorious things of thee are spoken…"

New pitfalls seemed to open at his feet, as if he was not safe on a pinnacle but balanced precariously on a verge. The distant doctrines hammered into him in boyhood, boiled together with all these hymns, suddenly chilled him with superstitious dread. He was going to die here. Salvation or damnation opened before him, and he had to choose. He was in Hell, but the path to Heaven lay open to his feet.

God, that train of thought led to madness for certain! Was he flinging himself back into delusion, or was he cunningly marshaling his resources? Time would tell. The truth would out.

No, he knew the truth. Some day he would be gloriously justified. The hymns were in some sense about himself. "All praise to thee for thou, O king divine..."

Wors must be dead. He had not failed in a killing for many years now. The old woman clutching the rosary—he remembered clearly now giving the order to the Special Guard. "Truncheons, my lads," he had said. "No use wasting charges on oldsters and trash." They had grinned back at him with simple boyish pleasure and turned avidly to the work.

No, Wors was dead. But there was Toda, and Noben, and Monton, and so many other loyalists and supporters, an invincible host. Why, he was the lord of all he surveyed from this high place. Eternity could overtake him and he would be standing here, unchangeable as trolls are said to be when the sunrise overtakes them.

Enough of this mopery! He rose to his feet. Ten paces each way, and no way to keep count. But his resources were infinite. He raised his voice in song: "A mighty fortress is our God..."

Who Killed Science Fiction

Jennifer Stevenson

"I love this bookstore. You know? I guess I must spend five afternoons a week in here."

"At least that."

"It's dark, it's quiet, there's never anybody else in here. I can browse for hours if I want."

"That you can."

"What are you doing?"

"Ringing in used books."

"Oh, hey, any Bark Dangerly in there? I'm looking for—"

"Volume ten, *Bark Dangerly*—"

"*And The Möbius Machine*. I guess I've asked before."

"Only every day, Pushme."

"Well, I'm a collector. It's guys like me keep guys like you in business."

"Mm-hm."

"I've got every Bark Dangerly in every edition printed. I have the whole set. Every volume except—"

"For volume ten. I'm watching for it."

"You sure it's not in this box of used books? Maybe somebody brought it in. Didn't know what it's worth."

"If they shop here, they know what it's worth."

"Why? Are you telling them?"

"No, you are."

"Me? Oh. I guess you mean they might overhear me asking for it."

"It's possible."

"I don't want that moron Pullyu getting it before I do. His collection isn't complete either. We've both been after it—"

"For forty years, ever since your mothers threw out your old books."

"I guess I told you about that. We were in school, so we had no idea what they were up to. We came home from school—it was a half day—"

"Pep rally."

"Or some stupid thing—"

"And they'd thrown out all those old Bark Dangerlys."

"We never did have volume ten, you know."

"I know."

"So, if I get mine first, I'm not gonna show him! That'll teach him to sell all his Batmans without offering me first refusal. I helped him build that collection, you know."

"Hey, what do you know? A third edition volume six! You already have a couple, though, don't you?"

"Let me see that!"

"Pullyu doesn't have a duplicate copy. I'm pretty sure he said so."

"Gimme!"

"You've read it already."

"Only four hundred times. It's my favorite! *Bark Dangerly*—"

"*And the Spleens of Rigelius*. Pretty good condition, too."

"Let me look at it. I won't sweat on it, I promise."

"Why? You already have three copies."

"Four. I had to buy that last one so Pullyu wouldn't get it."

"Well, you'll have to buy this one because I'm not letting anybody else touch it. It's losing value just being looked at. See? The cover's not even in good condition."

"I'll buy it."

"A fifth copy?"

"Sure."

"It's worth forty-eight bucks."

"Sure, sure, gimme."

"No reading it in the back of the store and then trying to sell it back to me all sweated on."

"No, no. Here."

"<ka-ching!>"

"Oh, baby. I love this volume. I'll just go skim through it in the corner by the reading lamp."

"You do that. I'll ring up these books."

"Oh, did I mention I have three boxes of books in my car?"

"Uh, no. It's kind of late."

"That's okay. You can ring them up tomorrow and tell me what you owe me. I've got an Edgar Rice Burroughs mint *Mastermind of Mars* and some Heinlein juvenile first editions. That ought to offset what I owe you for this volume six nicely."

"Are you going to read it now?"

"Huh? Oh, yeah. Yes, I was, wasn't I? I'll just take it over to the reading lamp."

"How about you take it home? I think I'll close early."

"You can't do that! What if somebody wants to buy a book?"

"DID YOU KNOW JAKE LAPIEDIS only wrote twenty-one of the original thirty volumes?"

"That's right, Pullyu."

"And for some reason, volume ten is the only one nobody can find anymore. The story is that the paper was defective."

"Yep."

"Disintegrated in the warehouse. Piles of mouse nests when they finally got the boxes open."

"Uh-huh."

"Lapeidis was mad. He fired his agent over that."

"I know."

"Say, you don't have any leads on a volume ten, do you?"

"Nope. Sorry, Pullyu."

"I bet that duppus Pushme is still stewing about all those volume fours I bought out from under him at that estate sale. Eight copies! And he didn't even get one! Hyok-hyok!"

"Mm-hm."

"Lapeidis was a very moody guy, you know. He never talked to anybody. Just grunted. And he owned about a million old science fiction novels from the twenties and thirties. Never opened 'em. Just kept 'em. Swore he would open a bookstore one day, if he ever got writer's block."

"Ugh."

"Say, would you like some help going through those boxes?"

"Nope."

"I see Pushme brought in another batch. Dope. He never has anything good to sell. Maybe he's going broke. Maybe he's starving to death, eating cat food in that moldy old house of his mother's, selling off his collection a box at a time. Doesn't that sound likely?"

"Mm-hm."

"Maybe he made a mistake and brought in something good. I'll just toss through these real quick and see—"

"Thanks, but I'll handle it."

"He's so old now he's probably half blind. Probably wouldn't even know if he did have a volume ten. Might toss it in the box to bring over here and not even notice."

"But I would notice."

"I guess you might."

"Trust me. Did you notice we have that old prequel to *2010* on the shelf up front? Might want to take a look at it."

"You know, I'm getting so impatient to see volume ten, I wonder if *I'm* not going to die before I get my hands on it."

"Terrible."

"Exactly. So, I'll tell you something. But it's a big secret, okay?"

"Sure."

"I mean, you can't tell Pushme. The stupid jerk will probably laugh. Not that he's got a creative bone in his body."

"Maybe you better not tell me."

"This is it. But it's a secret. *I'm writing volume ten.*"

"You still writing that trilogy?"

"No! I'm writing the missing Lapeidis!"

"You're kidding."

"No, I'm not. I'm fed up waiting for a copy to turn up. It's going to be a little longer than the original, mind you. Probably the real volume ten is only a hundred and sixty pages, maybe hundred and sixty-eight. This one will be slightly longer."

"How much longer?"

"Well, I'm up to the first time paradox and I'm only in chapter three. Two hundred and twenty pages."

"My God."

"I know. The sweat! How Lapeidis did it I'll never know. It's going to be called the same thing, of course: *Bark Dangerly and the Möbius Machine*. I like to think I'm writing it in the authentic voice. Plus a couple of improvements of my own."

"Improvements."

"Yeah. Like, instead of Ponto, his faithful robot assistant, he's now got a girl working for him."

"Imagine that."

"Yep. And she has big tits, and she can shoot the eye out of an Aldebarani ski-piglet at fifty meters. And she has five PhDs, and her name is Skeeter. Isn't that cute?"

"Adorable."

"I see Lara Crofts in the role."

"Sure."

"But the kicker is—you're going to love this, this is why I think I can actually sell it, if I can finish the damn thing."

"Sell it?"

"You don't have to sound so skeptical. Yes, sell it. I'm a very creative person, you know. I have lots of ideas. That's what this is, a literature of ideas. You can't stuff your head full of ideas all day and all night without getting a few ideas of your own, you know. It's why we're superior to dumb animals and romance readers."

"Oh, right."

"Where was I. Oh, yeah. The kicker is, Skeeter is a feminist! Ain't that a kick in the pants? Those snotty New York editors will go for that in a heartbeat. They love ballbusting girl action heroes."

"I've heard that."

"You can't buy a book without one of the damn things in it anymore."

"True."

"Part of the reason why I'm a collector. I can't stand how political correctness has screwed up the literature of ideas."

"Exactly."

"I mean, how many ideas do feminists have?"

"Pullyu, I think you should look through this box now."

"Why? You got all the good stuff out already?"

"Okay, never mind. I'll do it myself later."

"No, no. I'll do it. I don't know why you would want me to—he-ey, look at this! Volume twenty-eight, mint condition!"

"Not quite. Creased back cover."

"Still! And it's one of Sorenson's Dangerlys. He did the closest copy of the authentic Lapeidis voice. I mean, none of them can really do justice to vintage Lapeidis. Volumes one through eighteen, that is. After that he kind of fell off."

"After that he kind of had a ghost writer."

"You believe that filthy canard, do you? Tsk. And you a bookseller! Lapeidis was a great man, and he could write the ass off a donkey, and you are not worthy to lick his friggin' boots."

"Fine. Do you want volume twenty-eight? Because I'm going to bag it and tag it if you don't."

"Oh, I'll take it. Pushme's only got three of these. They're a drug on the market, really. But getting scarcer. Another fifteen years, these will sell almost as well as the really good Bark Dangerlys."

"Really. Good."

"You'll never guess what I've been doing."

"What, Pushme?"

"Corresponding with Jake Lapeidis's daughter! And what do you know, she's a fan!"

"Are you going to buy those books?"

"What? Oh, these? No, I was just holding them. You'll never believe this, but *she's read volume ten*! Practically nobody has, who's talking! She told me all about it."

"Imagine that."

"It's all about a time paradox, of course. It's a true möbius. That's where it starts at one end and twists in a figure eight and comes right back to the beginning—"

"I know what a möbius is."

"And it's as big as a building. It's huge. That's why nobody knows what it is. They think it's just this badly laid-out building."

"Plausible."

"So Bark Dangerly becomes his own worst enemy. And then he has to fight himself. And of course he outwits himself, I mean, he's Bark Dangerly, right? He's the hero! This ain't one of your high modernist science fiction novels of valium and betrayal and nothing happens until the moujik hangs himself in the barn on page three hundred. Nosirree! So he licks his bad self, but good! But he can't leave it there! Because that means, the past wins! Get it? If the good Bark Dangerly beats the bad Bark Dangerly he has become, then he never becomes the bad Bark Dangerly, and they never have the battle. Or worse, he kills *off* the bad Bark Dangerly, and he has no future!"

"Complicated."

"You betcha. So I bet you can't guess what Dangerly does."

"I'm afraid to."

"C'mon."

"Pushme, I'm trying to pay bills. That's painful enough."

"So what he does is, he *deliberately* goes bad! Yep! That's right! Bark Dangerly becomes a villain *on purpose*, so he'll have someone to outwit when he comes along to stop his own nefarious plans! And then, and *then*, this is so brilliant, he lets his past self *reform* him! Get it? Then he can move on to the next adventure! God, I love it."

"You have lunch yet, Pushme?"

"Yeah. Liver and onions."

"I thought so."

"Isn't that the best Bark Dangerly plot ever? I can't wait to read it. If that book comes in here, I'll buy it. Any price. I don't care. I'd do anything to read it before Pullyu can get his greasy paws on it."

"I know."

"I mean, anything. Make no mistake, he'd do the same to me. If he found two copies, he'd *destroy* one before he'd share. And let me tell you I'm never lending that jerk a book again as long as I live. Did I ever tell you—"

"Yep."

"—about the time I lent him my entire first edition Lensman series to read, and he *never gave it back?* Well, after that, I can tell you, I'm going to taunt him with this. I'm going to post it to the Barklist. Not the whole story, mind you. Hints. To torment him."

"You'll never guess what that bastard Pushme did."

"Posted on Barklist he knows something about volume ten?"

"He posted on Barklist he knows something about volume ten!"

"The bastard."

"And you want to know the creepy thing? He's almost kind of got it right."

"I thought you haven't read volume ten."

"I mean *my* volume ten. It's done, you know. I sent it off yesterday. I sent it to the same guys who are putting out the reprints now. Say, seems like all they put out these days is reprints. Not that I mind having *Dune* in a clean copy. One I can read, not a collector copy."

"You didn't buy one from me yet."

"Uh, didn't I? Are you sure?"

"Yep. I bought four copies, and they're still over there on the new books rack."

"Boy, it used to be half the store. What's up with that?"

"I dunno, Pullyu. Maybe I can't afford to buy new books."

"C'mon, I bring in tons of used books. You must sell 'em to somebody."

"I guess I must."

"There wouldn't be room to swing a cat in here if you didn't—oops, sorry about that. I'll pick 'em up for you."

"That's okay, I have to re-alphabetize them anyway."

"You don't want my help for that. With my darn dyslexia, I put books back wrong on the shelf all the time."

"I know."

"So I don't bother trying anymore. It's a kindness, really."

"Thanks."

"This way you know it's done right."

"I LEARNED SOMETHING NEW ABOUT Jake Lapeidis."

"Oh, hello, Pushme."

"You going to eat all of those fries? I don't care if they're cold. I like 'em cold."

"They're hot. It's my lunch."

"That's okay, I can stand 'em hot. Add more ketchup. In her last email, I heard from Lapeidis's daughter, you're not going to believe this."

"If she says it, I might not."

"Get this. He might still be alive."

"Nuts."

"Truth."

"She doesn't know that."

"She thinks, anyway."

"Why? The guy would be a hundred and ten."

"Yeah, but science fiction writers live a long time. Think of it! He could still be writing!"

"Oh, I doubt that."

"No, seriously! What if he is? What if he, like, burnt out and became a beachcomber or something for a while, but then he started writing again? You should have got vinegar for these fries. They're too thick for ketchup."

"Beachcomber. Why didn't I think of that? I bet they never have to look at a book."

"He could be Elmore Leonard and we'd never know!"

"Sure, Pushme."

"What if he, like, got a wild hair one day and wrote some more Bark Dangerly? Wouldn't that be a gas?"

"Total gas."

"And here's a rumor that'll knock your socks off."

"Mm."

"They're talking about reprinting volume ten! Somebody leaked it out of New York."

"Imagine that."

"Imagine that! I can't wait. And by golly, if they do, I'll buy it new this time!"

"Oh, my God. Oh, my God. You're not going to believe this. You are *not* going to *believe* this. I don't believe it myself. I'm hysterical."

"You certainly are, Pullyu."

"They did it! They bought my book!"

"No kidding! Which one?"

"They bought my *Bark Dangerly and the Möbius Machine*!"

"They *paid* for it? How long was it?"

"Five hundred and fifty manuscript pages. I thought it'd kill me. But you know, once you sit down, seems like you can't get up without writing at least a couple of pages, and then you get interested and before you know it your cocoa's cold and it's bedtime. I think I could really get into this. They offered me—this is so incredible—they offered me a four-book contract!"

"How much?"

"Not very much, actually. If you spread it out over the four books with basket accounting, it doesn't come to a lot of money. But who cares? I'm a writer! I'm gonna be published! I'm so happy I might have a heart attack."

"Not in my store, please."

"Seems the market for Golden Age reprints is really strong right now, well, stronger than for new stuff, and they want to bring out *all* their old Lapeidis titles again. Only expanded. They really liked how I did the Lapeidis voice. I guess people want fat books now. Thank goodness! Because *I'm* going to do the expanded reissues! That's publisher talk for newer and fatter."

"I know, I know."

"My name will be on the inside cover, and the front cover will say, 'From the Jake Lapeidis Universe™.' Kind of a big word, Universe. Makes you realize how big publishing really is."

"Ah."

"They want each volume to come up to at least five hundred manuscript pages."

"Yikes."

"I wish I knew what to do with the money. Seems stupid to put it into groceries. If I could think of a book I don't have that I re-eally want. I want to blow it all in one wad. Treat myself. Celebrate, you know? I feel like I deserve it."

"Hmmm."

"But which book would I get? What one single title is really worthy of the occasion? Or even two?"

"Maybe you should buy *all* the books, Pullyu."

"Oh, I don't have that much money."

"You could buy all the books in this store."

"With my advance? Naaw."

"Seriously. I'd sell you the store for the price of your advance. Building and all."

"It's not that much money."

"Cash down, hand you the keys, walk away."

"It's only a thousand dollars."

"A *thousand dollars*? For four five-hundred-page books? Basket accounting?"

"You think I got rooked?"

"You need an agent, Pullyu. You have to expect the first contract to be a sucker bet."

"That's probably true. Besides, I just know I'm going to love writing these books."

"Expanding."

"I mean, expanding."

"By the time you hate it, Pullyu, they'll have to pay you more money."

"Is that how it works?"

"That's how it works. So. How about it? Buy the store?"

"I—I don't know what to say."

"Try saying, 'Sorry, Pushme, I don't have volume ten in stock right now.'"

"'Sorry, Pushme—sorry, Pushme'—oh wow."

"Wow is right."

"Oh, my *gosh*."

"That, too."

"He'd have to sell his used books to *me*."

"That's right."

"I could write right here in the store. Nobody ever comes in here. It would be perfect. Write all day in my own store—in my own science fiction bookstore—people bringing me collector's items instead of me coming here—and when that bastard Pushme comes in here with his pathetic box of rejects, he has to talk to *me*!"

"If you have time for him. With all the books you'll be writing."

"If I have time. Wow. 'Sorry, Pushme, but I'm on a deadline. Leave the box and I'll tell you what it's worth tomorrow.' *Wow*."

"A thousand dollars. When the check clears, you get the keys."

"We can go across the street and I'll withdraw the money right now. How about cash?"

"Let's just say, I won't accept used books in trade."

"Hah-hah! Wow. A bookstore. Hello, I'd like to make a withdrawal. You want a cashier's check?"

"Cash, thanks."

"No problemo. Here. Gosh, my hands are trembling."

"Pretty exciting, eh?"

"Man, my life changed, just like that!"

"Mine too, Pullyu."

"You look a lot older out here."

"It's the daylight, Pullyu. I never see it."

"You're looking pretty tottery. I can't believe you let me have the store for a thousand dollars! What are you going to do with the money?"

"Spend it fast."

"Maybe you oughta see a doctor."

"I'm going to see a bartender. If I live, I'll become a beach-comber."

"Hey, it won't offend you if I change the store name?"

"Why not? It's yours. What you going to call it?"

"I was thinking something '*in*,' you know? So only *our* kind of people would get it."

"Like?"

"Something like, 'Who Killed Science Fiction?'"

About the Authors

Alma Alexander's life so far has prepared her very well for her chosen career. She was born in a country which no longer exists on the maps, has lived and worked in seven countries on four continents (and in cyberspace!), has climbed mountains, dived in coral reefs, flown small planes, swum with dolphins, touched two-thousand-year-old tiles in a gate out of Babylon.

She is a novelist, anthologist, and short story writer who currently shares her life between the Pacific Northwest of the USA (where she lives with two obligatory writer's cats) and the wonderful fantasy worlds of her own imagination. You can find out more about Alma and her books on her website (www.AlmaAlexander.org), at her Amazon author page (https://amzn.to/2N6xE9u), on Twitter (https://twitter.com/AlmaAlexander), at her Facebook page (https://www.facebook.com/AuthorAlmaAlexander/), or at her Patreon page (https://www.patreon.com/AlmaAlexander).

C. L. Anderson, a.k.a. Sarah Zettel, is an award-winning science fiction and fantasy author and one of the founding members of Book View Café. She has written fourteen novels and a roughly equal number of short stories over the past ten years in addition to practicing tai chi, learning to fiddle, marrying a rocket scientist and raising a rapidly growing son and helping found the Book View Cafe website. She is very tired right now.

Her first novel as C.L. Anderson, *Bitter Angles,* was released in September 2009 from Bantam Spectra.

C. F. Bentley sprang into the Space Opera arm of publishing in 2008 with her popular Confederated Star Systems, *HARMONY, ENIGMA,* and *MOURNER,* now available on Book View Café: https://bookviewcafe.com/bookstore/book/harmony/ A spiritual journey with a literary twist in a space opera landscape. The story in this volume takes the story one step further…

Maya Kaathryn Bohnhoff says that "Ask Arlen" was "actually inspired by another science fiction story about an intergalactic advice columnist. I loved the idea, but wondered (as I often do) what would happen if I brought alien sensibilities to the task." "Ask Arlen" was first published in *Analog Science Fiction Magazine* in 1997. It was a Nebula Award nominee.

Maya is addicted to speculative fiction. For this, she blames her dad, Ray Bradbury and a robot named Gort. She's authored novels of science fiction, fantasy and mystery (*The Antiquities Hunter,* from Pegasus Crime), while her short fiction has appeared in *Analog*, *Amazing Stories*, *Interzone*, and others, and been short-listed for the Nebula and British SF awards. She's also co-authored three Star Wars novels (*Patterns of Force, Shadow Games,* and *The Last Jedi*) with Michael Reaves.

Maya is half of Maya & Jeff, a Pegasus Award-winning musical duo. They've collaborated on three amazing children and live in San Jose. Find Maya's work at http://www.bookviewcafe.com. Her personal blog and links to her other books are at http://www.mayabohnhoff.com. She is a founding member of Book View Café.

Chaz Brenchley has been making a living as a writer since the age of eighteen. He is the author of nine thrillers, two fantasy series, two novels about a haunting house and three collections, including the Lambda Award-winning *Bitter Waters.* He has also published fantasy as Daniel Fox, and urban fantasy as Ben Macallan. He lost count of his short stories long ago; a "best of" collection, *Everything in All the Wrong Order*, was published by Subterranean Press in 2021. He is also currently publishing a series of girls' boarding-school stories set on Mars; the first of these, "Three Twins at the Crater School", is available now, and a lot more may be found on his Patreon page. His work has won multiple awards; it has been translated into languages from Chinese to Estonian. In his fifties he married and moved from Newcastle to California, with two squabbling cats and a famous teddy bear.

He can be found on Facebook, Twitter and Patreon.

Marie Brennan is a former anthropologist and folklorist who shamelessly pillages her academic fields for inspiration. She recently misapplied her professors' hard work to *The Night Parade of 100 Demons* and the short novel *Driftwood.* As half of M.A. Carrick, she is also the author of *The Mask of Mirrors*, the first book of the Rook and Rose epic fantasy trilogy. For more information, visit swantower.com, Twitter @swan_tower, or her Patreon at www.patreon.com/swan_tower.

Brenda W. Clough is the first female Asian-American SF writer, first appearing in print in 1984. Her novella 'May Be Some Time' was a finalist for both the Hugo and the Nebula awards and became the novel *Revise the World.* Her latest time travel trilogy is *Edge to Center*, available at Book View Café. *Marian Halcombe*, a series of eleven neo-Victorian thrillers, appeared in 2021. Her complete bibliography is up on her web page, brendaclough.net

Sylvia Kelso lives in North Queensland, Australia, and was telling stories almost before she could write. Her poetry has appeared in North Queensland and Australian Women's Poetry anthologies. Her short stories have appeared in *Antipodes: North American Journal of Australian Literature*, *Neverlands and Otherwheres* (from Susurrus Press), and *New Ceres Nights* (from Twelfth Planet Press), and two of her novels, *The Moving Water* and *Amberlight*, have been finalists for best fantasy novel in the Australian Aurealis genre fiction awards.

Katharine Kerr was born in Cleveland, Ohio, in 1944 to a family which considered itself British-in-exile far more than American. Since she was taught to read on British books alone, these sentiments resulted in her inability to spell properly in either system, British or American, though fortunately there were no other lasting effects.

Jay Lake and Shannon Page wrote many stories together before Jay's untimely death in 2014. **Jay** lived in Portland, Oregon, where he worked on numerous writing and editing projects. His books for 2012 and 2013 include *Kalimpura* from Tor and *Love in the Time of Metal and Flesh* from Prime. His short fiction appeared regularly in literary and genre markets worldwide. Jay was a winner of the John W. Campbell Award for Best New Writer, and a multiple nominee for the Hugo and World Fantasy Awards. **Shannon** is a Pacific Northwest author and editor, working in both fiction and nonfiction. She practices yoga, gardens, and has no tattoos. Website: www.shannonpage.net.

Vonda N. McIntyre wrote science fiction. You can find a bio for her (which contains few facts but much truth) by Eileen Gunn at https://vondanmcintyre.net/the-real-story/.

Steven Popkes is a software engineer, private pilot, and Nebula nominee for "The Color Winter." He lives in Massachusetts where he and his wife raise turtles and bananas.

Irene Radford is a founding member of Book View Café. You can find a number of her books, both reprints and original titles, at the café, including the entire *Whistling River Lodge Mysteries* Series. She has been writing stories ever since she figured out what a pencil was for. Editing, as Phyllis Irene Radford, grew out of her love of the craft of writing. History has been a part of her life from earliest childhood and led to her BA from Lewis and Clark College.

Mostly she writes fantasy and historical fantasy including the best-selling Dragon Nimbus Series and the masterwork Merlin's Descendants series. Look for her writing new historical fantasy tales as Rachel Atwood, a different take on the Robin Hood mythology in *Walk the Wild with Me*, from DAW Books and the sequel *Outcasts of the Wildwood* due out in January 2022. In other lifetimes she writes urban fantasy as P.R. Frost or Phyllis Ames, and space opera as C.F. Bentley. Lately she ventured into Steampunk as Julia Verne St. John.

If you wish information on the latest releases from Ms. Radford, under any of her pen names, you can subscribe to her newsletter: www.ireneradford.net. Or you can follow her on Facebook as Phyllis Irene Radford.

Jennifer Stevenson has far, far too many friends who own bookstores, so she can testify that they really do live a long time, even on half-orders of french fries. Their message to the world: Be careful what you wish for.

Sarah Zettel is an award-winning science fiction and fantasy author and one of the founding members of Book View Cafe. She has written fourteen novels and a roughly equal number of short stories over the past ten years in addition to practicing tai chi, learning to fiddle, marrying a rocket scientist and raising a rapidly growing son and helping found the Book View Cafe website. She is very tired right now.

Copyrights & Credits

Spawn of Rocket Boy and the Geek Girls

An Anthology of Short Fiction
Phyllis Irene Radford and Shannon Page, editors

First digital edition Book View Café 2010
Second digital and print edition Book View Café 2022
ISBN: 978-1-63632-039-7

Production Team:
Cover Design: Marissa Doyle
Proofreader: Shannon Page
Formatters: Jennifer Stevenson (ebook) and Shannon Page (print)

This is a work of fiction. Names, characters, places, and incidents are the product of the author's imagination, and any resemblance to actual events or locales or persons, living or dead, is entirely coincidental. Any real persons or places mentioned are used in a fictional manner.

Book View Café
304 S. Jones Blvd. Suite #2906
Las Vegas NV 89107

BOOK VIEW CAFE

www.bookviewcafe.com

About Book View Café

Book View Café is a professional authors' publishing cooperative offering DRM-free ebooks in multiple formats to readers around the world. With authors in a variety of genres including mystery, romance, fantasy, and science fiction, Book View Café has something for everyone.

Book View Café is good for readers because you can enjoy high-quality DRM-free ebooks from your favorite authors at a reasonable price.

Book View Café is good for writers because 90% of the proceeds goes directly to the book's author.

Book View Café authors include New York Times and USA Today bestsellers, Nebula, Hugo, Lambda, Chanticleer, National Reader's Choice, and Philip K. Dick Award winners, World Fantasy, Kirkus, and Rita Award nominees, and winners and nominees of many other publishing awards.

www.ingramcontent.com/pod-product-compliance
Lightning Source LLC
LaVergne TN
LVHW091023080826
845145LV00002B/341

* 9 7 8 1 6 3 6 3 2 0 3 9 7 *